THE BEST CHRIS✝IAN SHORT STORIES

EDITED AND WITH AN INTRODUCTION BY BRET LOTT

WESTBOW
PRESS

A Division of Thomas Nelson Publishers
Since 1798

visit us at www.westbowpress.com

Published in Nashville, Tennessee, by WestBow Press, a division of Thomas Nelson, Inc.

WestBow Press books may be purchased in bulk for educational, business, fund-raising, or sales promotional use. For information, please e-mail SpecialMarkets@ThomasNelson.com.

Scripture quotations are from the Holy Bible, New International Version®. Copyright © 1973, 1978, 1984 by International Bible Society. Used by permission of Zondervan Publishing House. All rights reserved.

And from *The Living Bible*, copyright © 1971. Used by permission of Tyndale House Publishers, Inc., Wheaton, Illinois 60189. All rights reserved.

Publisher's Note: This book is a work of fiction. Names, characters, places, and incidents are either products of the author's imagination or used fictitiously. All characters are fictional, and any similarity to people living or dead is purely coincidental.

Library of Congress Cataloging-in-Publication Data

The best Christian short stories / edited and with an introduction by Bret Lott.
    p. cm.
    ISBN 1-59554-077-6 (softcover)
    1. Christian fiction, American. 2. Short stories, American. I. Lott, Bret.
PS648.C43B47 2006
813'.60803543—dc22

                        2006009607

Printed in the United States of America

06 07 08 09 10 RRD 9 8 7 6 5 4 3 2 1

THE BEST
CHRISTIAN
SHORT
STORIES

CONTENTS

INTRODUCTION

My name is Bret Lott, and I believe in God the Father Almighty, Maker of heaven and earth. And in Jesus Christ his only Son our Lord; who was conceived by the Holy Ghost, born of the Virgin Mary, suffered under Pontius Pilate, was crucified, dead, and buried; he descended into hell; the third day he rose again from the dead; he ascended into heaven, and sitteth on the right hand of God the Father Almighty; from thence he shall come to judge the quick and the dead. I believe in the Holy Ghost; the holy catholic Church; the communion of saints; the forgiveness of sins; the resurrection of the body; and the life everlasting. AMEN.

That's where this collection of stories by Christian writers begins, a collection that, I hope, will begin to fill a gap in the world of fiction: that between popular Christian writing and that of literary art.

But please don't worry about those two words, "literary" and "art." Too often they make us think of the dry, scholarly notions most of us suffered through in high school and college English courses, those lectures when it seemed that all the teacher cared about was *irony* and *symbols* and *theme*, having missed the fact that what we'd all been assigned to read for class was, finally, a *story* about something that had happened to *people*.

Neither will these stories be sermons, in which the writers collected here hold forth on the evils of the world we as Christians are assailed by every time we walk into a bookstore.

Rather, what follows is proof positive that the phrase "Christian literary fiction" isn't an oxymoron.

What really is "literary fiction"? When my students ask point blank what the difference between popular and literary fiction is—and they ask this question a lot—I tell them that literary fiction is fiction that examines the character of the people involved in the story, and that popular fiction is driven by plot. Whereas popular fiction, I tell them, is meant primarily as a means of escape, one way or another, from this present life, a kind of book equivalent of comfort food, literary fiction confronts us with who we are, and makes us look deeply at the human condition. Henry James said that it wasn't "the rare accident"—the plot—that made a story worth our attention, but the "human attestation" to that plot: how people deal with their histories, rather than those histories in and of themselves.

At least I *think* that's what is meant by literary fiction.

I started with the Apostles' Creed because I do believe in Christ's divinity, in His resurrection, in His being precisely who He claimed to be. That is, I believe in a supernatural God, one who loves us, cares intimately and deeply for us, so deeply that He gave His only begotten son to die for us. And I believe in a supernatural God whose wrath, as my life's reference book—the Bible—tells me, will be inflicted upon this world so fully that John saw in his revelation "the kings of the earth and the great men and the commanders and the rich and the strong and every slave and free man, [hide] themselves in the caves and among the rocks of the mountains; and [say] to the mountains and to the rocks, 'Fall on us and hide us from the presence of Him who sits on the throne, and from the wrath of the Lamb, for the great day of their wrath has come; and who is able to stand?'"

That, dear readers, is the God I believe in. The loving God who loves us on His terms, and His only.

And now begins the rub of this all, the clash between the Christian worldview that says there is a supernatural God, and the world of contemporary literature that preaches relentlessly, *The world is what we make it, and we are on our own,* the mantra by which it seems most all contemporary art lives, eats and breathes. For this is the difference between literary art and *Christian* literary art: the fact of hope the writer has *not* in the world to save itself, but in a God *who has already saved us.*

The writers collected here believe in a supernatural God who loves us, who asserts Himself outside of our hands, outside of our control, outside of our concepts of time and space, to actually show Himself to us.

For that reason, the book you are holding in your hands is about the most radical book you can read: We are writers who, by the power of Christ, are trying to smash the gates of serious literature with the joy and light and hope of a personal, saving, supernatural God.

But I'm sure some of you reading this are thinking, *what does he mean by* supernatural?

Let me tell a story now. Or two. Maybe three.

A few years ago I worked my way through the book *Experiencing God,* by Blackaby and King, that book everybody and his brother was carrying around church back then. I'm betting this small piece of news—I worked through *Experiencing God*—might disappoint some of you out there who hold the romantic belief that writers wear berets and wait for the muse to strike while sipping cappuccinos at Starbucks. Next thing you know he'll tell us he's read *The Purpose Driven Life*, some of you are thinking. But I'm afraid it's even worse than that: For nine years I was an adult Sunday school teacher at East Cooper Baptist Church, a Southern Baptist church in Mt. Pleasant, South Carolina, and I *taught The Purpose Driven Life.*

The fact is, I am about the squarest person you will meet. I was a Cubmaster for seven years, Assistant Scoutmaster for three; I was an assistant soccer coach for eight years too. For five years I played baritone sax in my church orchestra—not in the hip and cool Praise Band, but the orchestra. For four years my wife, Melanie, and I ran our church's Wednesday night supper. To reach even further back, and to see perhaps how *really* pedestrian my faith story might appear, I was born again after a Josh McDowell rally when I was eighteen years old and a freshman at Northern Arizona University, and I met Melanie—we've been married for twenty-six years now—in the College and Career Sunday school class at First Baptist Church of Huntington Beach/Fountain Valley in Orange County, California.

We are talking square here.

But to *Experiencing God* and what it means to say *supernatural*: one day the book instructed me to pray for an opportunity to share Christ in some way. I was told to pray specifically for an opportunity—and then instructed as well to keep my eyes and ears open, to look for that opportunity, rather than simply to pray it and forget it.

Later that day I was in my office at the college where I taught, and received a phone call. It was from one of my students, a genuine slacker who hadn't shown up for class that day, a kid I had written off weeks ago. And of course you know already how this story will end.

But I want to underscore what a slacker this kid was, and the attitude I had toward him. I don't dislike any of my students—I love them. Really. But there are certain kids who show up in your classes, and you know by their actions how much they want to be in the class, and so you begin to adjust your own views of them to reflect theirs of you. That is, this wasn't a kid with whom I would have gone out of my way to build a relationship. He was simply marking time in my class, so I was simply marking time with this phone call.

He was calling to say he was sorry for missing class, and had some lame excuse for not having been there. I remember leaning back in my chair and putting my feet up on my desk, listening to the story and, the phone to my ear, rolling my eyes. I really remember rolling my eyes at this kid.

And then he said it: "Mr. Lott," he said, "if I were to read a book from the Bible, which one would it be?"

Just like that. Out of the bluest blue you can imagine, me already shining this kid on, rolling my eyes, marking time with him.

And I sat up, then stood at my desk, hit square over the head with the two-by-four of God's answer to my prayer that morning: to receive an opportunity, and to watch for it. Sadly, I had just about dozed off at the wheel, but was blessed enough to have been awakened in time to recover myself, and begin to talk about the Gospel of John, but also about the book of

Acts, my favorite. Oh, and James too. But John. The Gospel of John.

And I saw, because I had been caught unawares, that this prayer wasn't about my giving to someone I had signed off the message of grace, but about my having signed him off: it is the *being ready* that mattered, I saw. The message of salvation saves in and of itself; opportunities abound every minute we are awake to share.

But it is being ready to take those opportunities that matters.

Of course the world's enlightened people will chalk up the outcome of that story to chance, to coincidence. Maybe even to a conniving kid who, knowing as most every kid on my campus does that I am a Christian, thinks he has found a way to appeal to my forgiving side if he intones inquiry into the Bible while asking to be excused from a class he has missed. Don't think this all hasn't occurred to me.

But none of that rationalizing matters. What matters is that that morning I prayed for something—an opportunity, and an awareness—and was provided with both when I was least expecting it. That kid had no idea, I saw, that I was praying for this, and though I have to this day no idea if he really read John or not, he was given by a willing messenger—me—an opportunity.

That is all God asks, I saw. That willingness from us.

And this opportunity given was a supernatural act, God's answer to prayer.

But here are the other two stories. A little more dramatic, I think, than the possibility of coincidence.

I have been on church missions trips to the eastern European country of Moldova twice now, the first trip with my older son, Zeb, to help build an orphanage for kids in the town of Telenesti, the second time to help run a Bible camp for kids in the same town. Moldova is the poorest country in Europe—the average income there is $30 a month, this in what had been an industrialized Soviet bloc country.

My job for the second visit—Melanie and both our boys came this time—was to be the activities director for Bible camp, all that Cub Scout expertise coming back to haunt me. The job, given to me by acclamation, was to herd 140 children ranging in age from 4 to 18 into four groups, and then to entertain them for four one-and-a-half-hour blocks each day for a week—all in translation, either to Romanian or Russian, depending on the age of the kids. My team and I organized games and sports for them all. The last day we did wacky relays—silly games such as standing directly over an empty soup can on the ground and dropping a clothespin into the can from your forehead, or skipping rope ten times, or kicking your unlaced shoe off your foot to see who could launch it the farthest. We'd brought our own supplies: those clothespins, empty cans, all sorts of arts and crafts supplies, everything from Polaroid film for pictures of the kids, to T-shirts—140 of them—for the children to tie-dye one afternoon. The mission group—there were sixteen of us, all from East Cooper Baptist—spent an entire afternoon a week before we left, parceling out all these supplies evenly so that no one was overburdened. There were even entire sets of Old and New Testament flannelgraphs, too, for the nationals to use once we got to the camp in Moldova, all parceled out.

One of the relay games was a goofy thing in which a kid runs to a paper bag, next to which are two garden gloves. The kid has to put on the garden gloves, then reach into the bag and pull out the pack of chewing gum inside it, and then extricate a stick of gum from the pack with these garden gloves on, put the stick in his mouth, take off the gloves and run back to tag the next person on his team, until everyone is done.

The problem we were facing all week, though, was the kind of problem we all wish for: there were simply more kids than we had been told would be allowed to participate. Simply too many kids. The first day we opened up, in a ruined school that, in America, would have been featured on national news for the scandalous fact that its broken and filthy shell still housed kids for classes, we had 170 kids show up.

And I'd packed only enough gum for 160 kids, thinking that twenty extra pieces—we were told there would only be 140, remember—was, in fact, planning ahead. So on that last day, going into the relays, I knew we didn't have enough gum. I knew it. But there had been no place to buy more, and so we had no choice but to go ahead with the game.

Zeb and Jake, my younger son, served as monitors, helpers of a sort for the smaller kids once they were down at the bags and trying to put on those gloves. And late in the day, once we were working through the last batch of kids, Zeb hollered out to me, "Dad, we're going to run out of gum!"

I hollered back to him the only thing I knew to do: "Pray!" I said, and prayed myself that somehow there might be more gum, that this would work out.

Zeb prayed too. As did Jacob, and Skip McQuillan, the other dad along, and his two sons, Sam and Mac. We all prayed there, on the spot, that somehow there would be more gum, enough for all of them.

And there was enough gum. To the person: precisely enough pieces of gum, at the end of a frantic day of wacky relays, just a crazy day spent doing crazy games as a means to entertain kids who were being brought the Gospel message elsewhere in the school by the nationals for whom we were helping with this camp.

It is with a kind of wonder and joy that I tell you this story, no matter the cynic in me—Satan, actually—who rationalizes that perhaps not every kid participated that last day, and maybe not every kid did the relay. But there were more kids that day than any other, and they all did the relay.

And if there had been some single kid who had come up to the bag and found there was no gum for him, where would God have been, finally?

I believe in a supernatural God.

One last story, this from that same trip. There's a little fact I left out of all this: two of our team lost their luggage altogether, traveling from Charleston, South Carolina, where we all lived, to the capitol city of Moldova, Kishnau. So even though we had spent all that time parceling out all our various supplies, it didn't really matter: we didn't have enough of what we needed.

Sure, Debi McQuillan, Skip's wife, had brought some extra Polaroid film, more than she'd passed out to us all, and there were, finally, plenty of ice-cream sticks for the frames they would make for those photos. There was enough glue and glitter, enough of that Dayglo plastic string to make lanyards for them all. We made do with a couple of softballs and a baseball bat less than we had planned to have ready.

But the big craft event the last day was the tie-dyeing of

T-shirts. And we'd packed 140 T-shirts. Enough for the number of kids we'd been told would be there. There wouldn't have been enough, not by a long shot, even for the number of kids we'd planned for. That is, there weren't even 140 T-shirts. Plain and simple.

And here's what we did: We prayed over the T-shirts. We knew we didn't have enough, and we prayed over them, and then stepped boldly into that last day's craft activities, faithful that somehow we would have enough T-shirts, though we knew we had less than we needed.

And at the end of that long day of messy crafts—imagine, to begin with, trying to guide that many kids at dyeing T-shirts twisted and rubber-banded into knots, and then not being certain who would get one and who wouldn't—at the end of that long day of stepping out in faith, *there were precisely enough T-shirts for every kid who was there—more than 170 children.*

In the book of Joshua, God instructs Joshua to choose twelve men, one from each tribe and to have each one carry a stone from where they crossed the Jordan and place it where they were camped on the other side. "Each of you is to take up a stone on his shoulder, according to the number of the tribes of Israel," Joshua instructs them, "to serve as a sign among you. In the future, when your children ask you, 'What do these stones mean?' tell them that the flow of the Jordan was cut off before the ark of the covenant of the Lord. When it crossed the Jordan, the waters of the Jordan were cut off. These stones are to be a memorial to the people of Israel forever.'"

Let me tell you that these stories I have just given you are only a few of my own standing stones. They are reminders to me and to those who come after me—you reading this—of the supernatural power of God.

Because I cannot explain to you how we got the right amount of gum, or why a kid called me to ask what book of the Bible he should read on a day when I'd written that kid off, or how we got enough T-shirts to make each kid at that camp feel a part of that camp at the end of a week in which they were presented the Gospel message. In the town of Telenesti, in the country of Moldova, there is no running water; there are no flush toilets. Needless to say, there is no Wal-Mart to which we could repair and purchase bundles of T-shirts to save the day. But in Telenesti, there were orphans, kids whose parents had left them outright simply to go somewhere else and try to live. And there were also kids who lived with their parents and who showed up unannounced and unplanned-for to that Bible camp.

And not one of them went wanting. No one was missed.

I can only tell you that these standing stones point to a supernatural God, one I can't explain by logic or rationalization. I can only bear witness to Him.

So, do I really believe that God reached out His hand to us and, as those five thousand people who'd gathered at Bethsaida on the shore of the Sea of Galilee were given food from five loaves and two fish, gave us some extra gum and a big wad of T-shirts?

Yes I do. Count on it.

For if I, as a believer in Christ as God on earth, can find a way to explain away a phone call or a pack of gum or those T-shirts, then what is the point in my believing in the resurrection of a dead man? Plain and simple.

But I do believe it. Plain and simple. Our God is a supernatural God.

I have a friend who is a surgeon. He, too, is a believer, and told me one time that he has to be careful about talking about God and His role in my friend's life when he is around other surgeons. It's because no matter your skills as a surgeon, he told me, no matter what schools you went to, where you did your residence, *no matter how long you've been saving lives*, once your colleagues smell on you a belief in something outside of yourself, you will be thought of as a loose cannon. A nut. A surgeon's hands are his to maneuver, a doctor is taught, and to believe that there is any sort of supernatural element involved in your being a successful surgeon is to admit into the OR an unaccounted-for entity, and hence the possibility for error. It is to admit a vulnerability.

I believe the same thing happens in the world of literary art. We have become so primed to believe in the self that there is no room for anything else, that it seems preposterous to have characters whose lives are altered by a supernatural God. James Joyce took that word *epiphany*—the "shining forth" or revelation of God to man in the person of Jesus Christ—straight out of the Church to slug in for his notion of the moment in a story when man's humanity, as it were, shines forth on himself, or on the reader. Ever since, when it comes to stories, that term "epiphany" has meant a kind of psychological reckoning of characters to themselves and their world.

But the stories collected here attempt to rectify that shift in meaning, and to return *epiphany* to its original intent: that shining forth of God's grace on the characters involved. The stories here—our memorial stones—point to a God who has saved us, but who has saved us on His terms, and His only.

Which brings me to a final word of warning about this book: don't believe that every one of these stories will be all about joyful triumph and tender reckoning. In her essay "Novelist and Believer," the writer Flannery O'Connor, one of my literary *and* Christian heroes, writes

> The Christian novelist [or writer] is distinguished from his pagan colleagues by recognizing sin as sin. According to his heritage he sees it not as sickness or an accident of environment, but as a responsible choice of offense against God which involves his eternal future. Either one is serious about salvation or one is not . . .

If what this book is attempting is a bridge between contemporary literature and Christian faith, then these stories must—and do—confront ourselves with ourselves, and because we are sinners, the fact of sin and its ravages must be faced.

I can only think here of how challenging the parables of Christ were to His listeners, of the ire raised by a story in which the hero is a Samaritan, or the strange mix of disgust and heartbreak at the story of the prodigal son's tending to swine, or the violence and depravity of the vine-growers who murder the heir of the vineyard in a deluded attempt to grab the land for themselves.

All of these stories were told by Jesus as a means not to comfort His listeners, but to confront them with their own sin.

No one was ever more serious about salvation than Christ Jesus Himself.

And because my job as a Christian is simply to bear witness to the power of Christ, the stories collected here bear witness— the "human attestation"—to the role of Grace in our lives.

Our God is a supernatural God, one of fish and loaves and gum and T-shirts.

Our God is a wrathful God, one who makes kings and slaves alike beg for the mountains to fall on them rather than having to face Him in His anger.

And our God is a loving God, who has given us the promise of a house with many mansions.

"What do these stones mean to you?" you may ask of the stories that follow.

And we will answer: God is good.

LOUD LAKE

MARY KENAGY

"Loud Lake" is a powerful story for its quiet voice, and its ability within that quiet to evoke the questions of faith, both in God and in those to whom we look for guidance in matters of our faith, that all believers must ask if we mean to live our lives inside the love of God. Pete is especially well-drawn as a young man who lives in the shadow of a loving father, and yet who feels the need, as we all do, to find his own path beyond that shadow.

—Bret Lott

LOUD LAKE
Mary Kenagy

I t was against camp rules to be out on the water before breakfast, but Pete guessed that his father would be secretly proud of him, and probably relieved too. In the east the sky was turning white, and the last stars were disappearing over the opposite shore. The sun would rise in half an hour, and a breeze had begun to wrinkle the surface of the lake. It blew Pete's hair back from his face and made him draw his hands into the frayed sleeves of his sweater as he walked out onto the dock. He wore shorts and soggy tennis shoes, and he carried a dingy sailbag. He was small for his age, twelve, but big enough to lift the removable mast of a Laser. He laid the mast on the dock, unpacked the sail, and shook it out. It was patched with tape and stained with lakewater, like the boats. In two minutes he had the Laser rigged and running before the wind toward the fading stars. He let the boom out and leaned to counterbalance its weight. Each wave reflected the white, predawn sky.

Pete squinted back toward the camp. He had gray eyes like his mother's, and his skin was tanned from summers on the water. His knees were scabbed and scarred, and also blotched with curious white patches, a harmless sort of cancer, the doctor had told his parents. He was supposed to watch the patches to make sure they didn't get bigger. Around his neck he wore a wooden cross on a leather thong, given to him by his father.

His father, Don Bonds, was the director of the summer

camp, a barrel-chested man in his late forties who still wore nylon sandals and printed T-shirts, and had an unhittable jump serve. He'd walk out past the back line of the volleyball court, pretending to hobble like an old man, then turn, make the high toss, take a slow two-step approach, fling himself into the air, and release all the force of his body into the ball. Then he'd laugh in the bewildered faces of the other team. "God breaks the rules all the time, just to get people's attention," he was fond of saying. "That's what miracles are." Loud Lake was a non-denominational Christian camp, and Pete's dad was a sort of stationary missionary. Kids came to him, or were sent. He was an impressive person, deep and gregarious at the same time. He was a great and competitive talker. "You can't force people to accept Christ," he said. "You can only show them that they don't have any other logical choice." He would sit for a long time after dinner and "argue philosophy" with the older kids, who loved him most of all, the boys especially. He was generous with his time and affection. If he had a fault, it was that his love of surprising people was mixed with a love for attention of any kind. He got up every morning at five to sit on the end of the dock and pray for an hour before calling the camp to breakfast over the public address system, using different comic voices. In the dining hall, everyone would beg to hear the voices again. Pete loved and respected his father, and assumed that he himself would eventually get on track and grow up to be just like him.

Pete didn't befriend kids at camp the way his father did, not even the ones who came back summer after summer. He tended to hang back and observe during capture the flag, bucket ball, and the counselor hunt. He spent a lot of time sailing the old Lasers, cruising the edges of the afternoon sailing lessons. He'd show off a little now and then. "Watch Salt!" the instructors would shout at their students. "There's a real rolling tack." Praise shamed Pete, because he knew he wasn't a great sailor, and he also figured the campers thought he was arrogant. In fact, he was shy. His father's charisma made his shyness more painful.

His father took the older boys on grueling, perilous hikes and did special Bible studies with them, for which he owned large dictionaries in unfamiliar alphabets and a six-volume concordance. Every summer the older boys were a little gang, and he was their godfather. This year's group wanted matching tattoos. At meals, girls and younger boys would gather around their table, and they'd tell how one of them had almost died rock climbing, and how another had saved his life. The one called Mike told Pete in a serious voice after dinner that his dad was the greatest human he'd ever met. They had just come back from a three-night survival trip. Pete said okay, thanks, and couldn't think of anything else to say. He wasn't sure he liked Mike.

That summer, Mike was legend. When he was six, his father had been killed on a fishing boat in Alaska. His mom had forbidden him to see the grave, and Mike would sneak out and go anyway, all the time, even though it made her scream. His friends spread the story around. "His dad left them right before he was killed," explained Brian, the friend who had brought Mike to camp, "and his mom still hates his dad, but Mike's not bitter like her." Brian's family had paid Mike's way to camp.

On the back of Mike's wrist was a bird-shaped scar. He told his table about it one night at dinner, and the story was all over camp before fireside. Pete heard it firsthand, since he sat at Mike's table whenever he could. "I was playing with a knife my dad left me," Mike said, "and just before Mom went to bed she said, 'Mike, don't do anything stupid with that,' so I did it, over the kitchen sink." The other kids leaned close, one forgetting the fork that hung in his mouth, and Mike told about carving the wings. It was a good bird, realistic-looking, a hawk or an eagle in flight. The healed skin was white and shiny as teeth.

"How come a stupid bird?" said Meg Holloway, the new girl. Everyone ignored her, as usual, and Mike described the blood going down the drain. Meg had come late to camp, and she made her cabinmates uneasy from day one. At her first breakfast she refused the greasy camp food and instead drank coffee from the counselors' table. Her cabinmates, seventh graders, were worldly enough to be put off by their waffles. They hesitated, making chicken scratches in their syrupy plates with the tines of their forks, until their beautifully sunburned, athletic counselor, Gravity, helped herself to bacon and assured them that girls had to eat too. They finished their meal, glancing at Meg, some with worry, some with disdain. At the far end of the table, Pete didn't eat a thing. He was sure that if he had, Meg would have thought less of him. He felt solidarity with her in fasting, and he wondered whether she had noticed.

Nobody but Pete seemed to like Meg, while everyone admired Mike. His father's death made him magical and tragic. Pete liked the story about the grave, though to him, defying parents only for the sake of defying them seemed mean. He felt sorry for Mike's mom, coming downstairs in the morning to find a ring of her son's blood around the garbage disposal. Mike was the first person Pete could ever remember disliking, and since

Pete had no one to talk to, he disliked Mike in a secret and festering way.

One evening after dinner, he overheard his dad telling his mom what a blessing Mike was. Pete was upstairs trying to get a radio station to come in, a hobby of his. His radio was large as a piece of furniture, made of fake wood, with an upholstered front and two aluminum dials that looked like bottle caps. It had been left in the attic by previous tenants. The camp was distant from any town, and the radio received only garbled spurts of noise, but the idea of a world of continuous, unheard voices and music always existing in the air around him tantalized Pete, and he spent hours trying to get the antennae in the right places, inching the needle across the dial, trolling for a signal.

When he heard Mike's name, he turned the sound down. "The one with the cheeks," his mom said. It was true that Mike had big cheeks, and Pete liked his mom saying it. Popular opinion held that Mike was very good-looking, if tough. Meg's cabinmates all said so.

"That kid is something," his dad said.

"He'd have to be, Vicar," his mom said. Her voice was warm and whispery, and the room went quiet. Pete turned the radio back up and wondered why Mike had to be something. Because he came from a tough home, maybe. Or maybe he was sick.

When Pete's mom married Don Bonds, her family was confused. They were cultivated people, faintly Anglican, and Don didn't seem like Joan's type at all. They were made restless by the long, heartfelt prayer he gave when he first came to dinner. After that, Grandpa Gayle started calling him vicar, as a joke. "Well, Vicar, did you win your softball game last weekend?" he'd ask. Behind his back he was the vicar. Pete's mom would call him that too, affectionately, when she disagreed with him. "Have it your way, Vicar," she'd say, closing her eyes.

Pete had once heard her tell him he should be careful how much he made the campers like him. "They're like Konrad Lorenz's baby ducks, some of them. They imprint on the first thing that catches their attention, and then they're yours for life," she said. "It can't do them any good. You'll be gone." Last fall, she had fielded the angry, embarrassed, and confused telephone calls from parents whose children had come home from camp and given all their possessions to the Goodwill, and in some cases some of their parents' possessions as well. Her husband had stood behind her chair, listening in and laughing. It took her the entire school year to convince him to be less exacting the following summer. "God gave me my wife to understand the world for me," he told people, and she sometimes joked that without her to weigh him down he'd rise straight up to heaven without even waiting to die. Then he'd correct her theology, and she'd pinch his ear. Pete respected his mom instinctively, but he didn't work at pleasing her like he did with his dad. She was always in the background. During the summer, she rarely left the house. She ate few meals in the dining hall and did not go to the bonfires.

On the fourth night of every week, Pete's dad gave an important talk in front of a bonfire in the amphitheater, and afterward lots of campers always accepted Christ. He would come home blustering and radiating, and talk with his wife for a long time. Though she never attended, she had never gone to sleep after a bonfire without hearing about it. They would sit in chairs side by side on the back porch, and he'd tell her how many, who, and what they were like. Pete would fall asleep with their murmuring voices drifting through his window.

Fourth nights spooked Pete a little. His father would stand in front of the fire, his long, flickering shadow falling across the benches and onto the pines. Behind him, a column of swirling ash rose from the blaze, the flakes floating upward into the dark. He would call kids forward by name, ask them questions, stare into their eyes, and pray with them. Kids cried, and other kids came forward to lay hands on them. Kids were filled with the Spirit, which made them stare and quiver and confront their friends with divine messages. Giving or receiving a message like that made a person act funny all week. That summer, Mike was first. Pete's dad put his hands on Mike's shoulders, and they looked into each other's faces for a while and spoke in low voices until they were both nodding and smiling together. Pete guessed it was a good thing. He had watched from the woodpile, picking at the ashy scars on his knees. The first time he saw a fourth-night bonfire, he wondered whether he was really saved, because no such thing had ever happened to him, and later he asked Jesus into his heart again just to make sure. After a while he decided that things were different for him because of his dad. Maybe his revelation was spread out over his whole life, a little at a time, so that it never seemed like a big deal.

He did feel, when he was alone, that God was there with him, interested in him, and this was an idea that gave him some peace and also some fear. On one particular day the summer before, he had been sitting by himself above the rock-climbing face, near the place where the lines were anchored to three wizened, stunted old trees that grew out of cracks in the rock slope. Below, he could hear climbers calling out to their belayers, and the belayers shouting encouragement up to the climbers, but he couldn't see anyone; the slope plunged into a face ten feet away, and all he saw were the tops of the trees, and farther away the roof of the cookhouse, and beyond that the other side of the lake. He'd been minding his own business, thinking about going back to school in a week or two, when it occurred to him as it did from time to time that God, who heard all his thoughts, was hearing his thoughts at that very moment, but instead of seeming fearsome and mysterious as it usually did, the idea seemed perfectly ordinary and natural. Pete felt as if he'd finally given up on trying to pull off a fantastic and increasingly complicated fib, and some deep, rustling movement began far away inside himself, but soon he felt afraid, and the movement subsided. His father had probably been praying for him again.

Lately he had tried to make the feeling come back. He would sit still in remote spots and wait, but nothing happened. Once, as he stood in the cedar grove at the far end of the farthest trail, Meg Holloway walked by. She came out of a part of the forest where there wasn't a path, and she said, "Hey," as if they were on a sidewalk and not at the loneliest spot in the wilderness. Pete couldn't think how to answer, and Meg shrugged and kept walking.

Meg Holloway made that summer different to Pete from any summer before. He tried to sit at her table whenever he could, and since she wouldn't eat, he didn't like to eat in front of her. He became thinner. Even his hands and feet got thinner, and he could see his own tendons and bones. Because she'd come one week late to camp, Meg was the new girl all summer. Word was that her parents were atheist psychology professors who had sent her to Loud Lake to observe Christianity in the field. She had a lot of curly hair and wore silver rings on all her fingers and some of her toes. She looked permanently bored, and her dense, baggy clothing concealed her shape. The other campers regarded her as a spy. Her counselor, Gravity, was forever hunting her down during activity periods, finding her in the empty kitchen with a paperback, or lying on a boulder by the lake. Pete's father had tried several times to talk to her.

One day she had turned up missing from leather bracelet-making, and Gravity was just going off to search, when Pete saw his father motion to her to stay put, and he went instead. On the back porch after dinner that night, Pete's father asked his mother if she knew who Meg was. Pete was upstairs in his room, almost getting a station on the ancient radio. He'd made extensions of aluminum foil for the antennae. The reception was best when he held one antenna, touched the wall with his other hand, and stood absolutely still. There were voices, a man's and a woman's, impossibly muffled by static. He let go and adjusted the dial. He heard abrupt fractions of words, a blare of music, then a white hiss.

When he heard his dad say Meg's name below on the deck, he turned off the radio and the light. The back deck was built on stilts over the water, directly below his window. "The one with the army boots," his mom said.

"The faculty kid," said his dad.

"They do mean well."

They were both quiet for a moment. "She seems special," his dad said. "Important to reach. There's something about the way she looks at you that's . . . Does she seem special to you?"

Pete went to the window. His parents stood close together in the half-dark below. "I don't know, honey. She seems like a normal kid, an outsider, but there's nothing odd about that. She's one of those people who need space." His mom's voice was whispery again. "You know people like that."

"I've been trying to get her to talk to me, but she's not having it," he said.

"Really?" She set her coffee cup on the rail and put her arm around him. Above, Pete drew back from the window.

"I've practically been stalking her."

"If you're starting to make her uncomfortable, you'd better leave her alone. I know you, but she doesn't know you. There's no telling what she thinks you want."

"Geez, I wasn't—" Something small and wooden clattered on the deck and rolled away. His father had dropped a napkin ring. "I hate it when you say stuff like that." Pete laid his folded arms on the sill. His arms had turned harder since he'd quit eating. Skipping meals made his whole body feel sharper and more adult. Meg still wasn't eating either.

"I'm just pointing out how it might look," his mom said.

"I don't like that you can even think that way."

"It's how most people think, Vicar," she said softly. Waves gently lapped the wooden pilings below the deck. "You should be glad you don't," she said. They were both upset. When his dad said Meg was important to reach, Pete knew he meant saving her.

A day or two later, coming back from the boat shed in the

afternoon, he met Meg walking toward the south trail with Mike. Since they were two and he was one, Pete stepped off of the path to make way and stood under some low fir branches. Though they passed only five feet from him, they never looked his way. Mike never took his eyes from Meg, who looked straight ahead, unsmiling. This was the first time Pete had seen her alone with anyone, and he remembered that she'd called Mike's scar stupid on her first day at camp. He hoped she still thought so. As the pair stepped into the thicker trees, Meg tucked an invisible strand of hair behind her ear and glanced at Mike, and Pete saw a quarter view of her face. Her smile was nervous, and he'd thought she breathed in excitedly.

That evening Pete made his plan to go out on the lake. He would go to the other side to sit and think and pray and watch the sun come up over the camp, and then come back while his dad was still on the dock. He knew that his dad would have to punish him for breaking the rule about being on the water before breakfast, and he knew that the punishment would probably be helping wash up. He liked working in the steaming industrial kitchen, slamming racks of dishes around, splashing water and listening to the cook's R & B. And his dad would not actually be angry. His dad said often that when you broke men's rules you had to take men's consequences, but better men's consequences than God's. Pete imagined what his dad might say at breakfast. He would boast by pretending to complain about how stubborn Pete was, and how committed, and he would think, just like me at his age. Pete wanted people to say that he was a spiritual boy, just like his father was a spiritual man.

Pete also imagined he'd have to hear his dad's praise and look stupidly into his oatmeal. He wasn't good with comebacks. At times like that, he knew he was letting his dad down. If only he could make a good story of his trip, the way Mike had with the bird scar on his wrist, everybody would like him. Pete's own scars, his congenital knee patches, seemed bland and incoherent by comparison. They weren't even scars really, just flat, blotchy discolorations. They had no story and no meaning, but there they shone on his brown legs, a stupefying pair of peeling white spots.

Pete was at the middle of the lake when the wind became stronger and the boat began to lift. He started scanning the opposite shore for a place to land. The sun wasn't up yet. He wanted to stay clear of the spot where a stretch of road was visible, where there was a restaurant, the only other building on the lake. He saw another boat ahead and glanced automatically at his watch, disappointed that anyone else was awake. It was quarter to five, still long before breakfast. He gained on the boat, which was also heading away from camp. It was a camp canoe paddled by one person, a girl. She had seen him and kept glancing back, but didn't call out or wave. She was paddling too fast, not taking the glide, and the waves rocked her. She seemed not to want anything to do with him, but the lake was big and empty, and it would be civil to see how she was getting along. Civil was his mom's word. Maybe the girl hadn't expected the wind. Rescuing someone when he had gone out to pray could be better than going out to pray by itself.

As he approached, he pulled in the sail. The girl's hair was tucked inside the hood of her sweatshirt, and he could see flashing silver rings on the back of her hand. Meg Holloway. She held the paddle too close to the blade, and half her sleeve was black with wet. She must have known he was alongside, but she didn't look. "Coming alongside," he said.

She turned. "He speaks." She'd been crying, and her face was wind-chapped. He pulled the sail in and coasted. In the bottom of the canoe were a large army duffel bag and a small backpack covered in black beads. He tried to think of something to say. "You're Bonds's kid," she said. He nodded. "You're out awfully early."

"Are you doing okay?"

She shrugged. "You have a camp name, don't you? Salt."

He picked at some splinters in the tiller. "My real name is Pete."

"You don't like your camp name?"

This was going all wrong. They were supposed to be talking about her.

"You should tell people if you want to be called Pete."

"That's the point of camp names though," he said lamely. He felt ashamed for letting people call him by the wrong name all those summers. "Where are you going?"

She began to paddle halfheartedly, and the wind pushed her off course. Pete offered to show her how to adjust her stroke, and when he reached for her paddle, she looked at him suspiciously and tightened her grip, and it occurred to him that she shouldn't have been running away from camp, and that if he took her paddle away he could grab her painter and tow her home. His dad wouldn't do it that way. His dad would convince her.

"I hate camp," she said.

Pete did not love his father's camp. He liked school better than summer vacation. His mom seemed more alive at the house in town. She talked more at dinner and smiled at his father more often. But Pete had spent every summer he could remember at camp. It wasn't something he hated or liked. It was home.

Meg went on. "I hate the singing, the praying, people going batty and crying all over the place, the skits. I'm not staying two more weeks. And my cabin. Nice of them to pray for me, but it's not like I need extra cosmic forces in my life."

Pete could see that Meg had Issues of Faith. His dad talked about how to help people with this. He would practice on his wife, and upstairs Pete would listen, with the radio off. His dad would prove loudly and articulately that there was a God whose very existence demanded praise, and then Pete's mom would cross-examine him. All Pete could ever hear of his mother's argument was a low murmur. He looked back toward camp and thought he saw his father on the end of the dock, starting his morning prayer. He tried to think of what his dad would say to help someone like Meg. He remembered something he'd once overheard. "How could the world be so beautiful if there's no God?" he said.

Meg looked at him as if he'd just appeared. "I never said I don't believe in God. And do you really think this world is beautiful?" She didn't miss a stroke.

His ears got hot, and they were both quiet. They had passed the center of the lake by now, and were nearing the other shore. Pete looked at Meg's left shoulder and inhaled deeply. "Still, Jesus Christ died for you on the cross, and you need to—"

"—accept him as my personal Lord and Savior." She paddled faster, tearing the water. "Listen, you're a very nice kid, and I appreciate your concern, but I know about it already. I've taken it under advisory." Pete felt crushed, and he must have looked it, because when she spoke next her voice was kinder. "But you're much nicer than some people. Nicer than everyone, actually, and if I were in the mood to listen, I'd much rather listen to you than any of them. But do me a favor and go home now, and when you get there, keep your mouth shut."

He continued to scull the Laser alongside the canoe. "Sorry," he said.

She pushed out her lower lip and blew her bangs out of her eyes. "I'm sorry too. It's becoming a sore spot. I know you're just doing your job." She paddled in silence for nearly a minute. Then she said, "Do you actually like living here?"

"We live in town during school. Mom likes that better." He wanted her to know all about his mom. They would have liked each other. "She's a teacher. Seventh grade."

"I've met her."

Pete wondered how Meg had met his mom, but this seemed private. His mom was a private person. "What are you going to do when you get across?" he asked.

"Going to stash the canoe at the restaurant, hitch to town, then back to the city."

Pete was impressed. "Are your parents there?"

"Yes."

Dark lines swept across the surface of the water ahead. The wind was beginning to dance and shift. Pete tried to imagine what atheists were like. "Won't they be mad you left?"

"They'll probably ground me, but my dad will brag about me to his friends."

Pete nodded. "My dad would do that too."

"He'd like it if you ran away?" Her voice was dull, unbelieving.

"He likes for me to break rules. I know it's weird." She

studied him more closely than before. "I'll have to do punishment for being out here, but I won't really be in trouble," he said. He cinched the boom down a little farther and tried to think of what his dad would say to Meg next. Probably he'd keep asking questions.

"Your dad will be impressed," Meg said. "He'll be glad you had this experience."

"I guess so. Are your parents really psychology professors?"

"My dad is. My mom teaches at the same school as yours." She was short of breath, and her teeth chattered. She must have been on the water much longer than he had. "They both wanted me to have this experience."

"Like an experiment?"

"No, not so perverse. They just wanted me to see it, in case I might like it." She let the canoe coast. "Except if I did like it, I think they'd be embarrassed." Pete didn't see why, but he wished he could help her feel better. She looked cold and miserable in the canoe.

"My dad gets embarrassed when I'm too quiet," he said.

She smiled a shivery, white-lipped smile. "Mine too. And my mom. They want me to be more of a tomboy. You know, no Barbies." She laid her oar across the gunnels. "I'll tell you something. I'm not leaving because of your dad. He's okay. I don't really hate camp. I'm leaving because of this guy Mike."

"I don't like him either," said Pete.

She smiled her shivery smile again. "I thought I was the only one."

"Mike is how my dad wants me to be."

"Mike's a fake." She looked as if she were weighing whether to say more. The canoe had stopped. He watched the water. She pushed her sleeve back and began to paddle again, slowly now. "I got tricked," she said, and that was all. Pete thought of his parents' talk on the deck, the vague, unmentioned things that upset them both. "That's all you need to know," she added. He realized he'd been staring.

The distant figure on the camp dock behind them seemed to be standing now, hands on hips, scanning the water. Pete wanted to stay out on the lake a little longer just talking with Meg, but he knew he wouldn't be able to say the right things before they got to the other shore. Only his dad could say the right things to her. "Just let me show you something before you go," he said.

She rolled her eyes and handed him the paddle. He'd known she would. She trusted him. Sadly, he released the sheet and shoved the boom leeward. The sail snapped full, and he began to overtake the canoe. "What are you doing?" she said.

The Laser swept forward. As he passed her he leaned out, and without meeting her eye, picked up the canoe's painter. "You absolute rat," Meg said. She looked up at the sky. "I am so flaw-lessly naïve that there is no hope for me." Pete cleated the painter to the Laser, watching the wind patterns on the lake's surface. When the line was taut, he came about hard toward camp and yanked in the sail. The canoe followed the turn and almost cap-sized. Meg clenched the gunnels. She didn't shout, but he could hear every word across the span of water. "I thought you were like your mom. Did you know she let me hide in your kitchen during bonfire? I bet your dad didn't know that either." But she was wrong. Pete was not surprised at his mom. She was that way.

Air roared across the side of the boat, cutting through his wet clothes. Meg crouched in the canoe's bow, trying to untie the painter's weathered knot. He could just hear her voice. "I should

have known he sent you. You're just like him. You and Mike both."
Pete felt like nothing, like a dry twist of lakeweed on a docked
hull, light enough for the wind to blow away. Towing the canoe,
the Laser moved sluggishly. He wanted to tell her all the ways he
wasn't like his dad, how hard he had to work to be even a little bit
like him, that the difference between him and his dad was way,
down deep inside, that really he was like her. He couldn't drag her
back. He didn't care whether it was right or wrong.

He released the sheet and let the air spill from the sail. Both
boats glided to a stop. They rocked and drifted, bumping against
each other gently, blown backward by the wind. Their hulls
made a deep thudding sound. Pete looked at his ash-colored
knees, and at Meg, who tore at the painter knot with white-cold
fingers, her face hidden by her hood. He watched until she
looked up. "I'm not like anyone," he said. The fierceness went out
of her face. She let go of the knot and sat back down in the
canoe. Her shivering had stopped, and she breathed hard, her
mouth open. They were exactly in the middle of the lake.

Crows flew overhead in a long, noisy line, wheeling and rising on the wind, falling out and reforming, flying east toward the
day. There were so many that their procession began and ended
beyond the horizons, spanning the whole sky like radio waves.
They kept coming and coming out of the west. Pete tilted his
head back until he saw only sky and crows. Something was moving over the water around them, like the wind but not wind, and
not crows, something he could nearly feel. It was right alongside
their boats, some shape or shadow beyond the periphery of his
senses. He wanted to look, and he felt sure that if he tried, whatever it was would disappear like a faraway radio station when he
let go of the antenna. He kept looking up, hearing the crows and

the hollow tapping of the boats. The cold air went right through his sweater. Meg was quiet, her breath calm. He remembered his dad saying that God is relentless, that he is always with us.

He looked. Nothing was there except boats and air. "It's a strange lake," Meg said. She put her hood back. Whatever it was had already begun to seep away. God would always be shy with him, forcing nothing. He uncleated her painter and threw it back into the canoe.

"It's real," he said. The thing was gone.

"A really strange place. Beautiful, though," Meg whispered, hugging herself and looking at the sky around them. She took the paddle and began to push the canoe away. Pete drifted, watching. She moved awkwardly, still not taking the glide, but the wind had shifted and was no longer interfering. The line of crows ended. The last of them crossed the sky and disappeared over the dawn horizon, circling and dodging each other in flight, rising on an updraft like bits of ash. At breakfast, he'd eat. He felt hungrier than he'd been in his life.

The wind came from the east, from camp, and the Laser keeled hard as Pete cut his oblique path home, heading first to the right of it, then to the left. He braced his feet under the strap and hiked his weight far outside. Without the canoe, the Laser rode high. As he neared the dock, he saw the outlines of three people hugging themselves in the cold morning. Mike and his father stood side by side, dressed and ready, as if they'd known this would happen. His mom was in her bathrobe. He cleated off the main sheet and leaned back, feeling the spray soak his clothes. He had nothing to tell any of them.

MARY KENAGY is the managing editor of *Image*, a quarterly journal focusing on the intersection of art and faith. Her fiction has appeared in the *Georgia Review, Image,* and *Beloit Fiction Journal,* and is forthcoming in the anthology *Peculiar Pilgrims: Stories from the Left Hand of God*. Her awards include an individual artist's grant from the Seattle Arts Commission and a special mention in the Pushcart Prize Anthology. She teaches fiction writing at Seattle Pacific University.

EXODUS

JAMES CALVIN SCHAAP

THE STRENGTH OF "EXODUS" LIES NOT JUST IN ITS CLEAR-EYED, matter-of-fact storytelling, but also—and more importantly—in the way a rough-edged father, clueless to what it means to truly love his wife and children, finds the faith and courage needed in this moment of crisis. That courage, not only to see his daughter and her husband as the lost souls they both are, but also to see himself as a failed father desperately in need of learning the love necessary to begin the healing of his fractured family, makes "Exodus" a story worth measuring against our own understanding of the ways in which we love those with whom God has blessed us.

—BRET LOTT

EXODUS
James Calvin Schaap

E ven though it came first, Nebraska seemed the longest
stretch, land so flat and ordinary, so dark green in August
along the Platte, but only the start of a long trip he and Eleanor
had taken—what?—ten times and even more. Coming up on
the silhouette of the Rockies was always a thrill otherwise, the
mountains in an outline of haze, Pike's Peak on the right when
finally you turn south to New Mexico. That pretty red rock he'd
missed in the darkness, driving all night, the dawn finally coming up in his rearview when he'd turned west again from
Albuquerque. Then, desert country so naked he felt forever
guilty about what the white man had done in giving it up like
some prize to the Indians. A whole day and a whole night he'd
spent on the road before that three-hour drop-off from Flagstaff
to Phoenix, a road where you spend more time footing the
brake than the gas. A long, long way he'd driven, even though it
didn't seem that far now that he was there, and he never once
got tired, because the Lord knows this was no pleasure trip and
he didn't spend a moment sight-seeing. It was a good thing he'd
bought that Travelall for the boat, because he needed the space
to move Janna's stuff back—and the kids.

Wilfred Staab had his own reasons why his daughter's
marriage had failed, and it had less to do with Craig's drinking than it did with what his son-in-law did for a living—
police work. Television said it all the time, how cops couldn't

25

come home without dragging the job along; *but it wasn't just that either*, he thought, since nobody worth his salt can go home and turn it off just like that, whether it was laying concrete or raising hogs or catching crooks. It wasn't just being good at what you did; it was what Craig did specifically— being a cop and always having to see so much evil. *That's what did him in*, Wilf thought. That's what made him drink, and that's what did in their whole dream of living in Arizona— Craig and Janna, who'd hardly ever been out of Iowa, and their two little ones, who, since their parents had moved to the Promised Land, had hardly ever been back home.

He parked the truck in front of a 7-11 across the road from the station where he stopped to refuel, then went inside and asked for quarters, five bucks' worth, even though he didn't mean to make a long call, just to tell Eleanor he'd arrived. Almost twenty-six hours, straight through, but he wouldn't have to tell her how long, because Eleanor would know the minute the phone rang.

The instructions were in two languages, one of them Spanish, but the place was full of Mexicans, jabbering just like Vietnamese used to back in Saigon, as if they were all hard of hearing. He knew what kind of target he made too—this old, overweight white guy driving a Travelall with Iowa plates—easy tourist pickins, and he'd heard far too many of Craig's horror stories, so many in fact that if Craig were his own boy, he'd have told him to cool it with the blood and guts. Back home, Craig could get a crowd in church or at the bowling alley or anywhere downtown inside five minutes, everybody wanting to hear what life was like for a big-city cop—all the gory details, how people are pigs.

Scared?—*yeah, darn right scared*, he told himself, just like

Vietnam. *I'm a fish out of water here*, and he'd have likely told the operator exactly that if those three hombres standing by the air hose had come any closer while he had the phone in his hand. Scared?—*sure I'm scared*, he told himself, but mad too, and full of hate, and not for them either.

Even the operator was Mexican. She told him that he couldn't use quarters on this pay phone, that if he'd like to call long distance, he had to use his card or else reverse charges. "I don't have a card," he told her. "Then reverse charges," he said; "make it collect," and immediately he felt dumb for not thinking of it himself. So now what was he going to do with a pocket full of quarters jingling in his pants like a come-on?

"Your name, sir?" she said. Behind her voice, the phone back home was already ringing. He glanced at his watch, then remembered Iowa was an hour ahead.

"Wilf Staab," he said, "S-T-A-A-B. But she'll know my name—it's my wife I'm calling."

The phone line bleated three times before Eleanor picked it up.

"I'm here," he told her after the operator let them alone. "You know where we always get gas? I'm across the street." One of the kids whipped an empty bottle into the air. It turned and gleamed in the bright lights and crashed in a dark parking lot next door. "She call?"

"Four, five hours ago or so. Wondered when you'd get there," Eleanor told him. "She's not crying. Seemed to me the kids were quiet—at least I didn't hear 'em."

"You okay?" he said.

"Worked my fingers to the bone on that couch of Eric and AnnLynn," she said. "You should'a let me come along, you know."

"A whole day in that truck with you, and I'd be dead," he said.

"You just make the nest. Keep yourself busy 'til you can't anymore, and then hit the sack. You can figure when we'll be back."

"What time is it?" she said.

"Hour earlier than it is up there," he told her.

"I'm not thinking well," she told him.

"Was *he* there?"

"What do you mean?"

"Was Craig there when Janna called?"

"No, but I don't remember, Wilf. I'm all upset. Now, you be careful—you hear me? You keep a civil tongue and all, and—"

"You know me. I can't talk. I'm just like Moses," he told her.

"Just bring her home, sweetheart," she said. "Make sure they got toys out when you leave so the kids got something to play with in the truck."

"Whyn't you make something out of those blueberries you bought?" he said. "Cobbler or something, something the kids'll like?"

"I got a ton of muffin mix all ready, and I canned some—"

"Just try to get some sleep, then," he said. "Everything's going to be fine. I'm going to bring your daughter home."

"It isn't fine, Wilf, and you know it," she told him.

"Well then, at least it's going to be better tomorrow than it was today. Think of it that way."

When he put down the phone, the first thing he heard was the whine of a siren, and he thought the same thing he always did when they visited their kids—how some people get used to that sound when they hear it all the time. He picked up the quarters and turned back to his truck in thick desert heat that always seemed to him unnatural.

The boys he'd seen at the side of the building were coming

his way—three of them, all of them taller than he was. He stood up straight like military. He hadn't dressed up for this trip. He'd gone home right away, as soon as Eleanor had come to where they were pouring concrete to tell him Janna said to come pick her up because she couldn't take it anymore. He'd filled up with gas, picked up some cash, and left town in a half hour—never even changed clothes, streaks of concrete still on his jeans. Right then he was happy about that. He'd have felt scared in Sunday clothes or a sport shirt. Work clothes were like fatigues.

"Mister," one of the boys said, "you got any cash?"

He'd already had his hands in his pockets, so he scooped out the quarters, all twenty of them, and rolled them in his hands until he had them in a stack, then grabbed the hand of the kid who'd asked and banged them in his palm. "Now, get lost," he said, "before I whale on your ass."

Scared?—*sure*, he thought, as he got back into the truck he bought just for fishing, but maybe he shouldn't have said what he did exactly.

He came back on the freeway from Grant Road, and wondered who could have ever guessed that after eleven years without kids, in a matter of days they'd have two back in town. Already a year after he'd started medical school, their son Eric had been courted by local doctors who wanted him to consider family practice in Neukirk. He and Eleanor hadn't tried to push him to come back—push *them*—because AnnLynn was a part of the decision, and it had to be what she wanted too. They wanted their kids back in town, but they wanted what was best for them first and foremost; and if Eric and AnnLynn felt some other town was a better option, then that was just fine too. Eleanor came home with the news even before Eric had called to tell them. She knew he'd signed because Doc Beckering told her. They acted surprised anyway when Eric called. Played the fool.

And now Janna. Not that they didn't know things were bad. Janna was always stubborn and hard, not one to complain but never one to throw in the towel. He pulled back into the traffic and remembered the night he and Eleanor had figured this boy—and Janna'd had her choices all right—that this Craig was going to be something special. They had lain in bed talking that night about how you couldn't choose your kids' mates, how really powerless parents were in such a big decision.

"You don't like this guy?" he asked her, looking up at the little glowing stars Eleanor had pasted on their bedroom ceiling years before.

"It's not that," she said. "It doesn't just come out of nowhere is what I'm saying. I can see why she loves him."

"What's he do?" he'd said.

"It's not so much what he does as who he is—"

"Okay, then what is he?" he'd asked.

She waited a minute. "He's a whole lot like her father," she said, laughing.

A long time ago already, when Janna didn't call and didn't write, and when finally both of them could tell she was faking the good times, when she seemed more blessed cheery about things than she'd ever once been, they figured it all for the worst. They weren't foolish, and they'd understood that at least part of the reason for leaving Iowa was this sense that maybe they needed a new start, some hope.

"He drinks too much," she told them a year ago. "Way too much, and I get mad too often," she said, her voice letting out words like steam. Wherever she'd leave gaps, Wilf filled them in with the worst—just as Eleanor must have on the kitchen phone. He had trouble trying to know who to feel for most—Eleanor, who was upstairs bundling Kleenex, or his only daughter, who probably had it worse than she was letting on, if he knew her.

"Maybe you ought to try AA or something," he said, because he knew Eleanor wasn't about to try to talk just then. "You talk to your pastor ever?"

Silence. "You know me," Janna says.

Nobody said a word.

"What am I supposed to do?" she'd said.

He's got the two women closest to him in all the world on separate ends of the phone he's got in his hands, both of them full of hurt, and the two of them leave it up to him to say the right thing, a man who can lay a three-car driveway in half a morning without a ripple but isn't worth a quarter at picking words out of the fray.

"You see if you can't work it out," he told her. "We're not asking for a miracle here, and if things don't get any better, you call. But he's your husband, and you swore to it." That's what he told her—something like that, only maybe not as pretty.

For a year, they'd never heard a word. Vacation came and went—the whole family back to Iowa. Nothing. No mention. Craig out with his old buddies, the three of them home alone at night, kids in bed, and still nothing. Janna could have spilled her guts right there in the family room where she'd grown up watching cartoons, and not a comment. So the moment she left, Eleanor cried.

"Just like my wife to think the sky's falling," he told her. They were standing at the door, the minivan barely out of the driveway. He had to take her in his arms.

"Never once the whole time did they even touch," she told him. "You see that, Wilf?" she said. "Never once."

"So?" he said. "They got two kids and they been married long enough. All that goosey crap is over."

She dug her face into his shoulder.

Kurtis is awfully young for glasses, Wilf thought, but cuter than a bug's ear anyway. So studious, he looked like his uncle Eric, the big-shot doctor. He sat on the couch with a book that looked way too heavy for a boy his age, never really said much when his grandpa showed up, just smiled. Right then, Wilf felt bad that he'd not changed; if he'd looked presentable the kids would have maybe taken a shine to him—although they hadn't seen their grandparents all that often, twice a year only since they'd been born.

Gracie was reading too, and it made him wonder about how all of this was affecting the kids, whether maybe they were hiding between the covers. She was a doll, toothless, that perfectly blonde hair falling light as down to her shoulders.

Janna was heavier again, not that he wanted to blame her. Everybody's got to take refuge somewhere. She was wearing a sleeveless blouse, the kind her mother wore around the house in the summer, and shorts that were too much a reminder of what she used to weigh. He hugged her, but it was awkward because it always was with Janna. Even when she was a baby, she didn't take to being held. Janna was a cat, Eric a dog. Janna had a mind of her own. Eric always tried to please—Eagle Scout, track star, whatnot. Janna wasn't a bad kid, but she'd never really given the sense that she needed her parents at all, not really. She had her share of hard times—seemed, sometimes, to choose them.

The first thing she did when he came in, after the hug and seeing the kids, was stick a cup of coffee in his hand and take him out through the dining room door and into the garage, where she already had the goods lined up—four suitcases, a Ninja Turtles duffel bag, two thick garment bags, and a pair of backpacks loaded with goodies for the trip.

"Where's *he*?" Wilf asked when they walked back into the dining room.

"Working."

"He knows?"

Janna ran a twist of hair back behind her ears and bit her lip. "He knows," she said. "You can bet he even knows you're here. He's got his buddies watching out for him."

"Cops?" Wilf asked.

Hate was in her eyes. "They watch me constantly—they do."

Behind her, up on the wall at the door to the garage, was a bulletin board full of kids' finger paintings, a list of numbers, and that ugly church picture of Grandpa and Grandma Staab Eleanor had sent.

"Don't tell me to stay, Dad," she told him.

"I didn't come all the way down here for nothing," he said. "I could'a told you that over the phone for a buck and a half."

She smiled.

"So what's the plan?" he said.

"You must be tired," she told him. "You must be shot."

"Not as young as I used to be," he told her. "It's too hot to lay cement anyway."

"I thought you quit for your shoulders' sake," she said. "I thought you sold the business."

"I did," he told her. "But Buddy's so busy that he can't do without me. That's how valuable I am, even with my shoulders shot."

"I thought you were going to do nothing but fish," she said. "Just dreams."

She shook her head like she knew about dreams. These little bits of the real her you had to pick up on—a smile once in a while, a tip of her head, a twitch in her eyes. That was her language, always was. She didn't give a thing away.

"I'm sorry about all this," he said. "Your mother and I—" He didn't know exactly how to put it. He looked up at that bulletin board. How in heck could he tell her how dead her mother felt about it, how she'd told him one night that she didn't think she could ever make love again, not with her daughter in the kind of big trouble Eleanor thought she was?

"It just didn't work, Dad," she told him.

"From the start?"

She shrugged her shoulders. "Maybe I shouldn't have married him. It was the big thing back home, you know—getting out of the house and getting married."

Up on that bulletin board she'd hung a picture of the Colorado Rockies with a little inscription—"Ain't no mountain high enough" and some Bible verse printed in such little print he couldn't read it without glasses. Had to be a Colorado mountain, Wilf figured, because no Arizona mountain was that kind of snowy beautiful.

"I can't anymore. I tried," she told him. "I just can't."

"I know you did, Janna," he told her. "You're our daughter."

"Mom told me once how mad she used to get at you. She told me about a time you had some kind of family picnic or something, and all day long, she said, how you played volleyball with all the men, while she had to run after kids and get this and get that, and put all the food out and whatnot, and how it wore her out, Dad."

Could have been a hundred picnics, he thought.

"She said you were coming home that night in all that heat—"

"In Iowa?" he said.

"Yes, in Iowa. It's worse in Iowa, Dad, believe me." That was the old Janna. "You were coming home on the blacktop from Neukirk. Mom says she can remember the exact spot. She says she'll never forget it. She says you turned to her and you said, 'Boy, that was fun. That was a great day.' And she says she was so mad she could have got out of the car and walked home. She says she'll never forget the exact spot on that blacktop, Dad, the exact spot where you said that."

"I did that?" he said.

"She says you never thought about her that day, chasing kids and keeping them happy. And I asked her how she could do it, and you know what she said, Dad?"

He shook his head.

"'You just gotta love him. I love your father'—that's what she told me." She looked him straight in the eye. "I don't love Craig," she said. "Not anymore anyway."

He couldn't get the garage door open because for a minute he couldn't figure out the lock. *Dang shame anyway*, he thought, people having to lock up garages. What kind of life you got when you can't trust the neighbors?

Once he got it open, he backed the truck up the driveway like a moving van, and inside a couple of minutes he had the kids' seats strapped in and everything loaded—whatever Janna had packed and plenty of room to spare.

"How come you took the bikes, Grandpa?" Kurtis said, flicking his glasses up on his nose.

"Your Grandma and I gonna want to try these things out," he told him. "These are beauties—"

"They're not for big people," the boy said, scolding him. "They're for kids."

He stopped dead in his tracks. "You aren't kidding?" he said. "Maybe we ought to leave 'em here then."

Kurtis pursed his lips. "Can I ride at your house?" he asked.

"All day long if you like—all over town too," he said. "Tell you what—why don't we keep 'em in the truck in case you want to tool around?"

"Okay with me," the boy said.

He picked up Kurtis and hiked him up on his arm. "Grandma says she's got blueberry muffins just growing in the kitchen. She says you shouldn't be eating anything all the way back to Iowa, just saving up room for those muffins."

"I love muffins," Kurtis said.

"Grandmas know that. They got lists of what kids like," he told him.

The boy pointed over his shoulder. "It's Daddy," he said, and he scrambled to get down.

The tall blond guy getting out of the squad car didn't look like the Craig he wanted to see. He remembered what Eleanor had said the first time she saw him after he got the job: "There's something about a uniform." And what was worse was the way Kurtis ran down the driveway just to get to his father, so much like he loved him.

Right then he'd have given anything for a trowel and a pail of mush. Rather than face the talking he was going to have to do, he'd have traded places with any mason in the whole valley, even though it was hot as Hades. *Like Jonah, or Moses*, he thought. He got those two stuck in his craw because the both of them complained to the Lord they couldn't get the words out.

Craig was down at the end of the driveway, sort of nuzzling his son's hair and looking for all the world like the father Wilf figured he wasn't. "So much like you," Eleanor had told him— and not just that first night either, but later, at the wedding, at the reception, when Craig and Janna walked from table to table, greeting the families and well-wishers, Craig standing there straight as a beam, looking like for a dime he'd rather be out somewhere filling silo, while Janna—who really wasn't all that much better at being sweetheartish—led him around like a mule. "You were the same way," Eleanor told him that night at the head table. "I was so mad at you."

He'd pointed at Craig. "It's all he cares about is the honey-moon," he said. "I can't blame him."

It was blue, the uniform, full of badges and whatnot, his waist thick as a roofer's with tools of the trade, the gun leaning away from his hip on the right side, things hanging all over. But neat. His hair was cut shorter than Wilf remembered, even styled, and he didn't look at all like a drunk.

"Kurtis, you run inside now," Craig told his son. "Go see what Mom's up to."

Wilf wiped his hands on his pants and walked out the open garage to meet him. Scared?—*sure*, he thought. Give me the words, Lord.

"I been thinking," Craig said when he came up. "You're my father too, you know? Not just hers anymore."

Wilf lifted his cap and wiped back the sweat. "That's true in the books," he said.

Craig raised his eyebrows enough to let him know he didn't like it. "You don't know the half of it," he said. "You don't know anything but what your daughter tells you."

Down there around his belt there was belly hanging already, and he wasn't even thirty-five, Wilf thought. Without the uniform, he wouldn't have been such a big shot, doughy in the face, red in the cheeks like an alcoholic, a man who looked like he could have had a heart attack long before his time.

"You don't want to hear the other side?" Craig said.

"I'll listen," Wilf said, "but right now I'm bringing my daughter home."

Something came up in Craig's throat. "We can lick this," he said, choking something back, "but I can't do it without her."

Wilf shook his head. "Well, you're going to have to, because I didn't drive all this way for nothing."

"I won't let you," he said, his eyes jumping from the brickwork to the garage and the bushes, the landscaping. "I'm not letting you take my family."

"You aren't the law this time," he said, "even if you're wearing a uniform."

"Then who is?" he snarled.

Wilf looked at the truck. "I guess it's me."

"On whose authority?"

"My own." He thumbed at his chest.

The kid was ripped up. You could see it. "I'm in counseling now, all right?" he said. "Dang it, Wilf, I'm doing what I'm supposed to be doing."

"Aren't you on duty?"

"Yes."

"Then clean up these streets, all right? Get out of the way," Wilf told him. "I'll be glad to talk about this once we get back home. I'll talk forever. But right now I'm getting her out of here, and there ain't nothing more to say."

"Don't do this, Dad, all right? Stay over tonight. Stay in our house here and we can talk. We can start over. We can sit down over coffee, and you can hear me out for once. You must be tired—"

"I got a full tank of what I been running on."

"Don't do this to me, Wilf," he said. "Don't do this."

"It's nothing I'm doing to you, Craig," he said. "What I'm doing, I'm doing for her. What comes after this is what the two of you got to do together." He rubbed the sweat from the corner of his lips with the back of his wrist. "Don't fight it now, because it's a done thing."

That whole time Janna was loading the kids behind them, strapping them in the backseat, checking through the stuff Wilf had loaded in the back of the truck. She threw in her purse and whatever other goodies she'd tucked along. Craig stood there in his uniform, his hands in his back pockets, looking almost like a baby, Wilf thought, sadder than anything. Maybe there was hope.

"Where's Daddy going to sit, Mom?" Kurtis said, once she had him in good.

That question hung in the silence like the sound of a siren.

"Mommy's got plenty of books," she said, showing the kids the big shopping bag up in the front seat. She climbed in the front seat.

"Daddy?" Kurtis said.

"You got a map?" Janna asked.

"I know the way," Wilf told her.

"You got gas? I got money," she said.

"It's already filled," he said.

"C'mon, Daddy," Gracie said.

Somebody had to say something, he thought. "Your daddy's coming later," Wilf said. "He's got to work, and then he's coming by himself."

Janna pulled the shoulder harness around her and locked it in place. Kurtis reached out with both hands for a kiss from his father, and Craig obliged, crawling into the backseat to give both a hug. Wilf stood outside the driver's side, Janna acting like her husband was some kind of desert snake. Then he went back to the garage and pulled down the door.

Through the back of the van, through the handlebars of the bikes, he saw Craig hold on to every last minute, and he was struck with the sense that the kids, both of them, looked more like their father than they did like Janna. Craig pulled himself back a bit from Gracie, touched his lip with his pointer and tapped the tip of her nose.

Janna turned and ripped out the seat belt, then stepped back out of the truck. "Get him out of here, Dad," she said. "Let's go. Get him out of here."

He stood at the back of the truck as both of the kids wouldn't let their father go. "Good Lord," he said to himself, "give me a map out of this." *Maybe I ought to stay*, he thought. Maybe he ought to just sit here with the two of them until things settled down or something. Maybe hauling them off wasn't the right thing to do. Twenty minutes ago he'd been sure that the only question was going to be how long all of this was going to take, how much time to pack the car and have them aimed back toward the Midwest.

Craig slowly untangled himself from his kids and backed out of the seat, stood there with the door open, looking at him. "Look at what you're doing to them," he said, just like that, talking way too loud. "Look once what you're doing to my kids," and then he pointed at them, as if they weren't kids at all, nothing with blood and a heart.

He shouldn't have said something like that in front of the kids, Wilf thought. He walked around the passenger's side, stepped between his son-in-law and the door, and shut it softly. "Now, get back in that car or go in the house or do whatever you're supposed to do," he told Craig, "or else I'm going to call a real cop."

Just like that he was all words. Craig blew out a whole lot of things in a tone of voice he shouldn't have used, *words that could have been forgiven*, Wilf thought, if it hadn't have been for the kids right there beside him, their doors and windows closed, but his own door still open like a gash. It wasn't the words so much as the pitch of his voice that the kids wouldn't forget, the sound of an animal wounded, their father.

Big as owls' their eyes were when he got into the truck. He started the engine as quickly as he could and pulled it into gear, but Craig ran out front and stood directly in the way, the look on his face rock-solid. Janna said, "That son of a bitch," and Wilf reached across the seat and grabbed her wrist. "Don't let me ever hear you say that about their father again," he said.

"Well, look at him," she said, eyes like notched spears.

He wanted to cry, not for himself but for all of them and the darkness all around that, try as you might, you never could quite turn your back on—hate, pure and simple evil he could feel even in the way he was, right then, pinching his daughter's arm.

"You're not going," Craig screamed, and he put both hands up against the hood as if by force of will he could stop them.

The kids don't have to hear another word, he thought as he got out of the truck again and shut his door behind him, keeping hold of the handle. "I'll run you down, Craig, I swear it," he said as quietly as he could. "You better believe me when I say I'm right now bringing Janna home."

"You'll kill me for what *she* says?" He pointed at the front seat. At least he didn't scream. "You don't even know the whole story, and you'll run me down?"

"I ain't going to hurt nobody here if you get out of the way," Wilf told him, slowly, quietly. "What I'm saying is, soon as I get back to Iowa I'll call you and we can talk forever. But right now, I got to leave—*we* got to leave."

"Then leave my kids behind," he said.

"Who's going to care for them, Craig?" he said. "Who's got the time with you off to work? Don't be stupid." He pointed at the squad car. "Get back to work. Once things cool off here— tell you what, I'll pay for a ticket. You fly home."

Craig took his hands off the hood but stayed in front of the truck, backed off just enough for Wilf to think it was his turn to act, so he threw open the door and jumped in without looking at his son-in-law, as if trusting him to give it up. But when he got back behind the wheel, Craig still held his ground.

Janna should never have done it, but she did. She rolled

down her window and screamed at him. She said, "Get out of the way." That's all, nothing else at first, but it wasn't so much what she said either as the way she laced those words with hate. "You son-of-a-bitch," she screamed at him, "get out of the way." Right in front of the kids.

Whatever it was that set him off so fast he didn't even change clothes back in Neukirk, whatever force pushed him to drive down here as if going to Arizona was a trip to Sioux Falls, whatever fire was in his belly all the way down went out maybe because Janna didn't seem so much his daughter, someone who needed him, as someone who needed something a whole lot more than anything a father could ever begin to think about providing.

He reached over, but at that moment, she yelled, "Go ahead," and he looked back up at Craig, who had that service revolver out and pointed right at Janna, his elbows down on the hood, the gun in both hands like you see on TV. "Go ahead," she yelled again. "You don't have the guts," she said.

And just like that, Craig stood up from the aim he'd taken, stood straight and tall, and turned that gun on himself, swung it up toward his mouth, and in that flash, that half-second, Wilf finally did exactly what he'd threatened, without even thinking. Even before Craig got that barrel in his mouth, Wilf hit the gas and the truck lunged forward like some tethered beast and knocked him down. There was no sudden clunk because Craig wasn't so much smacked by the force as he was shoved hard to the cement.

"You stay in the truck," he yelled at his daughter, and in those few seconds—three maybe—that it took for him to get around the hood to the front, he thought of so many possibilities that it seemed almost as if he might be the one about to die.

Concussion—and he saw Craig in a hospital bed like some swami, head in bandages. Pinned beneath the truck—he'd have to call on the Lord for the great strength, like farm women lifting tractors miraculously off their husbands. And even as his mind was riffling through scenes, he waited for a shot from that pistol that would have ended it in the way Craig had threatened.

What he saw before anything else was the pistol, maybe three feet from Craig's right hand, and the first thing he did was stick it in his pants. Craig was up on one elbow. His face seemed turned at an angle, like a dog who hears something strange in the wind, woozy as if he'd hit his head. "You're my son, all right," he told him, "and I'm not going to forget it." He picked him up by the shoulders and dragged him across the driveway and laid him in the grass. Then he got back in the truck, slammed the door, and the Travelall bumped softly down the end of the driveway as he turned it right, toward 35th Avenue.

"He okay?" Janna said.

He didn't dare look back at the kids, but he knew he couldn't let Craig lie there in the grass, helpless. He reached for the sweatshirt he kept beneath the seat, stopped the truck when he was alongside the police car, jumped out once more. "I'll call you, I swear," he said as he lay the sweatshirt over his son-in-law's shoulders. "We got to make something out of this," he said. "It can't end this way."

Craig pulled himself up and held his head with both hands. Wilf got to his feet and went to the car. If he could operate the radio, he'd call something in, he thought, so he opened the door and picked up the handset, tried clicking it, making it squawk, but there was nothing. He looked up and down the dash for some kind of switch for the lights, and when he found it, he snapped it on so red and orange flashes danced across the panel on top, sending colored lights banging off the front of the houses up and down the street.

He wasn't thinking so much about the kids when he got back inside because Janna was crying now, and for that he was thankful. He came up to the traffic on 35th and pulled into the right lane, going south toward Thunderbird. If he'd taken his work truck, he could have used the CB, but he figured the lights would pull in a crowd and somebody would see Craig there on the street, somebody would help him. Hadn't Janna said that his cop buddies were always looking out for him? It was all he could do now to get some distance on the whole mess, separate them for a while, cool the whole business down, bring some silence.

He saw Janna sneak a peek at her kids as they came to the freeway entrance, and he turned right into the cloverleaf and took that long curve so slow it seemed they weren't leaving all that trouble behind in the dust and the darkness of the desert. A pair of courteous eighteen-wheelers swept into the left lane to give him room, and he was on his way home.

The lights of the north suburbs gradually tailed off with each mile they passed in the silence outside the big city. He didn't have a thing to say to her. If there were some way he could draw a partition up between them, like a taxi, he'd have done it, because he didn't have a good thing to say to his daughter right then, nothing sweet. It wasn't at all like he imagined it, he thought, wasn't at all like Moses taking people out of trouble, wasn't that way at all, he thought, not the kind of joy he thought he'd feel doing the right thing.

Ten miles north of 35th and Thunderbird, the lights from the city finally stayed behind them, the tail-end of a long clear desert day still glowing over the ridge of mountains west, a ridge cut jagged by the purple dusk. The only thing lit in front of them now were green Interstate signs and here and there a billboard. He looked over the gauges in front of him. Tank was full. The truck rolled heavily, the engine pulling a bit, the gas pedal low to the floor beneath his boot, even though they weren't speeding and not about to, not with Craig's friends in uniform. They were going uphill, he remembered. All the way to Flagstaff it was a climb.

Perfect silence in the truck. Just so there'd be something, he turned on the radio and something country and western came up with so much volume he turned it down so there wasn't much more than a beat and faintest hint of melody. The faint reach of the interior lights wasn't enough for him to see anything of the kids in the rearview mirror, little more than a shine off Kurtis's glasses.

So he tried to run away for just a minute. He looked out to what was left of a sunny day. Somewhere out there west, he thought, if you go far enough into that ridge of mountains that wouldn't disappear, if you climbed high enough to get out of the desert cactus and those thick bushes that crawled all over the hills, up high enough somewhere, you'd find pines probably, and somewhere a lake, perfectly blue, like the sky above it, and about a thousand trout or walleye or pike or whatever, a little lake so still it'd be a shame to start a motor. You could take a canoe out there, pack some bait in, and a couple of rods, and spend a day talking to nobody whatsoever, nobody but worms and some fish and the Good Lord of peace in the wind and the stillness.

"Grandpa," Kurtis said.

He turned just slightly and laid his eyes on his daughter, who looked hard and cold. "Whatcha want, honey?" he said.

"I think it's okay if Grandma tries my bike," he said. "But maybe you ought to buy her one that's for her."

"We can do that, sweetheart," he told his grandson.

"But it's okay if she tries it. She'll probably like it," the boy said. "It's got three speeds."

"You're kidding," Wilf said.

"I got a horn, too, for beeping."

"For beeping, huh?" Wilf said.

"It goes *real* fast," Kurtis said.

"Maybe too fast for Grandma," he said to his grandson.

"May-be," the boy said.

Wilf Staab had prayed before in his life. In Vietnam, often enough. And when Eleanor had some female problems Doc Beckering had to explain in a tone of voice that made him worry far more than the words. Sometimes in church—often enough for Janna and Craig—and the kids, too, in the middle of all this darkness.

But here he was, going uphill in the darkness with just the faintest glimpse of day's end over the mountains west, and in his mind the words of his grandson who was starting to do what all of us want to do, he thought, what all of us try often enough: hide—starting already at five years old, the kind of dumping people try when they can't bring themselves to think about what it is that stands so directly and awfully in front of them. *It's in all of us*, he thought, *me too*. We all do it. And that's why he prayed what he did in the darkness, one little sentence to a God a man or a woman almost *had* to believe in. Inside his head, with nothing above him in the bright and clear desert sky, not even the roof of his fishing truck, he said, "Good Lord, make me, please, a whole lot better than I am."

It was almost thirty hours of driving, and he still wasn't tired. For an old mason with shot shoulders, he thought that wasn't all bad. But he knew that sooner or later, Janna would want to talk, and once again the good Lord would have to give him words to say it all just right.

JAMES CALVIN SCHAAP grew up in the small town of Oosburg, Wisconsin. He has two older sisters, and is proudly Dutch American and is part of the Dutch Reformed community. He has been a teacher and professor of English throughout his professional life, and has been an English professor at Dordt College since 1982. He has published several books, including novels, historical short fiction, meditations, essays, and stories, and has also had numerous short stories and essays published in a number of magazines, literary journals, and newspapers. He has two children and lives with his wife in Sioux Center, Iowa.

THINGS WE KNEW WHEN THE HOUSE CAUGHT FIRE

DAVID DRURY

THIS MANIC AND DELIGHTFULLY CLOSE-TO-THE-BONE STORY tells the truth of what it means to be a kid, from the accepted norms of brutality inflicted one on the other to the wonder and awe at unexpected joy and mercy and peace, no matter one's station or status. In his indictment of the Bainer family, the narrator indicts himself and every other kid on the block, and every parent too, but it is Alleray's tangible expression of faith—and her generosity to a neighborhood that doesn't deserve it—that resonates even in the deepest recesses of the heart.

—BRET LOTT

THINGS WE KNEW WHEN
THE HOUSE CAUGHT FIRE
David Drury

When the neighbor's house burned down, the massive motorized doors on the firehouse would not open. Why the doors jammed, why the fire trucks never rolled out, we of Magnolia Park Drive did not know. But we saw it all. The firehouse was less than a block away.

They were the Bainers, and while their house blazed and smoked, the rest of us gathered on the safe side of the street. It was morning, early and cold. First light in the sky early, frost quivering on the grass in anticipation of the sun. And as the adults took their positions, tightening bathrobes and blowing steam off coffee mugs, the newspaper delivery man came rattling around the corner in his station wagon, right on schedule, steering with one hand, launching papers from his window with the other. Fabulous terror on his face. I was just one kid, but speaking on behalf of all the neighborhood kids, we couldn't have been more ecstatic.

Calamity, tragedy, houses afire. You see, these are the daydreams that children dream. High-flying motorcycles, ninjas wielding samurai swords, the playground bully falling backward from a kick to the neck. Godzilla versus monster trucks. Bank robbers with two guns apiece. High-speed car chases that end with police vehicles lifting off the ground and spiraling through the air, lights and sirens a-blazing. Explosions that end with money raining down out of the sky. Wolves fighting bears. And houses burning to the ground. Even if those houses belonged to the Bainers. Especially if those houses belonged to the Bainers.

They were the bad neighbors. That was the thinking. But let me back up.

Here is a list of things:

BMW (him)

Sport utility vehicle (her)

Franchise coffee (whole bean, bought by the pound, kept in the freezer)

A Martha Stewart garden that you pay someone to tend

A clean house, brightly lit

A divorce

A family who downhill skis (with helmets on) and participates in organized community sports

A sixty-hour work week

A daycare you pay overtime

A babysitter who sleeps over

A dog with a new leash, who eats biscotti

The perfect suburb is a delicate thing. It takes a careful balance of ingredients—all the perks of being near to the big city without all the ugly side effects that would turn it into a strip mall or ghetto: crime, traffic, malt liquor billboards, diapers, and dog-food cans blowing around in the street like urban tumbleweeds.

Larkspur, California, was a cozy "high-income" community one bridge-length north of San Francisco, tucked in the shadow of Mount Tamalpais. The schools all won national awards; the streets were kept clean and safe. Then came the Bainers, tracking mud inside our paradise.

The family inherited the house from an aunt, and rather than sell it through real estate agents, they picked up and moved to California from one of the states in the middle. Brought their yellowing RV and parked it right out front. Because of an addendum in the "General Unsightliness" parking ordinance, they were forced to move it within three days, but not before the tow truck actually showed up.

Mr. Bainer brought daughter Allaray and son Kendall from his first marriage. Mrs. Bainer brought sons Kennel and baby Glen from hers. At eleven years, Allaray was the oldest and shrewdest. Kendall and Kennel, made brothers by the union of parents, not only shared nearly identical names, which would have been strange enough, but they had been born on the same day nine years earlier. We thought of them as twins. Baby Glen, old enough to walk but young enough to slobber, was born of giants. He was huge. A freak of nature. We clung to the belief that he outweighed his siblings.

The Bainers did not fit. You needed only catch sight of them to know it. Dirty bare feet. Tattered corduroys. Little-House-on-the-Prairie dresses worn over jeans. T-shirts with stretched-out neck holes and peeling iron-ons: The Incredible Hulk, E.T., Heroes of Motocross. And there was never a time they didn't have Kool-Aid-stained faces and purple-popsicle tongues. By comparison we must have looked like model citizens or department store mannequins, decked out in our squeaky white Reeboks and designer backpacks. We even accessorized.

They didn't look the part, and it was our duty to make them aware of it. What did I know? I was just a kid among kids. None of us tall enough yet to see that the world was bigger than Magnolia Park Drive. Each and every one of us with that secret desperate longing to fit. The transition from childhood to adulthood is one long freeze-frame moment when the needle has been pulled off the record, and there aren't enough musical chairs for everybody. Scrambling for a seat, everyone frets that it will be only a little while before he or she is squeezed out, exposed, rejected, the die cast, the number up, and the parents stand around ever-smiling in party hats, unaware of the magnitude of this.

There's no time for conjecture. You don't stop and ask why the need is so strong or how you will meet it. It's the law of the jungle. Survival instinct doesn't pause for introspection. It moves too fast to be held to the scientific method. It is spirit-material. It floats in the air. But fitting is everything. In high school, it would express itself in want of popularity or scholastics, or jackets with square letters and sports accomplishments sewn on so no one will forget. But for now, while we ourselves were searching to fit, we felt a sense of place in at least knowing that the Bainers did not.

They didn't look right, they didn't play right. They were mischief makers, always up to something. Digging holes in the neighbor's yard, walloping the sidewalks with golf clubs. Clearly they exerted their will over the Bainer parents. From our vantage point, they were never spanked, never put on restriction, never punished. They seemed happy, but had they earned it? Not on our Swatches. We wasted no time in finding opportunity to let them know it.

When we approached, all four Bainer kids were sitting on the curb, smashing worms with a rock. "You better not do that." We said with a scowl. "Why are you doing that?"

Allaray shrugged as if it didn't matter why.

"Because it's fun," one of the boys said without looking up.

"Where are you from? Why'd you move here? Can't you talk? Are you retarded? I guess you must be retarded then. Ha ha, you're retarded." Our volley of inquiries came so quickly, nobody could actually answer them. We laughed and pointed until we were oxygen deprived and had to catch our breath.

"We just moved in," said Allaray, biting at a hangnail.

"Didn't you hear us? We already knew that. Are you going to our school? We have a tree house, but you can't come. We have Atari, but you can't play. How much is your allowance? Where'd you get those clothes?" No response. Now they were absorbed in flattening a Hot Wheels convertible with the rock, after placing a worm in the front seat. When they were finished pounding, they smiled up at us as if we would be pleased to share in their accomplishment. Baby Glen licked the worm-smashing rock clean and squealed.

It was no use. We failed to coax out of them the tears we were looking for. No crying. No running home to Mommy. No swearing. No giving the finger. It was only as we walked away, when we threw rocks at their feet and told them to dance, that we got a response. Little Allaray picked up the rocks and, with a naive joy in her face, threw them back at us with deadly aim.

Allaray might have been a skin-and-bones little girl, but she also had the best rock-throwing arm we'd ever seen. A major-league-baseball arm. A catapult. She could have taken out a first-grader at forty yards. A kindergartner at fifty. And as she fired on us, she was smiling. Giggling. Hopping up and down holding her sides, stringy blond hair bouncing in her face, her brothers clapping behind her. She didn't throw like she was vengeful or afraid. She had no fear. She threw rocks for the fun

of seeing us run scared. Like our insults had been the anticipated opening volley in some time-honored game, some ritual
of glee, and now it was her turn to play. She was the happiest
rock thrower we knew.

Of course we ran away laughing victoriously, but beneath
the shelter of our little arms covering our little heads as the
rocks rained down upon us, we secretly felt cheated. Like the
sword got knocked out of our hands.

A day later, we tried again. The three oldest children were
riding their Schwinns in the street. We pedaled past them on
our lightweight shiny racing bikes. After a few passes we popped
wheelies. A few more passes and we were whistling inches from
them. We circled like vultures, teasing them, throwing insults to
the air, calling attention to their duct-taped banana seats, goosey
handlebars, and mismatched reflectors.

We reconvened, conceived a new plan, and dispersed again.
One of us called out that he had found a wounded bird in the
gutter. We all dropped our bikes and went running. The Bainers
followed suit, curious to see the find for themselves. That was
the cue. Three of us, myself included, made a dash for their
bikes, hopping on and pedaling away furiously. Not for our
own, not to steal or destroy, but just long enough to gloat and
play an innocent game of keep-away.

They stood there contemplating whether they would take
the bait and run after us. We passed back and forth, faces hot
with insults and wind. The Bainers just watched. They didn't
take chase. We made closer passes, swerving as if we might hit
them, making more direct our insults. They turned and ran into
their garage. To get their parents. Ha. They folded, I thought.
They would come back, sucking their fingers to stop the tears,

forcing their parents to intervene, opening new avenues of insult and humiliation for weeks to come.

But when they returned, it was not parents they dragged with them, but something else, down the driveway and into the middle of the street. A wooden structure pounded full of nails. A plywood ramp nailed to a stack of two-by-fours. And the Bainers looked back at us to see what we would do. They didn't have to say anything. We were suckers. We went straight for it, pedaling like mad for liftoff. It was only when my front tire hit the ramp that I wondered, What if this is a ploy? The collapsing ramp trick, the perfect revenge, and they would have the last laugh as I went sprawling in the street? But then I was airborne, my buddies right behind me, and on my wobbly landing, it was the Bainers, clapping and jumping and whooping like we were the Heroes of Motocross ironed onto their T-shirts. Our own cheering section. "More! More! More!" they squealed. "Higher! Faster! Farther!" I bit my smiling lip into a straight face. And hit the jump again.

The Bainer family stood on their lawn, fixed like pegs in a sundial, and watched their home go up. Only their shadows moved, flickering and lengthening as the house burned toward the ground. Their dog, Furler, stood beside them and whimpered. And we all sensed a final justification. Retribution. Revenge. We could barely contain ourselves. What goes around, man, it comes around.

"Move out of the way, kids!" Mr. Stuckey barked out the window as he frantically backed his Cadillac Seville from the street onto the driveway and into his garage, afraid, in his paranoia, that the fire might spread to his luxury sedan. Then he said two words—one started with a capital *G* and the second one ended with "it." Until Mr. Stuckey, I had believed that all old people went to church and never sinned.

Ash and cinders swirled around the Bainers, settling in their hair and on their sleeping clothes and obscuring them nearly from view at times. They were frozen there, like plastic figures in a giant horrible snow globe, the kind you shake vigorously to see white flakes swirl around a pleasant little cityscape and settle to the bottom. But the snow was black, and their expressions lacked that Christmas spirit that is always captured so well in plastic. They were the anti-carolers in a snow globe of shame— and it was God who did the shaking. For the eleven months leading up to this day, when the house was not on fire, the neighborhood adults had muttered similar sentiments with the same folding of arms and tsk-tsks in their appraisals that they were muttering now. That they didn't appreciate having a squalid unkempt wreck of a home framed in their picture windows. Unsightliness is next to ungodliness.

As the newspaper delivery man came upon the unsettling scene, his sense of duty must have been throttled by the pandemonium. He leaned on the gas pedal as he passed. We know because we heard the engine gunning. And in his confusion, his arm already crooked out the window with a thousand rubber-band bracelets waving in the wind, he let fly a paper with force and trajectory such that it sailed up onto the Bainers' roof. The paper promptly burst into flames and fell into the living room through the collapsing ceiling. We children were so enthralled at all the chaos, we cheered and did jumping jacks in our pajamas and bed hair.

We wanted to see the Bainer kids suffer. Just a little. No more than any other person. Just general panic and loss-type suffering. Learning life's lessons. We had been under their curse forever. We wanted fairness. Balance. But we weren't alone. Our parents were in on it too. They had their reasons.

Apparently the Bainer parents, who were rarely ever seen by us, were also rarely seen at community meetings, council sessions, and parent-teacher events. They attended no church, they gave to none of the local charities, they didn't frequent the local businesses. They seemed fine with letting their children wreak unsupervised havoc in public view. But improprieties in lawn care were the greatest of their sins.

If measured in terms of devotion and attention, the Bainers ranked among squatters, recluses, and heroin junkies when it came to lawn maintenance. They let the grass grow. They let the weeds take over. The front sidewalk was consumed, the path to their door impeded. The tallest weeds tickled their windows. The "It-Gets-the-Corners" sprinkler that was on the lawn when they moved in, hose snaking back to the house, had never moved and was soon swallowed in the undergrowth. A cloud of pollen and dander hung in the air. Allergy season hit our street hard. Something finally appeared on the town council agenda, and no wonder, considering that the moniker "Our Town Is a Clean Town" took larger billing than "Welcome to Larkspur" on the signpost erected at the edge of town. At first the council issued an official request that the Bainers cut their lawn, but nothing changed. Except that dragonflies came to nest.

In a show of smug solidarity, we local kids, with the trickle-down politics of our parents, came wielding scissors (household, fabric, safety, toenail). We stooped down and snipped at the grass, taunting with gestures that we intended to carry out the council ruling. At first, Allaray, with that silly smile, charged at each one of us through the weeds, a child torso coming at us like a cartoon ghost, driving us back and knocking us off our balance. She blasted a third-grade boy so hard he rolled backward, right off the sidewalk and into the street.

When we started closing in, Allaray improvised her reign of terror. She ducked down, out of our line of sight, then reemerged with the long-buried hose and sprinkler. She gripped the hose halfway back to the spigot. She lifted it up over her head and began swinging it around, the bulky sprinkler out in front, churning like a helicopter blade. Faster. Rustling the tops of the waist-high weeds. Her brothers, who were behind her, dropped to the ground. The rest of us moved back with a ripple, knowing that stitches and ugly scars would be branded on anyone who came in contact with the hunk of metal at the end of the hose. She swung it around. Faster, higher, letting out slack. You could hear the hose beating the air with a heavy hum and the sprinkler warbling and whistling its warning. There we were, gathered on the outermost edges of the lawn, the corners, out of the death radius, but still on the lawn when one of us realized the truth and yelled out, "It gets the corners!" immediately scattering us in a panic. Except me. I held my ground. I was not willing to let this undernourished girl rule us with fear.

I postured. I sneered. I tried to look undaunted, even though my muscles were prepared to bolt at the last possible second. I lurched forward a step as if I might take the offensive. That's when my foot came down wrong, on some toy or ball hidden in the thick grass, and I fell hard, flattening the weeds below me. The breath went out of me. On my back, looking up—that was the moment when I KNEW. The momentum, the trajectory, the angle of her arm and the arc of the sprinkler coming around like brass knuckles on a right hook. There was no stopping it. I would get what I deserved. In that half second I made eye contact with Allaray. And though I knew she could hardly change the laws of momentum now, much less want to, I'd like to think I saw a brief softness in her eyes, the slightest tweak in her wrist, a kink in the affectation of her rotor, the delayed release that saved my life. Instead of lodging in my temple, the sprinkler turned a few degrees north, whistling through the air, smashing through the Bainers' front window and landing on their dining room table. My buddies ran home, their siren cries of "Ooooh . . . You're gonna get in TROU-BLE" fading down the street behind them. Allaray Bainer stood staring at me. Our half second of shared silence lasted long enough to make me wonder if she really had missed me on purpose. And Kendall and Kennel shuttled through the weeds giggling, racing to see who could turn the spigot on first.

The council eventually exercised a more reasonable and effective tactic when it came to cleaning up the overgrown lawn. Volunteer firemen were handed weed whackers and clippers on a Saturday afternoon in August, paid from an emergency fund to give the house a once-over. The neighborhood came out, even set up lawn chairs to watch.

The firemen could have walked the few hundred feet from the firehouse at the end of the block, but they loaded up the big red fire truck with lawn mowers, trimmers, and the rest and pulled up out front. They went right to work on the yard. The tactic would have been an embarrassment to any other family in town, but the Bainers acted as though they had won a prize. At least the children did. They joined in the work. Kendall brought out very sharp adult scissors and stabbed and cut at the grass, until he swung too wildly and nearly stabbed a fireman in the knee. The other Bainer kids ran in circles through the grass, pulling up fistfuls of it and throwing it above them in a ritual dance. The Bainer mother came out with a tray of lemonade, gushing as though the volunteer landscapers were truly there of their own goodwill.

One of the firemen gathered the kids together. We could see him talking to them and shooing them toward the fire truck, and that was the moment our hearts dropped. The most undeserving kids in the whole county, and they get an invite to play on a million-dollar playground. The daydreams that children dream, when they are not dreaming of houses burning to the ground, are of living in the toy store and playing on fire trucks without adult supervision. To scramble unfettered and free over the smooth red surfaces, leave your breath on the shiny chrome gadgets, make fingerprints on the mirrors, tug on the handles, climb over the step-ups, slide behind the wheel, burrow and nestle in the hiding places. It was the Promised Land on wheels. We couldn't have been more jealous.

Meanwhile it was hot, and the firemen, now freed from ambling children, were ready to work. They pulled off their heavy coats and hats and set them on the sidewalk. They didn't seem to notice or care when the kids came off the truck to try on the heavy garments. Allaray struggled to button one of the coats while it was freestanding on the sidewalk like a big yellow teepee. Kendall's thin greasy head popped out one arm of the coat, Kennel's out the other. Finally Allaray slid underneath and her head came out the top. They looked frightening, like a melting girl giant with two heads for hands. Allaray reached out between buttons in the coat to grab a red helmet and put it on her head. Furler, freed for the day from his backyard collar, barked and growled at them while they stumbled up one side of the driveway, down the other, and into the street, where they eventually fell apart. Baby Glen saw all of this and tried to mimic them, but his head got stuck in the sleeve and he began screaming. While the two older brothers pulled him free, Allaray abruptly crossed the street and came over to all of us who had been watching. She was holding something in her hands and offering it to us. She had found a stash of candies in one of the pockets of the fireman's jacket, and went up and down the row of neighbor kids, placing them in our begrudging, outstretched little hands until they were gone. She crossed back and joined her brothers as they all donned fire helmets and head-butted each other.

When the firemen finished their exercise, the neighborhood folded up its lawn chairs and went inside to escape the heat. Disdain by way of yard irreverence was abated for a time. But yard irreverence would rear its head again and reach blasphemous new levels against a backdrop of cardinal neighborhood virtues that blossomed during Christmas season.

Our town was one of those communities where extravagant displays of light and sound and decoration were a matter of homeowner pride. A matter of communal pride, where a dizzying display of lights and Santas and angels and reindeer and holiday exclamations meant that the Christmas spirit lived here, and more so than elsewhere. We expected, I think, the Bainers to bow out of this to-do, owing to the notion that they probably didn't believe in Christmas, much less participate in neighborhoodliness. And for the first half of the month their property looked like a black tooth in our street's Christmas smile. But the Bainer kids finally caught on. Their first plan, since they didn't have their own stockpile of holiday regalia, consisted of stealing one item of decoration from each house and placing it on their own. That worked until 8 a.m. the next morning when all the neighbors came by and loudly snatched up their absconded items. The next plan was to utilize that which they did have. They spread their toys out over the yard, inside a corral made of Legos, army men, Hot Wheels, stuffed animals, and a Barbie with burned hair.

"Those are the shepherds," Allaray told us, first pointing to the army men, "and those are the wise men, and the animals, and that is Mary," pointing to the Barbie doll. Then she ran in the house and returned with the baby Jesus, a Cabbage Patch doll with crayon all over its face. She laid it in the center of the yard, gently resting its head on the sprinkler. Creator of Heaven and Earth, Savior of Lost Souls, Teacher of Army Men, Son of Barbie. The boys were busy tying flashlights to the shrubs to shine like spotlights on the nativity scene. At night, the Bainer crèche looked eerie, especially in the glow of all the rest of the lights on the street. But the biggest blow was yet to come.

Coordinators for Larkspur's annual Christmas Craft Fair were raffling off a delicate blown-glass Baby Jesus this year, hand-painted and detailed, wrapped in silk swaddling clothes. Blemishless Jesus. With jewels for eyes, and a hole in his back for lighting purposes. Everyone who came to the event got one ticket, and you could buy more for five dollars each. The elementary school was raising money for a new playground with scientifically engineered tanbark—the kind of tanbark that won't give you slivers and that makes you something-percentage safer from breaking your spine or neck, or someone else's spine or neck. The glass Jesus was the creation of a world-renowned glass-blowing artist, one of our most famous local residents, a man who never came around really, but spent a lot of time in Europe and drinking wine on his yacht. Baby Jesus raised the eyebrows of more than a few. The latest trend in holiday yard-spirit was to prove you knew more of the "real meaning" of Christmas and employ a manger scene with hay and life-size or mechanical moving animals and figures. A throwback. The glass-blown baby Jesus was going to make a nice prize pony for anyone who wished to not just one-up other yard display participants, but blow the competition out of the water. It was appraised at a value of between $5,000 and $9,000, and came with a motion sensor alarm, so that thieves or Bainers would be discouraged from selfish urges.

When the ticket was drawn and the number announced, bounding down front were none other than the Bainer children with the winning ticket in hand. The artist made the presentation and handed Jesus to them, pleased to the core of his philanthropic ego to see the jubilation of the recipients. Had he known the Bainers, he would have hesitated. Kendall grabbed Baby Jesus by one foot and hoisted him up over his head like a carnival prize. He ran around the room with the other kids chasing. We all sat stunned. They were going to break Jesus into a million shards or value him at less than he had been appraised. They had no consideration for the quality craftsmanship, value, and beauty of the piece of art with which they ran whooping with joy, shoelaces untied and flapping behind them.

The Bainers didn't sell Jesus. Maybe they didn't realize they could. It would have been for the best. The parents let the kids have him, and the kids went bouncing up a ladder and tied him to the chimney with lengths of yellow rope (stolen, we believed, from both tetherball poles at school). The ascending Jesus, with a flashlight in his baby backside.

Now, by holy and cleansing fire, God was bringing the hammer of justice down, and saying, "No more!" Parents shook their heads at the prospect of having a burnt-out black shell on their block for weeks and months to come. They whispered back and forth that they had seen this coming, what with the way the Bainer parents kept the house, and the way they probably let their children play with matches.

"It's too bad," our parents sighed. "It's a shame, and at Christmastime." But they wouldn't have had it any other way. This was the great purging, a judgment handed down from on high, things being made right again.

Only none of us was convinced that even now—with their house on fire—the Bainers were getting it. Leave it to the Bainer kids to rejoice in tragedy. To wear it like the "S" on Superman's cape. Little Kendall lay down and made snow angels in the two inches of black gunk that covered the lawn. He had feared the delights of winter were a thing of the past, gone forever when his family moved to California. After watching the cast of Sesame Street do snow angels in Central Park, Kendall mourned out loud, yelling that *he* wanted to do snow angels. He hadn't stopped yelling it for fourteen weeks. Now he saw his chance to do snow angels, be it in snow or wet black residue from his burning home. His parents didn't stop him. Kennel jumped up and down with glee and sucked on all ten fingers. Baby Glen clutched his mother's leg with one hand, and with the other reached for the dewy ash, putting it into his mouth one baby fistful at a time. Once he discovered that it turned his baby-white skin black, he rubbed it all over himself, on his face and diaper and up and down his mother's leg. Mr. Stuckey was swearing out loud again, fumbling with a ladder and tugging on the garden hose in his yard. He propped his ladder against the roof, careful not to set the legs in the garden plot beneath his window, and began climbing with the hose looped over his arm and tucked into his belt. He was shaking as he made his way up, trying to keep his balance as best an old seething man can, and his ladder rattled against the rain gutters. With his head cocked to one side, he yelled for someone to turn on the hose, and he began spraying his roof.

We squirmed with delicious excitement, and while our house-socks and pajama bottoms soaked up morning dew like thirsty trees in the grass, we listened for sirens. We never heard them. The firehouse doors did not budge. The shiny red fire engines did not come.

Mr. Stuckey noticed it too, convinced his roof would catch fire before the firemen ever arrived. He pulled hard to get a kink out of his hose. He yanked once and then again. The water barely trickled. He cut the air to one side and then the other as if he was doing karate with his old arms, a series of epileptic seizures aimed at unkinking the hose. Finally, with one mighty yank, reeling in an imaginary two-hundred-pound fighting sturgeon, he tore the hose right at the spigot and water gushed out, instantly drowning his precious garden. The floodwaters spilled over, carrying potting soil and flower petals into the garage through the eight inches of cat space in the garage door.

We looked back at the fire station. Where were they? We could hardly contain ourselves. Our thoughts were malicious. That the firemen were playing a well-thought-out prank on the Bainers. For having to come cut their lawn. The Bainers were facing the music. Reaping what they had sowed. The world made sense again.

The firemen must have sat in their trucks for a full two minutes, waiting for the doors to go up, certain that they would at any second. When it was clear that there was a problem, they got out of the truck and tried to manually lift the doors from the inside. We heard something, even over the roar of the fire and the snapping of timbers. We heard banging, men yelling. Then we saw them. Firemen pouring out through side exits like bees from a thumped hive. Swarming around the doors. Scrambling and tugging at them from the outside. Trying to free their rolling fire-fighting machines. It was the trucks that gave them strength, that made them firemen. It was the trucks that held the tools and hoses and power to form water into the kind of H_2O canon that could put out a burning house. They were useless without them. But the doors were too heavy.

When the firemen finally gave up, they barely knew what to do. They turned and came sprinting down the street, pulling on heavy fire coats as they ran, gripping things tightly—small fire extinguishers, loose hoses dangling, large shiny axes. They were dedicated civil servants to the end, but they were in emotional distress. It was written all over their faces. Panic. They'd lost their cool. They'd broken the first rule.

A fireman on the verge of breaking down and weeping in the road is a confusing and sad sight to see. Something from the pages of *Life* magazine or on a heart-wrenching television documentary, but not on your own street. However, here they were. Large men who had trained and lifted weights and dreamed the daydreams that young men dream—being a life-saving hero in the face of danger. These who had practiced CPR on rubber corpses, ridden in parades, who led school assemblies on how to not panic in a fire. They were running past our lawn chairs, sobbing loudly, dragging equipment behind them, the most frightened faces I have ever seen. One lost a boot while running. Others nearly tripped over themselves. They were out of their element. Emotion blistered on the thick skin and moistened their old-world mustaches. The tears rolled back from their eyes, dripping off their ears.

Groaning, crying, screaming. Gnashing of teeth. Visible regret. Profound sorrow. We wanted all these things, but we wanted them from the Bainers, not the firemen.

And, though no one ever knew for sure why, in that moment of confusion, little Allaray Bainer charged back at her burning home. She disappeared into the thick smoke. The Bainers' dog, Furler, cited in police logs for noise and meanness, broke character. Sensing this new desperation maybe, he stood in and crooned his own sad siren laments while the house crackled like a record player.

We couldn't know if any of Allaray's family would have run in after her. The firemen were arriving now, moving the family back and dashing in after Allaray. The firemen kept running in and out, asking Mr. Bainer if anyone else was inside. He plainly told them each time that no, everybody was here. The firemen, still unorganized, ran wildly, fumbling with their equipment and bumping into each other. They circled the house, kicking in doors and yelling. One of them injured a shoulder knocking down a door. Another stepped through a floorboard and fell headlong into a smoldering section of wall, breaking his leg.

When the smoke cleared for a moment in front of the house, we saw Allaray. Our mouths fell open. She was standing beneath the chimney, gripping the bright green yard hose, spraying it up onto the roof as best she could manage in the blinding smoke. She was focused. We stared, frozen, making no sound, too shocked to gasp or pull her back ourselves before a wall fell on her.

If Mr. Stuckey was watching her from his rooftop, he was certainly regretting his eighty-six years of life on this earth, for he must have been forced to admit he couldn't handle a Sears garden hose the way Allaray did—thumb pressed over the ring spout for maximum velocity, sweeping back and forth. She stood her ground until a fireman ducked into the smoke and retrieved her under his arm.

The fire, which had burned so intensely, began dying down now. There wasn't much left to burn, and the firemen finally were getting hoses on the flareups and smoldering ruins. The Salvation Army arrived and put blankets on the Bainers' shoulders. Firemen sat on the curb, hanging their heads and passing around a cigarette, and while the medics gave Allaray oxygen on a stretcher, the Bainer boys threw off their blankets and tromped through the ashes, round and round the chimney. Allaray, by her efforts it appeared, had saved the chimney (non-flammable), the front window (badly melted), and a jagged halo of roof around the chimney. Was Allaray a hero? Saving what needed no saving? But there it stood, nonetheless.

At the top of the chimney was the true, confirmed miracle— Baby Jesus, swallowed in smoke but still hanging on, his ropes blackened and frayed, but not burned through. No way it could have been from Allaray keeping them wet. The ropes should have snapped, the delicate glass object smashed against the ground. And in any case, Jesus should have melted in the heat, like the windows.

It was one of the neighbor children who told me that Allaray spent a night or two in the hospital. She was so close to the fire she had breathed in smoke and suffered minor burns on her face. They said that the only part of her face not red from her burns were two thin lines from the corners of her eyes to underneath her chin where a small but steady stream of tears had protected her eleven-year-old skin.

When the Bainers came back one last time a few days later, they pulled up in their drab, clunky RV and parked it right out front. The kids ran around while the parents sifted through the mess, looking for anything they could salvage. The kids found the blackened aluminum ladder where the garage had been and hauled it to the chimney where they leaned it precariously. Up the ladder ambled Allaray, bandages on her face and all.

We kids had seen the emergence of Glass Jesus. Stunned when the smoke cleared, only then did we so fervently wish he had broken, or melted and dripped into the rain gutters. I know I did. In a moment like that, why did I continue to wish suffering upon the Bainers? Why even after their instances of unfounded generosity and the preservation of my life by Allaray? Why, after the example of the firemen whose civic love overlooked grudges? What did the Bainers ever possess that made me so jealous?

As soon as the Bainers and the firemen had left on the day of the fire, we had stood around with knowing looks, asking ourselves who would be the first to attempt it. We children, pirates till death, wanted to loot Jesus for his eyes. Those precious gems would wipe clean under faucet water. But who would dare? We all argued about it and did rock paper scissors a hundred times or more, and who won it I don't remember because in the end we knew we were still afraid to do it. For the risk of playing in a danger zone full of splinters, nails, and glass? Maybe. For the punishment we would receive if caught? Possibly. For fears unstated? Most likely. The idea of casting lots for Jesus' very eyes gave us pause. Especially in view of the miracle we had all been witness to. The glass baby survived an all-consuming fire, suspended for everyone to see like a supernatural exclamation point atop the heap of burnt-out home.

But now I gritted my teeth and burned inside and cursed Allaray when I saw her positioning the ladder. Mine! Mine! It should be mine! I wanted to scream. But the decision was no longer mine to make, nor the rest of the neighborhood kids'. She would lay claim to the prize, the image of her final victory over us. We could only hope those jewels were burnt-up black coals after all.

Up Allaray went, and I seethed. She pulled on the ropes. Still strong. Still tight. She spit on her jacket and rubbed Jesus' face. The visage of the baby emerged from the soot, and the two little shining jewel eyes came alive. Curse words! The eyes had survived the fire intact, brighter than ever. The Bainers would have the last laugh. Allaray reached around Jesus and fumbled for the flashlight that had occupied the hole in his back. "Still here!" she yelled down to the others. Allaray turned the flashlight on. She admired the display while descending the ladder, and then from the ground. And the Bainer kids ran around in the ash until their legs were black from it, and they looked like legless floating ghosts against the dark mound of their former home. Beneath the lit face and eyes of Jesus, eerily affixed above them, they floated like transparent spirits. And then they piled in their RV and drove away, leaving the charred, but illuminated face of Jesus behind them.

DAVID DRURY is a writer and editor in Seattle, Washington. He earned a Master of Christian Studies degree from Regent College in Vancouver, British Columbia, and a Bachelor of Arts degree in English/Creative Writing from California State University East Bay. He and his wife, Stephanie, have two children: son Judah Crutial and daughter Rilian Flannery. David has also released two albums with his indie-rock band, Tennis Pro.

THE RESULTS OF A DOG GOING BLIND

REBECCA SCHMUCK

STORIES COME IN ALL FORMS, FROM ALLEGORY TO DOCUMEN-
tary, from epistle to fairy tale. "The Results of a Dog Going
Blind" carries with it no overt Christian references, and reads
very much like a Middle-Eastern fable, but the soul of this
story—its spirit and heart—reveals the deepest of truths about
the Christian faith: that even when our attempts to make straight
our way for ourselves and our loved ones fails miserably, there
is available to us, once we confess the sin of our self-centered
lives, redemption, and the means by which, in our blindness, to
begin to see.

—BRET LOTT

THE RESULTS OF A DOG GOING BLIND
Rebecca Schmuck

I t was a great disappointment to Jusuf, his son's sudden descent into blindness. One moment Shan was running across the cracked-tile kitchen floor of the Empress Hotel in Medan, Sumatra, his nine-year-old form weaving around their familiar sweating figures: Farid, whose very skin reeked of coriander and mustard seed, whose chest hairs held the spices of a thousand exotic countries; and Jusuf, his father, the cook with the talent for birds.

The next moment the saucepan had dropped. The world clattered to a halt, his son dropped to the floor, and Jusuf thought at once of a dog.

Shan had found the dog—came home with it, even—years ago, after it had made an unfortunate appearance in the middle of the road. Jusuf knew the moment it opened its eyes that the dog was blind. It explained, actually, quite a lot—how else does one end up in the middle of Jalan Surakarta, after all—and it put to rest his suspicions, concerns. When the eyelids had slid apart, there could be no mistaking. It was the first bad sign, the blindness of the dog.

Now he sat in the hospital, waiting. The doctors were suspicious—concerned—so it was against Jusuf's wishes that a scant two hours later Shan awoke.

"I am here, Shan. It is evening," Jusuf said quickly—an attempt to explain any darkness. "Do you know what happened to you?"

"I was hit in the head."

"Yes. You are in the hospital right now. The doctors here are very good. They will have you better in no time, you will see. Listen," he rushed, "I was just thinking of your job. You must improve quickly so that you can continue with the chickens."

Shan nodded and they sat in awkward silence. The last vestiges of sunlight outside slipped away, and Jusuf felt his pupils widening, straining to see his son in the bed. Finally Shan said to him, "Papi, do you know, whatever happened to my dog?"

"The results of a dog going blind are these," said Jusuf. "He will stumble over objects, become hesitant to go places where he cannot see. Namely, he will not at first realize that he is blind."

"Papi, I cannot see you," Shan said, questioning.

"I know," Jusuf said softly. "You are blind."

A bruising of the cortical region of the brain, the doctors told Jusuf the second day. So sorry. Perhaps his sight will return. Perhaps not. You must emphasize the *not*, they said the third day, so as not to get his hopes in a whirl. By the fourth day Shan was home.

"I will put you to work feeding the chickens," Jusuf said, to not acknowledge the blindness. But by the second week, when the chickens were getting lean from Shan's scattering the feed to the winds, when Jusuf sensed the disturbance of the flock, he told Shan that perhaps simply to water them was best. He would take care of the rest.

Jusuf had worked at the Empress Hotel since the age of seven. It was then, when he was in the lobby one day, that a woman phoned from upstairs, desperate. "Go to the lift, boy," the desk operator had ordered him. "There is a woman frantic about chickens."

Young Jusuf walked quickly to the lift area and saw, as the metal box slowly emerged from above and ground to a halt before him, that the floor of the lift was covered with chickens. They were alive, clucking and pecking at their reflections in the burnished metal walls.

Quickly Jusuf slid open the grate. He dropped to his knees at the edge of the lift and placed his hands, thumb-to-thumb, on the lift next to the first group of chickens. Then, experimentally, he lowered his face on level with the birds. One hen, distracted from her reflection by his closeness, cocked her head and edged his direction. Others also quieted and followed suit. Seeing their attention, Jusuf rose to his feet and walked to the kitchen, thirty-four chickens falling into step behind him. He knew then that he had a way with chickens, that his talent for birds was in winning confidences from them. Only later would he discover his talent for cooking them too.

It was this talent that caused him to fear the dog Shan had brought home, the dog that now looked out at him through his son's sightless eyes. It, from the beginning, had shown an alarming liking for birds. He had said to his son, "A dog with a taste for chicken, quite simply, cannot be tolerated."

Birds were his livelihood, his calling—one Shan had not inherited. Jusuf had feared this since the moment he had looked at his infant son's hands and could not picture them thumb-to-thumb on the floor of the lift. He could not see in Shan's eyes the look of trusting birds. His fear had worsened with the coming of the dog.

"What is the relationship between a bird and a dog?" he had exclaimed to his wife angrily. "To put it plainly, Prava, the two cannot exist happily together." He had been relieved, actually, when the dog had gone missing in the night. Its blindness was an aberration in itself and, all in all, the dog was better off gone.

But Shan had missed the dog, had trusted it in a way that Jusuf only trusted his birds. They were reliably expendable. He could tell them things with the comforting certainty that they would be dead within the week, part of the never-ending stream of requests for *satay* and *soto ayam*, for rice served with his fried confidantes.

Mr. Andika, the hotel owner, spotted the new problem right off. "Jusuf, my friend, I hate to say this to you, but really you must find other work for Shan. With the chickens he is so *public*. The hotel guests see him, and the sight makes them uncomfortable. It is a purposefully sightless society we live in today," he sighed. "That is as it is; I cannot change people." He shrugged. "But Shan must work inside. Perhaps in the kitchen?"

"Perhaps," Jusuf allowed, and Mr. Andika went away pleased.

But Shan had no place in the kitchen. Even Farid said to him, "I have this thought in my head, Jusuf, that Shan is not meant for this place."

Jusuf looked at him and then said slowly, "He is not like us, Prava and myself. Shan is like—do you remember the dog he once had? The one that was blind?"

"Perhaps," Farid said, choosing words carefully, "he should go to University. He is intelligent, likable . . ."

"He is blind."

"Yes, but I have heard that there are things to be done. A guest at the hotel saw Shan with the chickens."

Shame burned through Jusuf. "You should not have listened to him."

"He says that there are animals that can be trained to limit Shan's blindness."

"And these animals are?"

"They are dogs," Farid admitted.

"Ah, there, you see? I have said it already. There is nothing to be done."

Farid shrugged, admitting defeat, and the two spoke of it no more. But after the evening meal, when Jusuf was transferring the remains of the night's chickens into the scrap heap, he was stopped by a man with a cane.

"Excuse me," the man said, "but I wanted to tell you, the chicken tonight was really quite good."

"Thank you," Jusuf murmured.

"Yes, and also, I wished to speak to you about the boy. Your son." As if sensing Jusuf's uneasiness, the man continued rapidly. "You see, I know some people south of here who are training dogs to lead the blind. It is their life's work, carrying guide dogs to countries around the world."

Jusuf laughed suddenly. "It must disappoint them greatly to carry this work here."

The man stared at him.

"Here," Jusuf explained, "dogs are eaten, run over by buses. Here dogs themselves are blind."

The man murmured in negation, but Jusuf continued. "Do you know what I did with the dog my son had? Sent it away! Wished it away. It was blind, you see."

He laughed helplessly, imagining Shan, blind Shan, led by that sightless dog through the streets of Medan, followed by thirty-four chickens.

The guest, embarrassed, bowed slightly and left, and Jusuf

collapsed onto the tiles. He looked up at the saucepans hooked onto the ceiling and laughed at the absurdity that one of them should have so perfectly fallen onto the head of his son. How utterly absurd that just like that, neatly even, his son had become like the dog with an affinity for chicken—how odd that only in their blind affinity were the three of them alike. He laughed until there was no more sound, until his diaphragm simply convulsed and convulsed and his wracking attempts to draw breath sounded more akin to sobs.

The next day he and Shan boarded the bus.

REBECCA SCHMUCK'S short story "The Results of a Dog Going Blind" won the 2004 WORLDview Fiction Contest sponsored by WORLD Magazine and WestBow Press. A native of Pensacola, Florida, she formed a love of travel from early family trips crisscrossing the U.S. and its borders. That, coupled with a love for learning languages, inspires her stories, many of which are set primarily in other countries.

LANDSLIDE

DAVID McGLYNN

"LANDSLIDE" IS AN ELEGANTLY TOLD STORY OF A PASTOR'S life weighed against a single moment out of his youth, when the prospect of a life in the ministry—and his first opportunity to preach—seems just within reach, and forever far away. Oftentimes in literature we see pastors rendered as stereotypes—either hypocrites or Bible thumpers or both—but in this story we have a pastor who seems perhaps as real as we will find: a man after God's heart, but fully and humbly aware of the missteps in his own life, and the loss that haunts him, no matter how "successful" he may seem.

—BRET LOTT

LANDSLIDE
David McGlynn

T he earth moved on a narrow bend in the Pacific Coast
Highway, about a half hour north of Cayucos State
Beach—the kind of place I had seen only in coffee-table books
on AMERICA'S GREAT SCENIC DRIVES. Cypress trees leaned sideways
over the cliffs' edges, which alone amazed me, and dark bushes
of chaparral speckled with yellow and purple carpeted the hills.
Driving that way had been Greg's idea, and when the traffic
backed up, I had no idea what we were in for. It was an El Niño
year, and a deluge of rain had saturated the soil and overfilled
the run-off channels. Down in Los Angeles, the concrete riverbeds
ran full for the first time that I could remember. A small earth-
quake, maybe 2.5 on the Richter, too small to feel, was all it took
to send who-knows-how-many tons of mud and rocks tum-
bling down the gulley. It blew through the guardrail, wiped out
the road, and poured over the side of the cliff to the little rocky
beach a hundred feet below. I have said, in the countless times
I've told this story, that the road was higher than that, more like
a thousand feet, but it was a hundred. I'm trying to stay true to
the facts. Debris piled up on the highway, sloping toward the
edge of the road in line with the hillside. A blond graft was
missing from the otherwise brown hill above. How anyone
could have survived getting buried beneath it is something I can
only explain as the grace of God.

However, people did survive, at least for a while, and had

somehow managed to call for help. This is one aspect of the story that seems improbable and I am not quite clear on the details. It was what I heard at the time, and being awe-struck by the mound of earth that I had walked nearly a mile from our parked car to see, I did not think to question it. Greg and I arrived to see people already digging, one man with a short-handled shovel and the rest, maybe a dozen others, using tire irons and buckets to pound and scoop away the dirt. A woman was bent forward with her hair in her face, scooping between her legs with her hands while a man in a green cap stood beside the open door of his Dodge Ram, talking into the square receiver of a CB, the cord stretched absolutely straight. I could see other people standing on the other side of the slide, a crowd mirroring ours, but I couldn't hear their voices. The slide was a consuming thing, and all that lay beyond it seemed like a different country.

We were there for two minutes before the highway patrol arrived, a single car driven by a single officer with close-cropped hair and a yellow windbreaker over his beige uniform. When he stepped up to the edge of the road and looked down at the beach, his sleeves flapped in the wind and pressed against his arms and torso, revealing the bulk of the bulletproof vest beneath his shirt. He appeared worried, which is an easy emotion to spot from far away; he rubbed his jaw with the heel of his palm and looked back and forth between the slide and the edge. He couldn't have been much older than I was at the time, which was twenty-one, but it was his responsibility to take control of the situation. He returned to his cruiser and sat down in the front seat and then spoke to us over the P/A, kindly asking everyone to get back. He even said, Please. Composing himself, he explained that the slide wasn't stable and that a simple shift could send more. He asked the people in the crowd to go back and wait at their cars. Those digging ignored him and kept right on with what they were doing. Greg and I wanted to help; it seemed better than just standing around. But despite every Good Samaritan impulse within us, every urge to sacrifice ourselves for the sake of strangers, neither of us was about to disobey the police.

A line of cars ahead of us tried to turn around and head back, but it wasn't long before a second officer rode by on a motorcycle and announced that the lane needed to stay open so emergency crews could get through. The road we were on was now closed and an officer was posted at the turnoff; anyone caught trying to go back before we were directed would be ticketed. At that point, people seemed to surrender to the wait, and though I was impatient to get home, I prayed I would surrender too. People unfolded chairs and blankets and set out food, intent on picnicking. It wasn't the worst spot for such things. I heard eight different radios tuned to eight different stations, at least two in Spanish. A few hundred yards ahead of us in line, four young boys stood shoulder to shoulder throwing rocks over the water, doing all they could to out-throw one another.

This gave Greg the idea to hit a few balls. He popped the trunk and unsheathed his three-iron and his grocery sack filled with chipped-up balls from the driving range where he had worked the previous summer. The balls were going to be thrown out; he would never have taken them without permission. The backside of our dorm faced a grassy slope, too steep to build on and which bottomed out at a junior-high soccer field. Greg drove balls from the hill whenever he was bored or had a problem he couldn't figure out, one of the many things about him I never fully understood. That morning I had played my first full round of golf at a tiny public course outside Pasa Robles, about a hundred miles west of Bakersfield where we had attended a wedding the night before. Golf was a sport I never had much talent for, and on that day especially I found that it required a much greater amount of patience and concentration than I had been prepared to give. But James instructs us to consider it joy when we encounter various trials, so I committed myself to learning, at least for the day.

I played with an old set of clubs borrowed from Greg's uncle; Greg taught me to grip the club with my thumbs down, to square my shoulders with my hips, my hips with the ball, and to return to this routine each and every time I stepped up to hit. One deviation and the ball went into the water or the trees, or into the grape vineyard beyond the course's perimeter. We ate lunch at the turn, two gigantic cheeseburgers spilling with lettuce and shredded carrots, and potato chips, and a dill spear that stained the paper plate green. Crop full and warm, Greg leaned back in his chair and closed his eyes, his spiked shoes crossed one over the other, his fingers interlaced across the stomach of his powder-blue golf shirt. I had seen him sleep this way in the library and in the Basilica, our study commons, and even seated at his desk in our dorm room. His sleep, even at night, appeared like a brief interlude between two greater, more consequential thoughts. I putted on the practice green while I waited for him to wake up.

The shoulder beside the car was six feet wide and covered in weedy grass. Greg chopped at it with the head of his club in high strokes like a reaper until he cleared a small patch of dirt. He dropped two balls in the grass and pulled one back toward him with his club head, then squared up, dug his shoes into the dirt, and did that thing that always made me laugh, no matter how many times I saw it: the little waggle of his butt that made him look like a duck. "Quack, quack," I said.

"Quiet." He kept his eyes fixed on the ball, then wound back and crushed it. The ball swam upward in the mist and carried forward against the stretched, blue horizon, a white speck that I lost for a moment in the sun and found again in time to watch it splash. The water near the shore was green-blue and full of rocks, fallen chunks of the cliff deposited by earlier landslides. I wondered how many God had placed there Himself when He created the earth, and on which day, and it gave me pause to think of the care that God took with each miniscule detail. Greg's ball landed in the dark blue. "Nice shot," I said.

"See the spot you want to hit before you even swing. Make the ball go where you tell it." He pushed the second ball my way. "Let's see what you've got."

"Haven't I seen this in a movie? Two guys hitting golf balls into the ocean?"

"It's a beer commercial," he said. "The guys are in business suits, playing hooky from work, or something like that. 'One more for old times,' is the slogan." He lifted an invisible beer in his cupped hand, and I did the same. We mimed the clink and swig. Then I tried to mime what I had seen him do only a minute before, the grip, the stance, even the waggle. I kept my head down and swung. The club nicked the top of the ball and sent it bouncing over the edge of the cliff. Greg fished another ball out of the sack, completely devoid of scorn or sarcasm. "Take a mulligan," he said. "That one never happened."

The mulligan was my favorite thing about golf. It was the perfect example of the first two verses of Psalm 32: "Blessed is he whose transgressions are forgiven, whose sins are covered. Blessed is the man whose sin the Lord does not count against him." Greg and I were seniors at Southland Pacific University, a Christian college perched on a hill on the south side of Los Angeles. Southland Pacific was an innocuous name for a conspicuous place. There wasn't a corner of the campus that lacked Christian intent or import. A wealthy judge had donated the land seventy years before to establish a school that would be "a light to the world"; our chapel was, in fact, shaped like a lighthouse. We joked that the water fountains were clean enough for baptism, and we had a thousand meanings for the initials SPU: Student Pastors' University, Sowing and Planting University, Savior's Pride University, Start Packing University (as almost every student spent time in the mission field). The list was practically endless, though most of us just called it SPEW, for more than Math, which was Greg's major, or History, which was mine, or any other discipline, we were taught the gospel, how to memorize whole New Testament books verse by verse, mnemonic exercises to help us quote it on command, ways to link the fifty major Messianic Old Testament prophecies to Jesus, techniques for sharing Jesus with everyone we met. Professor Tulliver ended each Pagan Psychology class with the admonition: "Love your neighbor, share your faith." While other college kids went to Santa Monica or to Tiájuana to drink and score, we went to witness. Our scores were measured not in phone numbers or drinks, but in souls, the tally of those I saved recorded on a sheet of paper taped to my closet door. One of my best lines was, "Heaven is like a party. God hands out invitations years in advance, and all you have to do is RSVP." It worked more times than you may think. I had a way with analogies, and anecdotes, though back then I didn't call them anecdotes. Back then I called them parables.

I practiced my parables on the youth at Fisher's Church, just down the hill from SPEW, where I interned my senior year. The name came from Pastor Dale Fisher, who founded the church in his living room, but also from Mark 1:17, when Jesus tells Simon and Andrew, "Come, follow me, and I will make you fishers of men." Fisher's was a church for the unchurched, an antidote to the hymn-bloated, wood-pew, fire-and-brimstone services that most pagans associated with religion. As Pastor Dale said, and which I have said many times myself, we weren't religious, we were relational. We came to church to be with Jesus. We didn't sing hymns; we sang praise songs, led by a band instead of a choir. Fisher's was already one of the largest churches in California, though in my lifetime I would see it become one of the largest in the country, and the complex that seemed so expansive to me then would become too small for Sundays.

Youth activities happened in a series of trailers on the northeast side of the church property, a square encampment that included several classrooms, an all-purpose room filled with sagging second-hand sofas and out-of-date movie posters, and a worship room where we held something of a pseudoservice during the second hour. I was focused and enthusiastic. Each week I regaled the youth with stories of God's presence revealed in daily life. I told the story of my neighbor in Escondido who scraped and saved to afford a hot tub so he could relax after work, and when it at last arrived, he gave it to his aunt who'd recently had hip surgery. It wasn't exactly true—my neighbor had plenty of money and in fact owned the house his aunt lived in—but as a story, it worked. Kids could be so consumed with themselves, with their hair and shoes and that month's brand of blue jeans, that a little airbrushing of the details could be justified if it led them to sacrifice for others as Christ sacrificed for us. Everyone understands that Jesus' parables were intended for this purpose, not as record of historical facts, as is true with the rest of the Bible. I spent the entire year looking for stories that I could shape into parables, watching the sun rise and set from the edge of SPEW Hill, watching students talk outside the library, watching hour after hour of television reruns for some plot line, some scene that would strike a relevant chord. I wrote everything down in a five-subject spiral notebook.

My internship ended with the completion of my degree and as a graduation gift, Pastor Dale had asked me to preach that Sunday at the ten o'clock service. Maybe it comes from living just south of Hollywood, but I felt that tomorrow would be my big break as a preacher, a giant leap in my pastoral career. I could just feel the Holy Spirit pointing me down my triumphant path. I told Greg that I should find a way to work this into my sermon.

"What's that?" He kept his eyes on the ball. The wind lifted the hair from his forehead.

"This," I said. "All of this." I waved the club handle at the sky and the sea, like Moses extending his staff. "Sometimes God blocks our paths to force us to wait on Him. Usually it means we have a lesson to learn, and until we learn it, we can't go forward. Sometimes that lesson is patience itself. If you hadn't taken that catnap at lunch, we could have been one more mile down the road. We should give thanks and praise for God's perfect timing."

"Sounds good," he said. He blinked, lost his concentration, and straightened his back. "Do you know why golf balls are dimpled?"

I shrugged, "So they'll sit on the tee?"

"They create Magnus lift, which keeps the ball aloft during the initial part of its flight." He picked up the ball. "Driven balls have backspin; Magnus force relates to the drag on the top and bottom parts of the ball."

"Balls have tops and bottoms?" I said, playing along. Greg was full of stuff like this. "They're round."

"At any one point in time, there is a top and a bottom. The top moves slowly and produces less drag. The bottom moves fast and produces more. This force creates lift. You've seen a golf ball fly upward, or slice to the side? That's Magnus."

"Something new everyday," I said, and spread my arms. "Our blemishes propel us toward God. Perfect." Unaware of anything I just said, he drew the iron up and over his head and swung hard, turning his hips when he made contact with the ball. A tuft of grass and earth flew up and disappeared off the side of the road, and Greg tapped the grass around the divot with the club head.

Greg was the only person I knew at SPEW who studied a science. I mean, the college had all the science majors, including chemistry, physics, biology, and several brands of engineering, but the vast majority who took those degrees did so to work in the mission field—either as teachers at missionary schools or else as missionary doctors. Karl Beckman studied biology in order to prove "evolution a crock," and spent most of his time reading books that declared Darwin an apostate. Greg studied math for math's sake, which didn't always go over well. Everything is for God's glory, we were told, not man's. What's more, the Math Department was conjoined with the Physics Department, and even though our professors were Christians, everyone knew that most physicists were atheists. Greg said that Einstein believed in a divine being, but Einstein was no Christian. Anyone could look at the starry sky and feel the echo of creation, but no one comes to the Father except through the Son. Worse was the fact that Greg studied abstract, difficult subjects that seemed to lead nowhere near Jesus, and worse, led no one else *to* Jesus. Students, in my time at SPEW, were known to shout out, "What does this have to do with Jesus?" in the middle of a lecture, and to tell one another before going out on weekend nights, "Think of Jesus." This was before those purple bracelets and bumper stickers became so popular and we thought ourselves both original and righteous, holding one another to a higher standard.

Greg's textbooks had queer titles like *First Course in Morular Forms, Calculus of Variation and Homogenization, Methods for Structural Optimization, Applied Complex Variables,* and *Asymptotic Methods.* I remember the titles because I remember leafing through the books, page after page filled with an alien typography. I know math is pure logic to those who practice it, but without the presence of a number, I failed to see the sense in any of it. Even stranger was watching Greg do his homework. He worked out problems on graph paper, his writing geometrical in its movements, boxy and square, but illegible on the whole, the kind of writing practiced by government code breakers and spies, at least in the way I imagine both. Ethan Prufer, one of the guys in our small-group Bible study, saw a sheet of Greg's on his desk and said it looked demonic. I said I thought it looked more like Aramaic, and told Ethan to be careful about accusing other Christians of demonism. Ethan apologized. He's not a bad guy.

More than one of our friends, and more than one of Greg's professors, suggested that he would have been better suited for an institution like CalTech. But like many of us, he had only attended Christian schools and his parents insisted that he remain close to the body of Christ when he went to college. They understood that college was a dangerous stop on the road of a Christian pilgrim. We all had friends who had lost their faiths at the public schools. And Greg did not dislike SPEW; in fact just the opposite was true. His senior year he rarely left campus. He did almost all of his coursework by independent study; he checked in with his professors once a week and spent the rest of his time in the Basilica. I always knew where to find him, and when I saw him there, he would be surrounded by pencil shavings and eraser bits, his hands sweaty and often in his hair, pages of graph paper stacked just beyond the bend of his right elbow, always in the same spot. He also began to write on himself, his skin merging with his paper as he moved across the page, just as one form of mathematics merged with another. There were nights when he came back to the dorm with bloody hands and knuckles, crimson rings in the cuticles of his fingernails, and pink streaks on his forehead and in his hair, which in the right light had a translucent quality. I used to joke that math gave him stigmata, which neither he nor I believed in. I saw the marks on his skin merely as the passion of a mathematician, a passion I have seen elsewhere only among missionaries who, in their resolve to reach the world for Christ, bought one-way passages abroad and took their coffins with them. Had Greg desired the missionary life, he would have probably had a lot more dates. Many women at SPEW were eager to marry, and to become, missionaries.

SPEW made it easy to set your thoughts on the noble, the right, the pure, and the lovely, as Paul tells us to do in Philippians. Stumble in your faith, someone was there to pick you up. Sin, and you had your Bible study to hold you accountable. No women in the men's dorms, no R-rated movies, no *Rolling Stone* or *GQ* or *Cosmopolitan* magazines with their lustful advertisements and perverted sex quizzes. Virginity is not so hard to keep if everyone agrees to it going in. We signed an honor code first day of freshman year, agreeing, among other things, to abide by 1 Thessalonians 4:3, to control our bodies in a way both holy and honorable. Love was a serious, grave matter and we knew not to fool with it. If two people were in love, it was best to get married, lest one begins to act improperly toward the other. That's Paul again, in 1 Corinthians, though I am paraphrasing a bit.

We all knew we couldn't stay at SPEW forever. We knew we'd have to descend the hill for good and live among the pagans, which nobody wanted to do alone. Senior year felt a little like the last call at a bar, when people scramble to pair up, wincing and dazed as the lights come back on and the jukebox shuts off. I saw this in a movie; I myself have never shut down a bar. There were a lot of engagements senior year, women hugging and crying after chapel, guys staying up late to talk about what it would be like to finally "get some." It was, as I have already said, a wedding that brought us to the landslide: Josh Rapenburg and Crystal McKnutt, whom everyone called McNuts, which made us all laugh, every time. Crystal didn't want to graduate an unmarried woman. She wanted her diploma printed with her married name, by which she would be known for the rest of her life—not an entirely unreasonable want. The wedding took place two days after classes ended, three days before finals week was to begin, at a un-air-conditioned, flat-roofed church in Bakersfield. Crystal's sister sang while her brother played the guitar, both off key. Greg and I wore jackets and ties, but not tuxedoes, and stood arranged by height on the steps leading from the floor to the pulpit. The ceremony included a sermon about Jesus' power to save; it lasted forty-five minutes and ended in an altar call. I stood the entire time, thinking about Kenna Stites.

Kenna sang in the praise band at Fisher's Church, and helped out some Sundays with the children. Though she was only nineteen and in school part-time, she seemed to me more mature than the other girls her age, the way she unabashedly filled the miniature chairs in the Sunday School classrooms and worked the tiny, dull-bladed scissors through sheets of construction paper. I liked her broad shoulders and soft chin, though my favorite thing was watching her sing. Her voice was true and clear and seemed to rise with the music; when a song like "Lover of My Soul" or "There is None Like You" would get to its high point, she would close her eyes and point her chin and lift one hand to the ceiling, palm flat and open. I'd watch the vocal cords vibrate in her throat, the quiver in the hand that held the microphone, the soft underside of her arm, which appeared to turn pinker and more flushed as the song built. It sounds like a small thing, and it was, but at twenty-one, it was enough to drive me crazy.

Rather than ask Kenna out on a date, I drove out to her parents' house in Whittier and spoke with her father. I arrived while he was mowing the lawn and waited in the dining room for him to wash his hands and change his shirt. I sat next to the head at one end of the table and imagined the years to come and the seat that would become mine, and when Mr. Stites came into the room in a flowered Tommy Bahama shirt, his thinning hair slicked back over his ears, I stood up and without any other small talk told him that I had feelings for his daughter. I said I believed she was a right, upstanding Christian woman who would serve a family as she served Jesus, and in due time I wanted to make her my wife. I didn't want to date, I said, as dating was practice for divorce; instead, I was there to ask his permission to court Kenna. Courting was the big thing at SPEW. I told him I would pursue Kenna in group activities that included both her friends and mine, and I planned to ask her to attend a couple's Bible study with me. He asked if I had shared any of this with Kenna, and I said I hadn't yet. I wanted his permission first. Then I promised not to kiss her until the wedding day. I wanted him to be the only man she had ever kissed before she kissed her husband. I said it just like that, to the man's face—I felt righteous in my intentions and spoke without fear. Mr. Stites hiked up his belt and touched the hairless spot on the back of his head, and stuck out his hand. When I shook it he said, "I appreciate you coming, son," which I took to mean that I had done the right thing. I have often told this story as an example for how other

young people and couples should conduct themselves in rela-
tionships. I have even told it on television. To this day I am
thankful that I was able to behave rightly toward women and put
first things first in matters of love and marriage.

The arrival of the equipment summoned us back to the landslide.
An orange frontloader came first down the road, followed by a
yellow backhoe with a shovel attached to a long hinged arm. We
hadn't waited long, maybe forty-five minutes. Because of the nar-
rowness of the road, both were driven in, rather than towed in on
trailers. A Caltrans crew in orange vests and white hardhats followed behind in the back of a pickup. The backhoe had to work
the corners, backing up, inching forward, rolling a tread up on
the side of the cliff. We practically walked alongside it. I whistled
"Onward Christian Soldiers." The highway patrol had taped off
the landslide and the area around it. Across the mound I could
see the flashing lights of an ambulance, the bay doors already
open, a fire truck behind it. A team of paramedics waited on our
side with a gurney, a tackle box, and an oxygen bottle. The highway patrolman spoke with the backhoe driver; the driver nodded
and pulled the levers in front of him and the backhoe began to
scoop, in its lurching way, shovelfuls of earth from the slide. After
each scoop, it backed up and swung its arm to the edge of the
road and emptied the shovel over the side. While it did this, the
frontloader pushed in and took away its own haul. It wasn't long
before the rear fender and taillights of a white Volkswagen Rabbit
appeared, like an egg buried in the dirt. At that point the backhoe
reversed and the crew moved in, working frantically to knife away

the dirt around the car. Greg, with his arms crossed, leaned close to my ear and said, "No way, not a chance." It took a few minutes more before I saw that the Volkswagen was rocked up on its right side. Greg looked at the hills above us, that blond slice grafted right out of the side of the hill, and then at the debris spread over the road, and then at the car. How the slide, with all its sudden force and gravity, did not sweep the little car right off the edge of the road was a mystery. "It's not possible," Greg said. "This thing would have taken a building over the side. I don't see how it didn't toss that car."

"Well, there it is," I said. I had not thought to question it. "Look and be amazed, for I am doing things in your own life-time that you must see to believe." That's from Habakkuk 1:5, the Living Bible translation, one of several verses I kept scribbled in my notebook.

Greg put his hands on his hips, then crossed them back over his chest. "Whatever. Call it a miracle, then."

I did. I trusted Greg completely when it came to matters of math and physics, and if this little car had defied the laws of physics, then a miracle was the only explanation. Not every miracle turns water into wine or fills the sea with frogs. I half-expected the dirt to be brushed away and the doors to be opened and for the people inside to simply step out, blink in the sharp sunlight, fill their lungs with sea-blown air, and wave to the crowd. I prayed I would have the courage to shout out "*Praise Jesus!*"

Of course, it didn't happen quite like that. When the slide buried the car, it crushed the hood and windshield and the front of the roof, and when the jaws of life at last managed to tear away the door and side paneling, and the crews were able to shovel out the earth, the man and the woman inside were both dead. No one told us; the highway patrolman never turned and announced it, but everyone could tell. The Caltrans crews removed their hardhats. People groaned and I could feel the air exit every mouth around me. Beside me a mother shielded her daughter's face, then closed her eyes and kissed the top of the girl's head. The woman in the passenger seat was extracted first and laid on the gurney and covered with a white sheet.

But then something happened that has kept me talking about the landslide ever since. The jaws of life wenched away the passenger seat and fender, and a crewman put his hardhat into the backseat; he yelled something, I couldn't hear what it was, and then he backed out of the car carrying a car seat, the bucket kind, the baby inside it still alive. The roll bar in the roof of the Volkswagen had survived intact; it provided enough space, and with the parents dead, enough air for the baby to fill its tiny lungs until help arrived. It came out of the car filthy, a long scratch on its forehead, and within a second the paramedics were upon it, papoose board, intubation tube, needles—but it was alive. The crowds on both sides of the slide went crazy. Some people cheered, but others sobbed and covered their mouths in fear, which is the right attitude when a miracle is witnessed, for the power of the Lord's intervening hand, His puncturing of the fabric of time and space, is filled with terror, with lightning and thunder, and death to those without the reverence to fall to their knees and touch their lips to the dirt.

Which I did not do. I stayed on my feet and did my best to memorize every last detail I could see, the waffled tractor treads in the dirt, the broken taillights on the Rabbit, the yellow tape flapping in the breeze, even the ropy outseam of the woman's jeans that I saw when the wind flapped the sheet up an inch. I turned and looked at Greg. His jaw was clenched and his eyes were narrowed into slits, his eyebrows knit together at the top of his nose, and he held his scabbed hands together in an odd way, the flattened fingers of his left hand pressed between the flattened fingers and thumb of his right. He had a strange look on his face. I slapped his shoulder, pumped my hand around the knob of the bone, and said, "I praise you, Father, Lord of heaven and earth, because you have hidden these things from the wise and the learned, and revealed them to little children."

Without turning to look at me, he said, "Sure. Right." He gritted his teeth. I heard them grind back and forth.

I didn't know it then, but this was the last day of our friendship. Although we talked some on the way home, most of it was spent in silence, looking long out the windows at the setting sun and the lights of Los Angeles when we came down into the valley. When we parked in front of the dorm, I went straight to the Basilica to rewrite my sermon, this time telling the story of what I had witnessed, working in Isaiah 25 and Ephesians 2 and the story of Jesus raising Lazarus from the dead. I preached with fire, God's voice on my lips, and after the service Pastor Dale shook my hand and said, "I didn't know you had it in you." Kenna's father invited me to lunch where I retold the story of the landslide with Kenna's fingers interlaced with mine beneath the table, and afterward, Kenna hugged me for the first time and whispered that she thought I had a gift. The smell of her shampoo and the bacon from her BLT, the warmth of her cheek and her breasts pressed against my chest stayed with me all through finals week and made it hard to concentrate on my papers and exams. Greg sequestered himself in the Basilica for the entire week, his bed undisturbed for five straight nights, his neck bent over his graph paper and books as though he didn't want to look up and find the week had ended. By the time we were face-to-face, we were donning caps and gowns, and Greg was rubbing Neosporin and Vaseline on his hands. We moved out of the dorms that afternoon, I just down the hill to an apartment with another Fisher's intern, he to his aunt and uncle's house in Pasadena.

I saw him one last time at my wedding. Before the ceremony I helped him with his cufflinks and saw that his hands were worse than ever, scabbed with crisscrossing lines and dark spots where ink and pencil graphite had imbedded beneath his skin. The marks disappeared up both sleeves, on both sides of his arms, like prison tattoos. He'd told me he was working at an engineering firm, but I didn't know which one and I didn't press him to tell me. The chairs beyond the door were full of my relatives, I was on the verge of kissing Kenna for the first time and the entire boundless frontier of marriage, and I didn't want to think of anything unpleasant.

Then life got between us. Fisher's hired me on full-time and by Christmas Kenna was pregnant. Pastor Dale asked me to preach one Sunday a month, and then every other, and when he retired, he tapped me as his successor. I saturated my life with God's Word as chocolate syrup saturates a glass of milk, and weekly encouraged my congregation to see the world the same way, to *open your eyes and look at the fields*, as Jesus tells the disciples in John. I was a good storyteller, as any effective speaker must be, and became known as the preacher who could see God in a ladybug crawling across a leaf, or in a dog at the end of a leash. Eventually my notebooks of parables and file drawer of sermons would get typed up and published in a book, *God Is Everywhere*, my half-factual autobiography told through a rosy lens, the climax of which was, of course, the landslide. "You too can emerge from disaster," I write, "you, too, can come out of your own grave and live again. Believe and God shall raise you up." It is a story I can tell when I am nervous or ill-prepared or needing to dazzle. I can thread it to any Bible verse, adapt it to every situation. For a long time, I believed God had shown it to me to do His will and to make disciples of all nations.

The only problem is that Greg is not in it. I tried at first to include him and the larger parts of that day, the cypress trees leaning sideways from the cliffs, his closed eyes at the turn of the golf course, his lessons about flight and lift. But space was limited—"Don't make people read too much at one time," my editor told me—and all that I knew of what had become of him I knew by hearsay, rumors filtered to me by an old SPEW acquaintance whose mother went to church with his aunt, or a friend of a friend in Salinas, where he grew up. I heard he was married, but isn't any longer, that he'd had a daughter who moved out of state with her mother, that he'd bounced around between jobs, his talents never quite matched with his employers' needs. I didn't know how to make any of that fit. I thought of his stacks of graph paper, and what Ethan Prufer said about them, and I imagined him in a sparsely furnished room in a shabby hotel rented by the week, unbuttoning his shirt at the end of his bed, his biceps and shoulders and chest and stomach inked black with a language no one else could read, and I deleted half of what I had written.

I could have tracked him down, found his parents, or his aunt, gotten hold of a number. I didn't have the courage. Instead, Greg found me. He called me deep in the early morning. This alone didn't surprise me; many people have my number and I am used to the phone summoning me from sleep. In a church the size of Fisher's, people leave and come into the world at every hour of the day. It wasn't until after I had said "hello" and "hold on a sec" and moved from my bed to my study and sat down behind my desk—that week's sermon drafted on four sheets of legal paper—that I realized who I was speaking to. His voice was far-off and graveled, a faint whistle through the line, wind blowing in the background. "Hello from Miami," he said. "I saw you on TV. You look good."

"Miami," I said. "How'd you get all the way out there?"

"I just did."

"Greg," I said. I hadn't said his name in years. "What's going on?"

"I'm in trouble."

"Trouble?" I said. "With the police?"

"No, nothing like that." I could hear a tapping on his end. "Things just aren't right." I wrote *not right* on the legal pad, out of habit. I circled it twice. "I can't make heads or tails," Greg said.

At first I thought he was just in a tough spot, confused and defeated, but then I thought about his hands again. I had seen enough sadness to know the difference. I said, "You need to get some help. Go to the Emergency Room if you have to. Write this number down." I scrolled through my file for the number of a pastor I knew in Miami. Then I took his number down, and his address, and I said I'd call someone on his behalf. I said, "Let's pray" and I rattled off Jeremiah 29:11–14, and prayed for God to grant him peace in times of calamity. I did everything a pastor should have done. I called the prayer chain, I mobilized resources, I set my elbows on the desk and my knees on the floor and prayed for him. But I didn't put on my pants and brush my teeth and get on a plane. I didn't go to him. Instead I went back to bed and told Kenna nothing was wrong as I stroked the plain of her back, and fell asleep. The next morning I dialed the number he gave me more than a dozen times, and each time I listened to a woman's voice, half-Southern, half-computer, tell me it was disconnected.

Ethan Prufer explained it this way, shaking his head: "He never was good at the basics. Plain speech, conversation, paperwork, the little ins and outs. I'm surprised he figured out how to dial in the first place. I wouldn't make too much of it." My phone calls to Miami had yielded nothing; the pastor I knew there had tried to visit, but couldn't find him. Ethan and I see each other every few months to barbecue—it surprises me sometimes that of all my friends from SPEW, I have remained closest to him. We talked about Greg while we stood beside the grill, turning over the burgers and waving away the smoke. "A merry heart is a good medicine," he said. "His problem is he never had a merry heart." I nodded because it is a good phrase, even though I knew that wasn't it. That's not the way I remember him.

I remember the paramedics disappearing over the landslide and the ambulance-bay doors closing, and the rig driving away, lights and sirens spinning, and the crowd dispersing back to their cars and the long wait that lay ahead. The highway patrolman shouted that traffic would be diverted to a service road that would take us back toward San Luis Obispo and the 101. When I told Greg I was heading back to the car, he gripped my wrist and said, "Let's go back to the golf course." His hand was shaking and hot against my skin. "We'll play one more round, spend the night in a motel, eat steaks tonight. I'll buy. I don't want to be on the road anymore."

But no way was I going to miss my shot at preaching. "Relax," I said. "Be not afraid." He pressed his lips together and looked down. The backhoe roared up behind us, spewing out a black puff of exhaust before digging its shovel into the earth. I slapped Greg's arm and told him the backhoe had the faith of a mustard seed—it could move the mountain from here to there. I couldn't fathom that anyone would see it otherwise.

DAVID MCGLYNN is Managing Editor of *Western Humanities Review* at the University of Utah, where he received his Ph.D. in Literature and Creative Writing. His stories and essays have appeared in *Image, Black Warrior Review, Northwest Review, Shenandoah, Ninth Letter,* and elsewhere.

THE VIRGIN'S HEART

A.H. WALD

"THE VIRGIN'S HEART" IS A SKILLFUL PORTRAYAL OF A woman's life lived in service to others, with the attendant triumphs and sorrows any life lived this way will have no choice but to encounter. Especially striking in this genuinely heartfelt character study is the manner in which Ms. Wald renders the tough landscape, allowing it to reflect the difficult life of Sharon Farley, a life, as with the countryside against which she lives, that is not without its own startling beauty and hidden joy.

—BRET LOTT

THE VIRGIN'S HEART
A.H. Wald

Sharon Farley had long since given up hoping for a child of her own. Visitors would notice her ringless fingers and with a draft of pity that made her stiffen, ask when she had come out to Tidderzane. That's how everyone in the mission spoke of it. Fifteen, nineteen, twenty-four years ago, she answered, trying to keep a boast out of her voice. She had determined that she would stay until she died.

In her twenty-sixth summer at the orphanage, she was hanging up the infirmary sheets and a tub of laundry for a family who had just taken in twins when she saw a man and girl trudging along the dirt lane below the property. It was late morning, and an oppressive cloud of heat had swelled over the dusty compound, pushing most of the children and all of the staff inside, except for Sharon and one energetic cluster of boys squealing over by the tire swings. From a distance, she saw nothing distinctive about the pair. The man wore a simple knit cap over his bushy black hair and an old jacket that hung below his wrists; the girl wore a faded print dress with a large tear hanging down in the back.

Sharon leaned past the sheets to get a better look, plucking her T-shirt with her fingers like clothespins to let in a spot of coolness. She knew most all of the locals and a good number of the mountain families who came down to the small village for supplies, but she didn't recognize either of them. When they came to a bored shepherd looking after his flock in the dry scrub, the man asked him something, and Sharon assumed they must be traveling through. It was not unusual to have strangers come by; the country was in the middle of a bad drought, and people migrating north to the cities often passed through Tidderzane. The shepherd pointed in the direction of the village around the other side of the rise, and when the pair disappeared behind a stand of anemic pines, Sharon's curiosity dwindled and she bent down for another sheet.

Around the orphanage, bald singular mountains puffed up out of the plains, and in the flat brown land in between, stones were the best crop. They bubbled up the size of baseballs and basketballs every spring after the freeze-thaw of winter and then were cleared by the local men into little stacks of three or four, like petrified prairie dogs. In the lower foothills where sparse groves of trees had managed to take hold, the ground was just as barren, with only a dull sage green scrub sowed with pebbles and rocks.

Everything changed in the years when the rains came and soaked the arid earth, softening the pods of minute seeds that lay buried in the soil like grainy ash. The sterile land suddenly turned green, and not just one shade of green but a lush palette of jeweled hues, emerald and celadon and malachite and jade. On the hillsides, the green would give way to tracts of wildflowers, their color spilling down the slopes like fresh paint: yellow tickseed, white daisies, purple lavender, orange hawkweed, flaming red poppies all spread out in an embarrassing extravagance. The children splashed in the water-filled ruts on the lane, and the new orphanage staff always stared dumbfounded at the miracle of what the landscape had kept concealed in its tight fist.

Even the old-timers would turn giddy at the sight of the brilliantly colored drops gesturing in the breeze, and the entire staff would make a holiday out of it with an afternoon picnic among the flowers. Someone was always sent to search out Sharon in the infirmary and urge her to join the others. "Who knows when the next chance will be?" But she could never be pulled away. She had promised to look after someone's baby, or the cook was sick and she said she'd help with supper, or the mattresses needed to be aired and she couldn't waste the sunshine. The envoy would hesitate for a moment in the doorway, but Sharon would shoo the person along. "Don't worry, I don't mind," she'd say, and the person would shake his or her head, admiring how Sharon could work so hard without taking time for herself. She pretended not to notice, but secretly she was pleased; it was one of the few indulgences she allowed herself.

She was not a natural nurse—she should have been a secretary; she was better suited for it temperamentally—but her mother had never been well and it seemed like a sensible course to follow. There had never been any marriage prospects back in Idaho. Her features, like her personality, were a notch below plain, with a high blank forehead crowned with frizzy brown hair and a shallow, mousy face that didn't hold an expression, and she had first been passed over by the girls who wanted sociable giggling friends, and later by the ranch boys who were looking for a dash of glamour or pizzazz. Then her mother died halfway through the program and the plans for her life deflated.

Sharon kept up with her studies anyway because she didn't know what else to do, and then on the last Sunday before graduation, the orphanage director came to the little Baptist church she attended in Boise and gave a presentation. As she listened to Bill Hudson, an idea took root, and by the time he finished speaking, the dream of sharing her life with someone was put aside for good and she decided she would go to North Africa and help. She had no great faith. If her mother had been alive, Sharon certainly would not have gone—her duty would have been with her. She might have stayed and doted on her nieces and nephews, but her two brothers were almost a dozen years older and she had never been close to them. She simply thought that taking care of all the children would be enough for her.

She examined the new babies, nursed the stomachaches and fevers, drove the broken bones to Boulem—the stitches she did herself. She washed the infirmary floors every day whether there were any patients or not, straightened the three beds and three cots in their rows, and kept the covers tucked in tight. She labeled the new bottles of medicine in small block letters, and lined them up in the locked glass cabinet behind the desk, along with the health records she kept on every child. It didn't bother her that Tidderzane was a five-hour drive from the capital without any bus service or trains—the French-built line ended on the other side of the mountains—or that there were no satellite dishes on the flat-roofed houses; despite the yearly promises that were made, the village remained outside the reach of electricity. She had one cramped room with leprous grayish-white walls partitioned off from the infirmary, bone cold in the winter and a sauna in the summer, with a bed, a dresser, and a few hangers of long, gored skirts that didn't flatter her tall, spindly figure. Yet all these difficulties she bore with an unwavering persistence; in fact she might have complained if things had been easier.

She had experienced only one real difficulty. From the beginning she discovered that it was much harder than she had expected to be single among couples and childless among orphans, surrounded by smiling toddlers running to their housemothers, and husbands and wives holding hands as they walked back to their quarters after dinner. There were other single women at the orphanage, but they always went back home in time to find husbands and raise their own children. New ones would come to take their places, and after a few more years they, too, would leave. Sharon was the only one who remained, and the daily reminders of her solitary condition blistered her patience, sometimes causing her to snap in irritation at another staff member or even one of the children. On the worst nights, she would go to her shoebox room and cry in shame because she was so lonely, and once when a houseparent came in unexpectedly with a sick child, Sharon had to assure them there was nothing wrong with her, it was only an allergy that made her eyes red and puffy.

Twice she had been tempted to ask for a child, and the first time, not long after she arrived, she scolded herself that the mission forbade single women taking on children. At her interview, the committee had specifically asked her if she could abide by the rule, and she had blushed at the question, quick to defend herself. The second time, during an unusually long stretch of good health at the orphanage that gave her too much time to brood, she had put aside her dignity and got as far as Bill's office door before she pulled herself together and turned around. She walked back to the infirmary, lecturing herself that she had chosen this life and she had to make peace with it, and when she entered her room, her heart was sealed with a vow to become the glue and the grease, the backbone and the finger in the dam, to turn her lack into her advantage.

"Let me," became her answer to every need she encountered. "I'll do it," was her response to every request. On Mondays, she did small errands in the village. On Tuesdays she drove thirty-five bumpy kilometers to Safik for the weekly market. She substituted for the teachers so they could take a few days' leave on the coast, and in the summers she was the one who always volunteered for the long, hot trip to the capital to pick up the new arrivals. She worked like the stubborn, bony donkeys carrying their heavy loads of kindling and flour and greens up the rugged mountain paths, allowing herself no rest, no letting up, and the virtue of sacrifice thickened layer by layer over her virgin heart until it was securely protected by a proud crust.

The more sensitive among the staff could detect a strain of condescension in her offers of help, and on occasion her zealousness turned meddlesome; she made sure that none of the thirteen-year-old boys escaped his turn washing the breakfast dishes, and she was always quick to point out to the houseparents the toys that invariably collected like dead mice by the dining hall door. She took over the annual updating of the staff manual from Bill's wife, Norma, so of course she was the one who remembered that orphanage funds couldn't be used for birthday candy. But who could fault her? Who could afford to criticize her when she was so willing and so useful?

When she looked up again, the man and girl had come through the orphanage gates and were headed for the main building. In one hand, the man clutched a frayed raffia basket that looked like it had come off an ancient donkey, and with the other, he kept a secure hold on the girl, who leaned to one side and dragged reluctantly behind him, her arm stretched almost horizontally. Sharon made a note to ask Bill at lunch if there was anything she could do to help, though she doubted it. The man was most likely looking for a handout or maybe an odd job.

But when she slipped into her customary seat at the end of the staff table and mentioned the pair, Bill wearily shook his silver head and said it was a difficult case. Normally, there would be no question—the girl was too old for them to take in. The father said she was five, but Bill suspected she was really six or seven, maybe even eight. The man's wife had died a few years ago, and he went back south so his mother could care for the child, but then she died too and now he was desperate. It was time for the girl to begin school, but work was spotty and he couldn't afford the books and supplies; he barely had enough to feed himself. Neighbors were willing to take the girl, but he was afraid that if he let them, they would find a family looking for help and pocket a fee. With a healthy girl like that who could start working right away, the money would be substantial.

There was a long, collective sigh from the others at the table. Out of the ninety-five children noisily eating in the dining hall, only twenty-eight were girls. Anyone who had driven through the middle-class neighborhoods in the capital had seen the child-maids in their turbaned scarves and aprons, opening the garage gate for the family car, or walking the dog, or bringing a carton of milk back from the store when all the other children were in school.

"What about the relatives?" Sharon asked.

Bill absently waved off the flies alighting on the platter of chicken and rice. "That's why he came here. It turns out the mother's half sister was from here."

"The village?"

"No, she lived here at the orphanage for a few years until an uncle took her. I told the father I'd see what we could do, but I just don't see how we can manage it."

Sharon lifted a plastic cup of water to her lips and surveyed the dining hall. Eight families were full, and the Roskers were due to go back for three months home leave. The week before Bill had reluctantly turned a premature baby away. If only she could take the girl.

"I could take her." The words slipped out of her mouth before she could stop them, and for an instant she hoped that perhaps someone else had given voice to her thoughts, but the others looked back at her in astonishment. One of the new teachers, wide eyed and scrupulous, blurted out, "But it's against the rules."

"Of course it is," Sharon said testily. "I was only thinking about the girl. Do you want her to become a maid?" She jerked up from her chair and made the legs grumble in protest against the floor. She started collecting the plates, struggling to hold down the redness she could feel seeping across her skin, while she kept arguing with herself. What harm would there be if she took the girl for a month or two until a space opened up? The girl could be kept clean and properly dressed, she would be able to go to school, she would have time to play, time to sleep.

"It would be such a shame," Norma said softly. "The girl has already had such a hard life. Maybe it's time to make an exception, Bill."

"Oh no," Sharon protested, the blush rising again to her face. "I—I didn't mean—I couldn't—it's not allowed."

But Bill pressed his fingers together in front of his mouth and sat motionless and silent for a moment. Then he lowered them and nodded. "Norma is right. It can't hurt to try. The girl is sure to end up as a maid otherwise."

The father stood up and greeted Sharon outside of Bill's office with a shy bow of his head, but the girl remained seated, her thin legs dangling from the bench without a twitch as she stared straight ahead at the wall. She was not a pretty child. Her head seemed too large for her slight frame, with gloomy black eyes bulging out from half-moon lids. A red ribbon had been skewered in the crudely chopped curls, and Sharon noticed the dirt smudged around her mouth and on her hands. The girl needed a haircut and a good wash, Sharon thought. And she wasn't overfed, but otherwise she looked healthy enough.

"*Shnoo smeetik?*" Sharon asked her. What is your name?

The father nudged her. "*Gooliha smeetik,*" he whispered. Tell her your name.

The half-moon lids did not flicker, and the curls lay still on the girl's big head.

"*Gooliha!*" he said louder. Tell her! "*Breeti tcooni bhel maaza?*" Do you want to act like a goat?

A hint of color came across the girl's sallow face. "*Smeetee Badra,*" she said to the wall in a broken whisper. My name is Badra.

"*Badra,*" Sharon repeated. The girl narrowed her eyes but did not turn to Sharon.

"*Badra, Breeti lma?*" Would you like some water?

The girl looked up at her father and he nodded.

"*Haji maya.*" Come with me. Sharon started off down the

119

hall without waiting; in another moment she heard the sound of Badra's plastic sandals slapping along the cement floor behind her. She stopped at the corner and pointed. "Over there is the bathroom. It's not a foot toilet. It has a seat. Have you seen one before?" Badra's big eyes did not blink. "Probably not. And if you come, you'll have to learn English. *Angliese.*"

Sharon knelt down at the drinking faucet. "When you drink, drink like this." She turned it on and leaned under it with her mouth open. She motioned for Badra, and the girl mimicked her perfectly.

"*Mezziane.* Good. Now you must be sure to turn the water off completely." Sharon made a turning motion.

Badra reached up and gave the handle a yank.

"*La.* No. If you turn it off too roughly, you'll strip the faucet. Slowly and firmly." Sharon turned the faucet on and then off. "Try it again."

Badra's head pointed at the floor, her eyes looking sideways down the hallway, and Sharon brought her hand up to the handle, but it rested limp and puppetlike. "Okay? *Wahkha?*" she asked. The girl remained still as if there was no life left in her. Sharon hesitated and then put her hand over Badra's. "If it is too hard on your own at first, we can do it together. Slowly and firmly," she repeated softly, turning the girl's hand, and then, like a lazy breath of wind stirring through a tumbleweed, the wild black curls floated up and then down.

Sharon was doubtful about the board; there was no reason to think that they would give her permission to keep a child after all those years, and in her first tentative weeks with Badra, she resolved to treat the girl like a patient who would be leaving after an extended stay. Together they searched through the orphanage clothes cupboard to supplement the few items of clothing in the black plastic bag Badra's father had taken out of his basket, and Sharon showed Badra how to fold them neatly and put them away in the bottom drawer of the dresser. Badra caught on quickly to brushing her teeth with a small pink toothbrush and then placing it in the holder with Sharon's, and eventually she learned to keep still while Sharon combed out the tangles in her thick curls.

Sharon was keen not to coddle the girl, but she felt it was out of the question for Badra to sleep alone in the infirmary, and she had a collapsible cot brought in that was stored under her bed and pulled out at night. And she couldn't help indulging her whenever Badra looked mournfully at an unfamiliar dish that was being served, as if the torture of eating strange food was too much for her to bear. Then Sharon let her eat all the wedges of the common round bread she wanted, and Badra would chew them slowly, savoring them like precious manna that might not appear again.

For a long time Badra barely spoke or showed any expression, and after meals when all the other children massed together in the yard, she would stay right by Sharon and walk with her to their room. But when Sharon finally began to send Badra outside to play during the day, she often had to rush out of the infirmary to stop Badra from throwing a well-directed punch at a child who had thwarted her or, if Sharon arrived too late, bring her over, scowling and unrepentant, to sit on the steps. Over time Badra became friendlier with the children and turned into a ringleader of sorts. From the window, Sharon would often see a group of younger children behind Badra, marching around the compound or following her as she jumped off the low retaining wall by the playground.

Summer gave way to fall, and there was still no word from the board. Sharon didn't bother to ask Bill about it; she assumed the refusal had gotten waylaid somewhere between the home office and Tidderzane, and she tried not to think about the future. She kept telling herself the only thing that mattered was the girl's well-being and what she could do to help her adjust to her new life. But at night, with Badra lying on the cot beside her, yielded to the peace of sleep, Sharon listened while the little room filled with a nocturne of wondrous sounds, the gentle puffs of Badra's breath, the dreamy murmurs, the wheezy whistle when her nose was congested, the rustle of covers and the squeak of the cot leg when she turned in her sleep, and then Sharon could not keep her thoughts from drifting to what she would do if Badra stayed with her. They would go up into the hills to hunt for fossils and bring back a few for polishing. In the spring they would go on the picnic when the flowers bloomed and later have a party—her birthday was in May, Sharon learned—and she would dig out her storage trunk and find the banana cake recipe her mother had always made. She would take Badra to an orthodontist in the capital for a consultation to see if her overbite would require braces, and when it was time for her to start college, Sharon might return to the states so Badra could study there. Of course it was dangerous to think like that. What if the board said no? How would she be able to go on? Better not to dream, better not to open her heart, she thought. But she couldn't help it.

Then the news came, the impossible, miraculous news. The board, considering the circumstances, agreed to make an exception, and Badra was now her permanent charge. When Bill told Sharon, all she could think to say were the words she had consoled herself with during the long months of waiting, "I'm sure the board knows what's best." Then she started grinning, and though she knew she must look like a silly fool, she didn't care. "Well," she said, tapping her knees with her sweaty fingertips. After years of sacrifice and denial, she had suddenly been rewarded with a child of her own. No more dead-end giving, no more short-sheeted offers to help; Badra's needs would be hers and hers alone to fill. "Well," she said again.

Right away she took Badra to the little photo shop in Safik. "My daughter and I need our picture taken," she told the man, and with that simple pronoun *my*, her life was doubled from half to whole. Together they went behind the frayed blue velvet curtain and sat side by side on the short, wobbly bench, Sharon giving one more fussy maternal run of the comb through Badra's curls before the bulb flashed. The picture turned out not to be a good likeness of either of them. Badra shared Sharon's tendency to freeze in front of the camera, and they both had stunned expressions that made them look worried, but Sharon didn't care. She replaced the old jaundiced photo of herself on the orphanage bulletin board and tacked up the new one with a slip of paper on which she had written, Badra and Sharon Farley.

Their days went on as before, walking to meals together,

working side by side in the evenings at the infirmary desk, Sharon on the orphanage accounts, Badra on her homework. But now Sharon proudly hung Badra's starred papers on the walls around their room, and in the late afternoons while the children played in the yard Sharon didn't hesitate to join the other housemothers who gathered together on the school steps and commiserated with them about the need for better playground equipment. Badra was still shy with her, but that didn't trouble her. She was the only one who knew of Badra's secret passion for raisins and how Badra tied the laces on her hand-me-down sneakers, one leg stretched out and the other drawn up to her chest, while her tongue skewed to the side, moving along with the tip of the lace. And when she spooned cough syrup into Badra's open mouth or took her temperature when she seemed warm, she felt happier because she was doing it as a mother, not a nurse. She was so delighted, so in love with this awkward, diffident child, that she hummed and whistled and smiled her way through her work, and right before Christmas, she made a special trip to the capital to buy a coffee-colored doll with two extra outfits.

Badra gave Sharon a necklace of green and red–painted pasta she had made and a card with the words, *Merry Christmas, Mother* in red glitter. Sharon immediately put on the necklace to show how nicely it matched the green turtleneck her sister-in-law had sent, and placed the card on the dresser. When Badra saw the doll, she stared at it in amazement. "Yes, it's yours," Sharon said. Badra named the doll Fatima after her grandmother and carried it with her everywhere, brushing its black curls with the little plastic brush and telling it not to fidget, exactly as Sharon told her. When school began again after the holiday break, Sharon told her she could bring Fatima once to show her class but the rest of the time the doll would have to stay tucked in her cot until Badra was ready to play with her.

Then one night after she finished her homework, Badra pulled out the cot and discovered Fatima was missing. She shook her head when Sharon asked her if she had taken her out to play with after school.

"Maybe she fell on the floor?"

Badra scurried under the bed but came up with tears in her eyes. She wanted to search the entire orphanage right away, but Sharon promised her they would look for Fatima in the morning when the light was better.

Badra woke Sharon early, and they turned the room upside down, looking under the mattresses, in the chest of drawers, taking out each piece of clothing at Badra's insistence. At the end of their search they had a stray sock and a pencil but no Fatima.

"Where is she? I want her." Badra hid her face in her hands and started to cry.

Sharon took a tissue out of her sweater pocket to dab Badra's tears and drew Badra to herself. For the first time, Badra did not resist her comfort; she buried her head in Sharon's chest, and Sharon put her arms around her and rubbed her back, feeling the sobs Badra inhaled like hiccups as the warm tears blotted her shirt. She knew it was pointless to offer to get Badra another doll, and she let Badra cry on without shushing her, as she murmured into Badra's curls, "I know, I know."

Badra finally stopped crying and folded her arms. "I'm not going to school."

"You have to go. But we'll pray and ask God to help us find Fatima."

"Are you sure he will answer?" Badra asked skeptically.

"Yes. We may not like the answer, but he will answer."

"Okay, then you pray, but tell him I want her back."

At breakfast, a houseparent came over with one of the ten-year-olds, and the boy held out Fatima to Badra. She carefully took the doll and cradled it in her arms for the rest of the meal, and when she came back to the infirmary after school, she brought a sticker to put on Fatima that said, GOD LOVES _____ and in the blank she had written, *Fatima, Badra's doll.*

The winter held on longer than usual, and it was still chilly when the early rains came, clattering endlessly on the tin roof, bringing a heavy dampness into the air. The sun barely came out of the clouds, and it took a week for towels to dry, but finally the weather turned warm and big spots of sunlight hit the upper fields. A tight green fuzz brightened the ground. But just as the first tiny wildflowers appeared, a vicious flu swept through the orphanage, and the infirmary filled with the most serious cases. Sharon was so busy she had to ask one of the teachers to stay with Badra in the evenings, though she always went back to their room in the morning when it was time for Badra to get ready for school.

One morning, she sat on the bed with her eyes closed in exhaustion and small rolls of shivers rippling through her. Then she felt a nudge. Badra was beside her, holding out her sweater. "Oh, Badra," Sharon said, fishing a tissue out of the sweater pocket to catch her tears.

"What did you lose?" Badra asked, looking at her with curiosity.

Sharon gave a little laugh. "I'm not crying because I lost something."

"Are you sad?"

"No, sometimes we cry because we're happy."

"You're happy?"

"Yes, I am."

"Okay," said Badra, satisfied, and she went back to tying her shoelaces.

As the flu raged on, school was canceled, and Badra spent the days playing outside with the other healthy children, their chaotic screams periodically bursting out across the yard and then falling away. During one of the lulls, Sharon stopped on her way to the storeroom and looked out the window. A group of children had managed to climb onto the peaked school roof and were slowly straddling their way across to the small bell that hung above the entrance. Even from the other end of the compound, Sharon recognized Badra in front, with her big head of curls tossing from one side to another and the boyish swagger of her shoulders as she waved a stick in the air.

She was afraid to call out and startle the children from their perch. She turned, and with long gulping strides she rushed through the infirmary, so she didn't see Badra lose her balance. But when she stepped out of the infirmary door and saw the children on the roof looking down in frozen disbelief, she knew instantly what had happened, and the nightmare billowed up in front of her. She bolted into it, flying in a panic to Badra, fumbling to brace her on the stretcher, honking the van around the sheep straying along the side of the thin road, gunning madly past the old rusty trucks balking up the mountain to Boulem while Badra drifted in and out of consciousness in the back.

By the time Badra was installed in an empty semiprivate room, she had slipped into a coma. The x-rays on her back were negative; there was a hairline fracture in her leg, but there was too much swelling on the brain, and the doctor showed Sharon where bits of Badra's skull had been pushed down. She wanted to know all the options: Could Badra be brought to the capital? Airlifted to France? The doctor dismissed her suggestions. It was too dangerous to move Badra. They'd shunt off as much fluid as they could, but there wasn't much else to do except to wait and see if Badra would make it out of the coma. "When she comes out," Sharon corrected the doctor.

"When," he conceded.

She pulled a metal-frame chair with a torn vinyl seat from the nurse's station into Badra's room and spent the night beside her, nodding in and out of a thick drowsiness and rousing herself every so often to check Badra's shallow breathing. During the day she sat and watched Badra in her calm, motionless sleep and wondered who she was dreaming of: the mother who had first cared for her, her grandmother, her father, Sharon? She was such a small part of Badra's life, but for her, Badra was everything. At dusk Badra's eyes fluttered behind her lids for a moment and Sharon spoke aloud, "It's time to wake up, Badra. Come on now." She stared at Badra's face for another twitch or a shudder and then at the bumps and ridges of her legs under the sheet, but there was no other movement, and she settled back in her chair for another night.

In the morning, two teachers came to give her a break, but she would not accept their relief; this was her vigil and hers alone. The hours rolled on, and there was no change except for the sunlight brightening the room and fading out again at night, and the shrieking wails that echoed down the corridor whenever a child in the ward died. To pass the time, she sang Badra's favorite songs while the thought spun around in her mind that this was not right. Badra would have to come back to consciousness, and even on the fourth day, when Badra turned paler and her breath became lighter, Sharon would still not let go of her hope.

She began to rock back and forth in the chair, trying to give Badra the strength to rally, and then she knelt beside the bed. She had never felt so powerless, and she prayed deeply, fervently for Badra to be healed, to have a chance to grow up, that she would do anything, anything to keep Badra alive, and she clasped her hands together so tightly they hurt. "Let this cup pass from me," she whispered, but she could not speak the rest: *not my will but your will be done.*

When night came, she stayed awake, massaging Badra's arms and sponging her forehead with a damp cloth, stopping every so often to bend over and whisper in her ear, "I'm here, I'm here," until Badra's legs punched at the sheet and she lifted up, gasping for air like a swimmer coming up from the depths, and then she was silent, and her body fell back dead.

"Bring her back, God, bring her back," Sharon whispered. She stared at Badra's still body, expecting to see her legs stir under the draped sheet or her finger begin to wriggle. She waited the rest of the night for the miracle, never taking her eyes off Badra. Only when a cart clanged down the hall did Sharon look up. Outside the sky was lightening to another day, and she finally slumped back in her chair. She squeezed her eyes tight against the salty burn; a nurse would be coming soon, and she did not want to fall apart in front of strangers. When she stood up, she touched the thin sheet and could feel the warmth of Badra's lifeless body. In that moment it seemed to her that death was as great a wonder as life. Then she took her hand away and the wonder turned to stone.

There were no arrangements to be made. She was not the legal parent; the hospital supervisor would only release the body to the father; otherwise Badra would be buried in the pauper's cemetery. Sharon tried to reason: she didn't know where the father was, she was the mother, she wanted to give her daughter a proper burial. But the supervisor remained adamant; it was forbidden.

She went back to her little room and gave the cot to one of the families who needed it for a visitor. Bill insisted she take a week off, but she refused and went back to work right away, as she had in the days after her mother's death, immersing herself in endless, heart-numbing, stubborn work. She launched into a thorough spring cleaning of the infirmary, dragging all the furniture out into the yard, airing every piece of linen, scrubbing the floor on her hands and knees, but it was not enough.

Every night alone in her room she cried as she had when Norma had put her arms around her in the hospital parking lot and she had collapsed, everything crumbling away at once, the muscles in her legs, the strength in her heart. The sobs flowed through her like a flood, carrying her down wild ravines, through vast interior expanses with nothing to stop the crushing surge as it traveled through the height and depth and breadth of her loss, every inch of it virgin territory. She had always liked the triumph of the verse, "O death, where is your sting?" but she had not known the answer. Now she knew exactly where the sting was. The thorn was plunged deep, slicing down all the way, and there was no protection against it. It would leave a mark in her.

Weeks went by, and her sorrow gave way to strange waves of bitterness at how she had been cheated. She had accepted all the hardships in her life, silenced all her complaints, and when love had been brought into her life, she had bent down before it, and now that too had been taken away. She did not know how she could go on. It was such a humbling for her, such an awful humbling to have sacrificed everything and have nothing left. She considered going back to the states; but when she thought about returning to her brothers' families, she realized it would not make a difference where she lived or what she did; she would never be the same again, and she decided she would stay.

When the bitterness finally wore out, her old pride was gone. "Please?" she would ask when she offered to help a house-parent. "Please let me?" Sometimes she would mention Badra to the children in the infirmary or make a reference to "my daughter" when she picked up a new teacher at the airport, and some thought she was boasting, but it was only how she kept her balance, like a hand groping in the dark. She kept the card and the necklace. She kept Fatima, too, though she wouldn't have been able to give a good reason why. At first, the doll lay on the shelf, and then, to keep her from getting dusty, Sharon put her in the trunk. The picture remained on the bulletin board, she and Badra sitting together sharing their awkwardness, and over time the edges curled and the colors faded, but it was never replaced. A stone was erected for Badra near the orchard, and Sharon went to it a few times, but she preferred to remember Badra when she turned the calendar and saw the anniversary of Badra's arrival at the orphanage. *Six years ago today*, she would think. *Nine years ago today. Fourteen years ago.* That was the measure of what she had been given and the measure of what she had lost, and out of the ashy shadows of her memory, the seeds of grief would bloom again, like the scarlet poppies that burst out of the barren ground for their brief season, bleeding with bright and colored grace.

A. H. WALD has lived in a variety of places and had a few jobs, some more quirky than others, "but nothing," she says, "that adds up to a stunning narrative." Currently, she writes full-time, and has had several short stories published. She lives with her husband in North Africa.

DOSIE, OF KILLAKEET ISLAND

HOMER HICKAM

IN THIS WHIMSICAL TALE OF AN OUTER BANKS COMMUNITY rallying to save its favorite daughter, Homer Hickam displays the essential traits of a great storyteller: an ease of language, engaging characters, and a plot that moves as surely as an incoming tide. But more important than the way in which the story unfolds is the nature of love this town has for Dosie, and its willingness to become a part of her grief in order to help stay her from what they believe she will do in the face of such sorrow. This is a portrait of a fellowship of believers, and their love for one of their own.

—BRET LOTT

DOSIE, OF KILLAKEET ISLAND
Homer Hickman

A mile down the beach from the great spire of the Killakeet lighthouse, a cottage sat amongst the sand dunes and sea oats, surrounded by a picket fence entwined with roses. It had a full-front porch (or "pizer," as it was called in those parts), a cedar-shake roof, and dormer windows in the island style. A sign on the cottage's front gate read *Dosie's Delight*, and on the pizer, shaded by an ancient fig tree, were several inviting rocking chairs. It was a peaceful little house, and very quiet except for the cries of gulls, and the rumble of the ocean, and the whisper of sand blown by a ceaseless breeze. In 1943, which was a time of war, a young woman named Theodosia "Dosie" Crossan lived here alone, not counting her beloved mare Genie who occupied the stable behind.

In those days, the people of Killakeet Island mostly cared about two things: fishing and raising their children (although they also clammed in season). Since Dosie didn't fish and was childless, there was a great deal of difference between her and all the other island ladies. Only a few Killakeeter women had ever traveled much farther than the mainland of North Carolina, which was a ferry boat ride across Pamlico Sound, but Dosie had been raised a rich man's coddled daughter and lived in many grand places, even Baltimore and New York City, and had traveled extensively in Europe. During her childhood, her wealthy parents kept a summer home on the island and the Crossans were the richest people Killakeeters had ever seen. Then change came, as it always will, and Dosie's father went bust in the great stock crash of 1929. The Crossan cottage was shut up for the next dozen years without a single member of the family returning.

One soft blue day in the Autumn of 1941, a woman arrived on the ferry, leading to the jingle of tack and the creak of saddle leather a big, brown quarter-horse down the plank onto Killakeet sand. At first, people didn't recognize this woman in jodhpurs, riding boots, and leather jacket, and were a bit astonished when she introduced herself as Dosie Crossan. But when they looked a bit closer, there was no doubt that this was indeed little Dosie, "all growed up." Gradually, it came out that Dosie had led quite the life since she had last trod on a Killakeet beach. She had discovered what it meant to be hungry and cold, she had loved a few men too many, including musicians, and she had not been loved back enough in return. In short, Dosie Crossan had left Killakeet a pretty girl of hopes and dreams, and returned to it a world-weary, though still quite lovely, woman of experience.

Dosie moved into her family's summer cottage (which, it turned out, her father had given her as a birthday present). When asked why she'd returned, she told people it was to find herself, which seemed a bit curious since she was standing right there in front of them. But Dosie knew what she needed, which was most of all to think and also rid herself of several phantoms, one of which was a trumpet player. While she was busy thinking and exorcising musicians, she also discovered, to her surprise, that she enjoyed creating art with the shells and beach glass and shark's teeth she found on her walks up and down the spindrift beaches. Before long, her fame as an artisan spread and she had herself quite the lucrative little business, her island-inspired jewelry coveted by the fine moneyed ladies along the coast even as far inland as Raleigh. As she hoped it might, the island had healed her. To her astonishment, one day Dosie realized she was content. That was when she made her sign, *Dosie's Delight*, and hung it from her gate.

Contentment, however, is a condition on this Earth that is not allowed to remain for long. Philosophers make much of this but the reason is simple: contentment and tedium are fellow travelers. So Dosie began to keep company with Ensign Josh Thurlow, the eldest son of the Killakeet lighthouse keeper, and a bit of a rough customer. Dosie and Josh had known each other as children but then Dosie had gone off to accomplish her years of wandering through the Depression while Josh joined the Coast Guard and shipped off on the Bering Sea Patrol. A few months before Dosie's return, Josh coincidentally had returned to Killakeet to skipper the 83-foot patrol boat *Maudie Jane*. Josh was a big bull of a man, and a widower with a reputation for being unreliable with women. Dosie, though blessed with a face and figure that tended to take a man's breath away, was cautious around men, and her tongue could be tart. From the start, their romance was like a Gulf Stream waterspout, dangerous and filled with spitting wind and tumult, but ultimately glorious and wildly beautiful. Appropriately, it was after an argument that they fell in love high on the parapet of the Killakeet lighthouse.

But then the war came, and Josh was sent off to the South Pacific, and Dosie became one of those women who also serve, by waiting. Faithfully, she wrote him a letter every week. Josh wrote back, occasionally.

It was in December of 1943 that the master of the ferry that made the crossing from Morehead City to Killakeet on Mondays,

Wednesdays, and Fridays came with a telegram addressed to Keeper Jack, Josh's father. Naturally, just in case it was bad news, the master had opened the telegram and read it, then tucked it inside his brass-buttoned coat where it hung as heavy as a lead brick. That was because the telegram was bad news indeed, an announcement from the Department of the Navy (which in those days included the Coast Guard) that Josh had gone missing and was presumed dead. "Poor Josh!" the master erupted, startling the mate who was at the wheel. Then, since he knew her well, the master added, "Poor Dosie!" In fact, so upset was the master that the mate had to steer the rest of the way, even making the landing, which was less than well-done, the bow crunching hard onto the beach. The master absently cuffed the mate alongside the ear but otherwise scarcely noticed. He thumped down the plank into the sand, chanting to himself, "Poor Josh, poor Dosie, and poor Keeper Jack too!"

The master took the cut across Killakeet that led to the lighthouse, meeting along the way Queenie O'Neal, the proprietress of the Hammerhead Hotel in the little settlement known as Whalebone City. He sadly apprised Queenie of the contents of the telegram, which, he knew, was tantamount to telling everyone on the island. By the time the master knocked on Keeper Jack's door and handed the telegram over, a mob was already charging down the beach toward the keeper's house.

With a cat curling around his legs, Keeper Jack stood on his pizer beneath the shadow of the great lighthouse and read the telegram with practically the whole of the island's population gathered in his yard. To discover that Josh had been killed on some Godless Pacific island or drowned in a patch of tropical sea was more than most folks thought the old man could stand. But stand he did, straight and proud. He read the telegram again, this time aloud so all could hear, then invited the folks in for coffee and sweet potato biscuits, and many took him up on it. After a biscuit well slathered with fresh butter from the keeper's cow, Queenie pierced the parlor with a great sigh, stopping all conversation. "Who's going to break this to Dosie?" was all she wanted to know.

"It's my place to do it," Keeper Jack answered quietly, and no one saw fit to argue with him.

"Poor Dosie," the master lamented, tears dribbling into his whiskers, and no one argued with him, either.

Later it was, some two hours later after his last guest had gone, that the keeper rode old Thunder down the beach to Dosie's cottage, finding her in her riding clothes leaning against a pizer post, a mug of fresh-brewed coffee in her hand, her big blue eyes placidly studying the white-crested sea. Wind chimes tinkled in the gentle breeze. A calico cat slept on the banister, its tail covering its eyes. As if occupied by ghosts, the rockers on the pizer moved in the gentle breeze. Dosie smiled at the sight of the keeper who looked so much like Josh, but when he climbed off Thunder, the expression on his face caused her smile to vanish.

"Is he dead?" she asked, straight away.

"Gone missing and thought dead," Keeper Jack answered, his hand on her gate.

"Did they say where?"

"The South Pacific is all they wrote."

Dosie gave that some thought. "Lots of islands out there," she concluded. "And Josh is an island boy."

The keeper took off his service cap and turned it in his hands. "Dosie, honey, men don't go missing in those waters and turn up too often."

"Our Josh isn't just any man, Keeper," Dosie replied, though the last words came out a bit choked. A tear trickled down her cheek. Defiantly, she wiped it away with the rim of her mug, then drank her coffee down in a single gulp. She nodded to the keeper and went inside, closing the door gently but firmly behind her.

Keeper Jack, knowing the kind of woman Dosie was, that consoling hugs and platitudes weren't her style, turned around and wearily climbed back on Thunder.

Just then, he saw Herman Guthrie, Dosie's "fetch and carry boy," walking barefoot along the sand dunes with a string of fish over his shoulder. He waited until Herman came alongside and told him what had happened. "You need to watch out extra special for your Missus," the keeper added. "At least for a little while."

"Oh, sir, I'm sorry to hear about Captain Josh, but don't you worry about my Missus," Herman replied, though he was trembling and tears curved through his freckles. Embarrassed, he used his white sailor's cap to wipe his nose. "I'll cook her up a pan of these sea trout for supper and fix some sassafras tea before bedtime so's she can sleep."

"You're a blessing to her, Herman," the keeper answered, then rode back to the lighthouse. The sun was sinking fast behind the land and it was nearly past time for him to light the light, to warn the ships at sea of the deadly shoals of the Outer Banks. Keeping the ships safe was what the Thurlows had always done. "But, Lord, who keeps the Thurlows safe?" Keeper Jack asked aloud as he climbed the two hundred and sixty-six steps of the black iron staircase that spiraled like a Nautilus's chamber within the inner wall of the high tower. He stopped on the third landing to read the brass plaque his father had placed there, inscribed as it was with the words from the old hymn, *"Let the Lower Lights Be Burning:"*

> *Brightly beams our Father's mercy*
> *From his lighthouse evermore;*
> *But to us He gives the keeping*
> *Of the lights along the shore.*

"Amen," Keeper Jack said and felt strengthened. Near the top of the lighthouse, the stairs led to the watch room and the keeper went inside and poured kerosene into the holding tank, then pumped it tight with air. A dozen more steps higher took him to the lantern room where the great lens sat like a massive glass beehive. He lit the kerosene-soaked mantle, then released a clockwork mechanism. Ponderously, the heavy glass structure began to turn on chariot wheels along a circular track, sending shafts of light flashing across the sea like spokes on a fiery wheel. Ships passing by would be safe as long as they heeded the warning, and as long as the keeper kept the light no matter what else might be happening in his life, including the death of a son.

Keeper Jack walked out on the parapet and looked down the beach toward Dosie's cottage. There was a lamp in the window, a single lamp, and that was all. "Poor Dosie," he said into the wind, which impishly snatched his words away, flinging them into the night across the pounding sea.

A day passed, then another and another. No more telegrams arrived. The government had stated the situation and what else, after all, was there to be said? Josh Thurlow was missing, thought to be dead, and there was a war to be fought and that was an end to it.

Dosie was a member of the auxiliary Coast Guard Beach Patrol, which meant she and Genie routinely rode up and down the beach, looking for German U-boats and saboteurs. Often alongside was Bosun Rex Stewart and his horse, Jubal Early.

One day, a pleasant sunlit day, nothing had been seen during the entire patrol except the grumbling ocean and an occasional seagull. At the beginning of the war, the Germans had been busy along the Outer Banks, but lately, all had been quiet. Rex was nearly asleep in the saddle when Dosie abruptly announced, "I can't go on."

Startled, Rex jerked erect. "You're turning around? But we got another mile to go."

Dosie replied with a sigh. "Oh Rex, it isn't the patrol I'm talking about. It's me. I can't go on like this."

"Like what?" Rex asked, completely mystified.

"This. Living, you might say," Dosie answered, and her tone was miserable. "I came to this island to find myself and start a new life, and I guess I did. But now with Josh gone . . ." She shook her head, unable to finish the thought.

"So what are you going to do?" Rex fretted.

"I don't know. I just know I can't go on like this much longer." And then she would say no more.

Rex worried over her words for a night, then carried the gist of the conversation to Queenie O'Neal, whom he found in her kitchen, cooking breakfast for the fishermen down from Hatteras and Ocracoke and up from Beaufort who had arrived to take advantage of the recent run of menhaden off Killakeet's shores.

After Rex told her what Dosie had said, Queenie threw her hands to her mouth, then spoke between her fingers. "That don't sound good, Rex, not good at all." Then she lowered her hands and wiped them nervously on her apron while frowning in thought.

"What are we going to do?" Rex asked.

Queenie reached a conclusion. "I'll talk to the women," she said.

Rex looked relieved, and was. In fact, as far as he was concerned, the matter was resolved. A few hours later, Queenie gathered the women in her parlor and, over yaupon tea and corn bread, they all put their heads together. Most favored sending someone, such as a fisherman's widow of which there were more than a few, to give Dosie a good talking-to, but then Herman showed up with more disturbing news. "That's what came out of her mouth, all you ma'ams," Herman said, finishing up. "She said she was going to get her affairs in order. And she asked me if I would like Genie for my very own, that is if I thought I could care for her."

Queenie and the ladies of Killakeet were shocked at this development. "I believe I'd best have a word with the preacher," Queenie announced, and all agreed it was for the best.

Preacher Hemphill was a tall, spindly young man with bad knees and a humped back, a little nervous with his hands, and from way out west somewhere, maybe Alabama. He stood bowed over in the sand outside his church while Mrs. O'Neal related Dosie's situation. Preacher Hemphill searched his mind for a suitable piece of scripture but failed to find one. Stumped, he asked, "Has anyone ever killed hisself on Killakeet, Mrs. O'Neal?"

"Not so we'd know, Preacher," Queenie answered after some thought. "There's so many good ways to get yourself killed here, what with the weather and the sea and leaky boats and all, people just kind of let it happen when it happens. But Dosie's a bit different. She ain't a Killakeeter by birth, you know, and she's only lived here full-time for a couple of years. There's still a bit of the landsman in her, and you know the strange ideas folks from over there tend to get, no disrespect meant in your direction, of course."

"Well, I could go talk to her, and get her to pray with me some and such," Preacher Hemphill suggested. "But I'm not sure what I'd say except suicide is a sin."

"She surely knows it's a sin, Preacher," Queenie replied, as tartly as she dared to a man of God. "Only maybe she's come to a point where she don't care. Romance is a powerful thing and it can cloud judgment."

Preacher Hemphill nodded gravely. "Then you should pray, Mrs. O'Neal, pray for poor Dosie and pray for guidance. That's all that can be done."

Taking the preacher's advice, Queenie walked to the dunes just east of the Coast Guard station. It was a lonely spot, with nothing there but sand and the sea and the everlasting breeze. Queenie bowed her head and said a few words, then sensed someone had joined her. When she opened her eyes, she saw standing in the sea oats a pelican. Queenie recognized him at once. It was the ancient and legendary pelican everybody called Purdy. Queenie's grandfather had told tales about Purdy, and so had his father and his father's father. For as long as anyone could remember, Purdy had showed up on the island when and where he wanted to, seemed to impart some silent wisdom, then disappeared. It was easy to imagine why some people said God sent messages through him.

"So, Purdy," Queenie said, pondering the snowy white bird who regarded her with quizzical eyes, "what do you think about poor Dosie?"

Purdy turned away, then hunkered down on the soft sand, made pink by the sun struggling through the clouds, and Queenie thought surely he'd gone to sleep until he suddenly shook his feathers and raised his wings. Then he looked at her and closed one eye, giving Queenie the wink, and that was when she knew what had to be done. "Thank you, old thing," she said but it was to empty air since Purdy had vanished as quickly and quietly as he had come. "I wish you'd stop doing that," Queenie muttered, then went on to do what needed to be done.

When Queenie got home, she woke up her husband who was taking a snooze on the parlor couch. "Pump, we're going to throw Dosie a party!" she yelled into his thin and unconscious face. Pump was so startled by the news he tripped over his boat-sized feet getting up and sprawled headfirst into a bronze umbrella stand. Queenie took no note of her husband's subsequent moaning. She was already off to give the women the glorious news.

For the next few days, Dosie's party was the prime topic of conversation and activity on Killakeet. It was going to be the grandest party the island had ever known and it was for the best cause ever, to keep poor Dosie from doing herself in. But then the ferry master came to consult with Queenie. He had carried Dosie into Morehead City, he related, and then followed her to a lawyer's office. Taped to the lawyer's window, written on cardboard, was his specialty: *Last Wills and Testaments cheerfully drawn*. After that, a number of ominous events occurred. The weather turned gray and stormy, not particularly unusual, but there it was. A dolphin stranded itself near the lighthouse. A gull on the church steeple started to moan, then flung itself into the bell and died. Then the menhaden disappeared, just vanished as if a giant hand had scooped them all up. Although the dolphin was pushed back into the sea with no injury done, everybody agreed these omens meant time was running out for Dosie.

The party was held on a Thursday eve and to celebrate it, the weather cleared and no more gulls moaned and died on the church steeple, and the dolphins stayed out in the ocean where they belonged. The menhaden, however, remained truculently absent so there was some trepidation that all was not resolved. As the sun set and the light began to flash at the tip of the lighthouse, the people gathered in front of *Dosie's Delight* and began to sing the old hymn Killakeeters had sung for ages:

> *Abide with me! Fast falls the eventide;*
> *The darkness deepens; Lord with me abide.*
> *When other helpers fail and comforts flee,*
> *Help of the helpless, oh, abide with me!*

Dosie, dressed in a pale blue frock, an embroidered shawl, and white pumps—her Sunday clothes—came out on her pizer, listened to the singing with her head tilted and her eyes closed, then invited them in, everyone. Of course, Killakeet being a very small island, she had divined for days that a party was being planned in her honor, although she didn't know its purpose. In any case, she was prepared with a huge load of food on her table and after the other ladies added their own, it was groaning beneath the weight.

The preacher said the grace and everybody took up plates and began to eat. After the roast merganser, fried mullet, clams, and oysters with sides of biscuits and corn bread and messes of greens and navy beans had been eaten, there was celebratory fiddle-playing and rigorous dancing. Dosie happily swung arms with old Doc Folsom, the island's physician. She waltzed with Keeper Jack, sharing a silence.

She did the Charleston with Pump O'Neal and clog-danced with Rex Stewart. Then, finally, after exhaustion had set well in, it was time for the speeches and the prayers and the praises to God, all made with heartfelt sincerity, all to tell Dosie how much she was beloved and not to be sad and all she should do was take her lumps as best she could like everybody else.

Dosie seemed attentive and everybody was certain they had accomplished their mission. A few wandered off home but most settled down where they were, in the parlor or in the rockers on the pizer or out on the sand to take themselves a contented nap.

It was morning when the people of Killakeet first got an inkling that their work was for naught. Dosie had made up her mind and nothing, including any number of speeches, prayers, and praises, was going to change her course. Herman woke and saw his missus come out of the kitchen and start up the stairs. For a reason he couldn't discern, he felt anxious. "Where are you going, Missus?" he asked, politely.

"Upstairs, Herman," she said, which was fairly obvious.

"What for?" Herman demanded because he didn't like the look in her eye.

"Among my other intentions, I am going to get my pistol," she answered and went on.

Herman found Queenie O'Neal sitting on the beach with her arm around Pump, who had his head on her shoulder, both admiring the ocean, remarkable in itself since they'd lived alongside that very same ocean for more than fifty years. Beside them sat the ferry master who'd recently showed up, wondering where everybody was. "Missus O'Neal!" Herman cried. "Dosie's gone upstairs to get her pistol and I reckon to put on her funerary clothes too!"

Queenie yelled and jumped to her feet, leaving Pump to fall over. She charged into the parlor and let loose with a screech that got everybody awake. "*Dosie's gone upstairs and she's got a gun!*"

There was a surge to the stairs, stopped by Dosie herself, who appeared at the top of it. She was wearing khaki breeches and riding boots and a blue denim shirt and her brown leather jacket. A canvas knapsack was slung over her shoulder. She was also carrying a big pistol, her father's somebody would later say. She stopped and looked at the crowd, then tucked the pistol in her belt.

"I hoped to go quietly," she said, "but I should have known I couldn't get away with anything on this island."

"Don't do it, Missus!" Herman cried out. "I'd miss you something fierce if you did!"

Dosie gave him an affectionate smile that made Herman's heart thump in his chest so hard he thought it would leap out. "And I'll miss you, too, Herman, but this is something I just have to do."

"No, Dosie," Preacher Hemphill intoned. "You mustn't. I looked it up in scriptures. *You are not your own. You are bought with a price.* It means you got to stay alive, don't matter how much you hurt."

"Pretty words, Preacher," Dosie answered, after a moment's frowning, "but they don't much apply to me."

"Well, they do, honey," Keeper Jack said, "if you're going to fly off to heaven because of Josh." He just couldn't say the word *suicide.*

"Is that what you all think I'm going to do?" She laughed,

and shook her head. "I don't plan on going to heaven any time soon."

"Then what are you going to do, dear?" Queenie asked.

Dosie came down the rest of the stairs and went out on her pizer, the throng following. "I'm going to find Josh and bring him home," she said, simply and emphatically.

There was a stunned silence for a long second. Finally, Keeper Jack said, "But Dosie, dear, he's on the other side of the world."

"That's why he needs finding, Keeper," Dosie replied. "Now, everybody on Killakeet has things they have to do. Keeper, you have to light the light, and Pump, you have to run the Hammerhead Hotel, and Queenie, you have to keep everybody apprised of what's happening on the island. Doc, you got to sew folks up, and Rex, you got to patrol, and Preacher Hemphill, you got to preach. All the rest of you have to catch your fish and raise your children. But me? All I've got to do is make my beach glass and shells and shark's teeth into art and I've got the rest of my life to get that done. Right now, I'm going to take the time to find my man. Herman, saddle Genie for me. I'd like a last ride. Ferry Master, I'd appreciate a ride across Pamlico Sound. That's the first part of my journey."

Keeper Jack's jaw had fallen open during Dosie's little speech. He managed to sputter, "But what then, Dosie? Where will you go? You'll have to cross the breadth of the country and then the Pacific Ocean. And there's a war on out there. It ain't like you can just catch a boat and go where you want to go."

"First thing to do is to get to Morehead City," Dosie answered. "Then I'll see what's next. That's the way I'll do the entire thing. Every place, I'll figure out how to get to the next place and so on. Herman, didn't I ask you to saddle Genie?"

Herman ran to the stable and soon had Genie standing by the gate. Dosie swung up in the saddle, then leaned over and softly spoke into the mare's ear, Genie answering with a low nicker. Straightening, Dosie said, "Well, Ferry Master, are me and the mate going to have to take your ferry across the Sound ourselves?"

The master thought not and off he went down the sand track at a fast pace. Dosie gave *Dosie's Delight* a last, fond look, then smiled down at the people of Killakeet. "You folks have been good to me, as good as anybody ever was, and I sure do appreciate your prayers and praise. I'll come back if I can." And with that, without so much as another glance over her shoulder, she clucked her tongue to Genie, and said, "Walk on, girl."

The people followed, silent, confused, but somehow hopeful. At the ferry, Dosie got off and handed over Genie's reins to Herman. "She's yours, Herman, if you still want her."

"Yes, Missus. Anyways, I'll keep her for you. And I'll look after the house, too."

"You'll find my will in the hutch," Dosie said. "You get the house if I don't come back."

"Oh no, Missus!" Herman cried. "I don't want your house!"

"Well, it's yours just the same," Dosie said, then gave Herman a quick hug and climbed aboard the ferry. The mate raised the plank and the master backed the little slab-sided vessel away. Dosie waved once and all the people on the beach waved back. Genie tossed her head and stamped her hooves. The men took off their hats and the women raised their aprons and dabbed at their eyes. For his part, Herman started to cry outright. Keeper Jack took Genie's reins from him and patted the big mare on her neck. "Good girl," he said, because she tended to be.

Herman was a snot-nosed mess. "Poor Missus," he sobbed. "And poor Josh."

"What do you mean, Herman?" the keeper asked. Then he said the strangest thing Herman thought he'd ever heard. "My boy Josh is the luckiest man I guess there is on Earth."

Herman couldn't believe his ears. "What's lucky about him?" he demanded.

Keeper Jack put his hand on Herman's shoulder. "Why, that he has a woman who loves him so much she'd go around the world to find him, even when nobody expects that she should."

All the men nodded agreement with wistful smiles. *Lucky Josh*, they all seemed to be saying although, them being men, no words were actually said out loud. Outraged, Herman threw off the keeper's hand and went to the women and told them the men's opinion. Queenie answered, "Herman, dear, you're right as rain. The men, as usual, have it all wrong. It ain't Josh what's lucky. It's that there girl on the ferry. Your Missus."

Herman was aghast. "But look here, Mrs. O'Neal, there she is all alone and she don't even know where she's going!"

"That's so true, Herman," Queenie answered with an odd little smile that all the women seemed to be wearing. "But it don't change that Dosie Crossan is as lucky as a woman can be. You see, she's fallen in love with a man she's willing to cross the world to find. Who'd of thunk it would have been the likes of Josh Thurlow, but there ain't no accounting for taste."

Lucky Dosie, the women sighed in unison.

Dizzy with confusion, Herman paced the sand, trying to find some sense in all that had transpired. He stopped and looked at the ferry, now nearly swallowed up in the pearly morning mists of the Sound. He looked at the people who'd raised him and they seemed like strangers. He kept trying to understand what they were getting at but he just couldn't. But then an answer of a sort began to form in Herman's mind. It was an answer he thought he'd heard in church. *Greater love hath no man than this, that a man lay down his life for his friends.* Herman said it out loud, almost without realizing it.

"And that goes for a woman, too, dear," Queenie advised.

"Well, I'll be blessed," Herman said, a glimmer of understanding settling into his soul. He was distracted by a ruffle of feathers and looked up to find Purdy perched on Genie's saddle. "I guess we're all blessed if somebody loves you and you love them back, ain't we, Purdy?" Herman asked. He got no answer, not directly, anyway, but it was the first time Herman realized a pelican could smile. And then something else settled into Herman's soul: a longing. He sought out his mama and told her what he had to do. The widow Guthrie looked hard at her son, then said, "Well, don't drown, and come back as soon as you can."

Herman hugged her, then sought out the keeper to ask him a question. "Will you look after Genie, sir?" he asked, and when the keeper said he would, Herman waded barefoot into Pamlico Sound. After a moment's hesitation, he tossed his cap into the air, threw himself forward, and swam as hard as he'd ever swum before.

HOMER HICKAM is one of the most popular authors in the world, his books translated into many languages. His best-known work is his memoir *Rocket Boys*, which was made into the movie *October Sky*. He has written two more memoirs: *The Coalwood Way* and *Sky of Stone*, and the nonfiction military history book *Torpedo Junction*. His novels include: *Back to the Moon, The Keeper's Son,* and most recently, *The Ambassador's Son*. He and his wife share their time between homes in Alabama and the Virgin Islands. For more information on Mr. Hickam and his books, please go to www.homerhickam.com.

AX OF THE APOSTLES

ERIN MCGRAW

A GOOD SHORT STORY IS NEVER ONLY ONE STORY, BUT TWO (AT least), just as the life of any of us consists of who we are in public, and who we are in private. "Ax of the Apostles" is a story that gives us a glimpse into the interior of a believer's heart and mind, a believer who, like most of us, is acclimated to his own sins, no matter how irritating the sins of others remain. What it is we as believers choose to do with the sin in our lives once we are made to see its lonely depth and corrosive breadth is what is at stake here, and why this story of a lost teacher and a searching student resonates so beautifully within the context of a life lived for Christ.

—BRET LOTT

AX OF THE APOSTLES
Erin McGraw

After four hours spent locked in his office, gorging on cookies and grading sophomore philosophy papers, Father Thomas Murray seethed. His students, future priests who would lead the church into the next century, were morons.

"Kant's idea of the Universal Law might have made sense back in his time, but today we live in a complex, multicultural world where one man's universal law is another man's poison, if you know what I mean." *So there are no absolutes?* Father Murray wrote in the margin, pressing so hard the letters carved into the paper. *Peculiar notion, for a man who wants to be a priest.*

They didn't know how to *think*. Presented with the inexhaustibly rich world, all its glory, pity and terror, they managed to perceive only the most insipid pieties. If he asked them to discuss the meaning of the crucifixion, they would come back with *Suffering is a mystery, and murder is bad.* Father Murray looked at the paper before him and with difficulty kept from picking up his pen and adding *Idiot*.

He had planned on spending no more than two hours grading; he would do well to go over to the track and put in a couple of overdue miles. But flat-footed student prose and inept, flabby, half-baked student logic had worked him into a silent fury, and the fury itself became a kind of joy, each bad paper stoking higher the flames of his outrage. He reached compulsively for the next paper in the stack, and then the next, his left hand snagging another of the cookies he'd taken last night from the kitchen. They were not good—lackluster oatmeal, made with shortening instead of butter—but enough to keep him going. *What makes you think,* he wrote, *that Kant's age was any less complex than yours?*

Still reading, he stretched his back against the hard office chair, which shrieked every time he moved, and started to count off the traits lacked by the current generation of seminarians: Historical understanding. Study skills. Vocabulary. Spelling. From down the hall he heard a crash and then yelps of laughter. "Oh, Alice!" someone cried. Father Murray closed his eyes.

A month ago one of the students had sneaked into the seminary a mannequin with eyelashes like fork tines and a brown wig that clung to its head like a bathing cap. Since then the mannequin had been popping up every day, in the showers, the library, at meals. Students mounted it on a ladder so that its bland face, a cigarette taped to its mouth, could peer in classroom windows. Now a campaign to turn the mannequin into the seminary's mascot was afoot. Savagely, Father Murray bit into another bad cookie, then stood, inhaled, and left his office.

At the bend in the hallway, where faculty offices gave way to dormitory rooms, five students clustered beside an open door. The mannequin, dressed in towels, half-reclined in the doorway to Quinn's room. Blond, morose Quinn, a better student than most, tugged the towels higher up the mannequin's bosom. The customary cigarette had fallen from the doll's pink plastic mouth and now dangled by a long piece of tape. "You should have seen your *face,*" Adreson was saying to Quinn. Father Murray knew and loathed the sort of priest Adreson would become: peppy, brain-dead, and loved by the old ladies.

"I thought you were going to faint. I thought we were going to lose you."

"Jumped a foot," added Michaels. "At least a foot."

"Went up like a firecracker," Father Murray suggested, and the seminarians turned, apparently delighted he had joined them.

"A Roman candle," Adreson said.

"Like a shooting star," Father Murray said. "Like a rocket. Like the *Challenger*. Boom."

The laughter slammed to a halt; Adreson stepped back, and Father Murray said, "You men sound, in case you're interested, like a fraternity out here. I would not like to be the one explaining to the bishop what tomorrow's priests are doing with a big plastic doll. Although I could always tell him that you were letting off some steam after your titanic academic struggles. Then the bishop and I could laugh."

"She fell right onto Brian," Adreson murmured. "Into his arms. It was funny."

Father Murray remembered a paper Adreson had written for him the year before in which Adreson had called Aquinas "The Stephen Hawking of the 1300s," not even getting the century right. In that same paper Adreson had made grave reference to "The Ax of the Apostles." From any of the other men Father Murray would have allowed the possibility that the citation was a joke. Now he looked at his student, twenty years old and still trying to subdue a saddle of pimples across his cheeks. "You have developed a genius for triviality."

"Sorry, Father."

"I'm giving you a piece of information. Think about it."

"Thank you, Father."

"Don't bother thanking me until you mean it."

"Oh, I mean it, Father." Adreson pursed his mouth—an odd, old-maidish expression. "Sorry we disturbed you. Guess we're too full of beans tonight. Hey—you want to go over to the track?"

Father Murray felt a plateful of oatmeal cookies churn in his stomach. "Another time. I've still got work to do."

"*Corpore sano,* Father."

Father Murray snorted and turned back toward his office. He cherished a measure of low satisfaction that the one Latin phrase Adreson seemed to know came from the YMCA slogan.

He should, of course, have taken up Adreson's offer. By ten o'clock his stomach was violent with oatmeal cookies; his error had been in eating even one. As soon as he'd tasted that first sweet bite, he was done for. He could eat two dozen as easily as a single cookie. Tomorrow he would have to be especially strict with himself.

Strictness, as everyone at St. Boniface knew, was Father Murray's particular stock-in-trade. Fourteen months before, his doctor had called him in to discuss blood sugar and glucose intolerance. "You have a family history, is that right?"

Father Murray nodded. His mother—bloated, froglike, blind—had had diabetes. By the end, she had groped with her spongy hand to touch his face. He had held still, even when she pressed her thumb against his eye. "Doesn't everybody have a family history?" he said now.

"This is no joke. You are at risk," the doctor said. "You could start needing insulin injections. Your legs are already compromised. You could die. Do you understand that?"

Father Murray considered reminding the doctor that a priest's job entailed daily and exquisite awareness of his mortality. Nevertheless, he took the doctor's point: Father Murray's forty-five-inch waist, the chin that underlaid his chin, his fingers too pudgy for the ring his father had left him. If he let the disease take hold he would deteriorate in humiliating degrees, relying on others to walk for him when his feet failed, to read to him when the retinopathy set in. A life based wholly on charity—not just the charity of God, which Father Murray could stomach, but the charity of the men around him. The next day he began to walk, and a month later, to run.

For a solid year he held himself to 1,100 exacting calories a day, eating two bananas for breakfast and a salad with vinegar for lunch. His weight plummeted; his profile shrank from Friar Tuck to St. Francis, and the waist of his trousers bunched like a paper bag. The night Father Murray hit one-fifty, ten pounds below his target weight, Father Radziewicz told him, "You're a walking wonder." They were standing, plates in hand, in line for iced tea. Father Radziewicz's eye rested on Father Murray's piece of pork loin, slightly smaller than the recommended three ounces, stranded on the white plate. "How much have you lost now?"

"One hundred twenty-four pounds."

"Enough to make a whole other priest. Think of it."

"I'm condensed," Father Murray said. "Same great product, but half the packaging."

"Think of it," Father Radziewicz said. His plate held three pieces of pork, plus gravy, potatoes, two rolls. "I couldn't do it," he added.

"It's just a matter of willpower," Father Murray said. "To the greater glory of God."

"Still, isn't it time to stop? Or at least slow down. Maybe you've glorified God enough."

"I've never felt better in my life."

The statement was largely true. He had never in his life been quite so satisfied with himself, although his knees sometimes hurt so much after a twelve-mile run that he could hardly walk. He bought Ibuprofen in 500-count bottles and at night, in bed, rested his hand on the bones of his hips, the corded muscles in his thighs. Out of pure discipline he had created a whole new body, and he rejoiced in his creation.

So he was unprepared for the muscular cravings that beset him shortly after his conversation with Father Radziewicz. They came without warning, raging through the airy space below his rib cage. The glasses of water, the repetitions of the daily office, all the tricks Father Murray had taught himself now served only to delay the hunger—five minutes, fifteen, never enough.

One night he awoke from a dream of boats and anchors to find himself pushing both fists against his twisting stomach. Brilliantly awake, heart hammering, he padded around the seminary, glancing into the chapel, the storage room that held raincoats and wheelchairs for needy visitors, the pathetically underused weight room. Finally, giving in, he let his hunger propel him to the kitchen, just so that he'd be able to get back to sleep.

Holding open the refrigerator door, he gazed at cheesecake left over from dinner. He was ten pounds underweight. He had left himself a margin; probably he was getting these cravings because he actually needed some trace of fat and sugar in his system. And the next day he could go to the track early and run off whatever he took in tonight. He ate two and a half pieces of cheesecake, went back to bed, and slept as if poleaxed.

Since then Father Murray had hardly gone a night without stealing downstairs for some snack—cookies, cake, whatever the seminarians and other priests, those locusts, had left. He stored his cache in a plastic bag and kept the bag in his desk drawer, allowing himself to nibble between classes, in the long afternoon lull before dinner, whenever hunger roared up in him. Twice he broke the hour-long fast required before taking Communion. Each time he sat, stony faced, in his pew, while the other priests filed forward to take the Host.

At meals he continued to take skimpy portions of lean foods, so stuffed with cookies even the plate of bitter salad seemed too much to get through. Father Bip, a Vietnamese priest he had often run with, told him that he was eating like a medieval monk. Father Murray slapped himself hard on the rump. "Brother Ass," he said. That rump was noticeably fleshier than it had been two months before, and he vowed again that he would recommence his diet the next day. That night, anticipating the stark hunger, he quietly walked the half mile to a drug store and bought a bag of peanut-butter cups, several of which he ate on the walk back home.

As he lay in bed, his teeth gummy with chocolate and peanut-butter paste, his days of crystalline discipline seemed close enough to touch. The choice was simple, and simply made; he remembered the pleasure of a body lean as a knife, a life praiseworthy and coherent. Yet the next night found him creeping back to the kitchen, plastic bag in hand, not exactly hungry anymore but still craving. Already his new black pants nipped him at the waist.

After his one o'clock Old Testament class the next afternoon, Father Murray returned to his office to find Adreson waiting for him. The young man, who had been absently fingering a flaming blemish beside his nose, held out his hand toward Father Murray, who shook it gingerly and ushered Adreson into his office.

"How was your class, Father?"

"We entertained the usual riotous dispute over Jerome's interpretation of 2 Kings." Then, looking at Adreson, he added, "It was fine."

"Your O.T. class has a real reputation. Men come out of there knowing their stuff."

"That's the basic idea."

"Sorry. I'm nervous, I guess. I want to apologize for making all that racket in the hallway last night."

"Thank you."

"I knew we were being—"

"—childish," Father Murray offered.

"—immature. I just thought you should know that there was a reason. Brian's mother has multiple sclerosis. He just found out last week. She's at home by herself with four kids, and she keeps falling down. I know it's killing Brian, but he won't talk about it. He just keeps going to class and services. It isn't healthy. That's why we put Alice in his room."

"He may find it comforting to keep up his usual schedule. This may be his way of coping," Father Murray said, autopilot words. Genuine surprise kept him from asking Adreson how a towel-wrapped mannequin was supposed to help Quinn manage his sorrow.

"He needs to talk, Father. If he talks to people, we can help him."

"You have a lot of faith in yourself."

"We're here to help each other." His hand fluttered up toward his face, then dropped again. "If it were me, I'd want to know I could count on the guys around me. I'd want to know I wasn't alone."

"He prays, doesn't he? He may be getting all the support he needs. Not everything has to be talked out."

"We're not hermits, Father."

"A little more solitude wouldn't hurt anybody around here."

A burst of anger flashed across Adreson's face, and Father Murray leaned forward in the chair, which let out a squeal. He was more than ready to take the boy on. But after a complicated moment Adreson's mouth and eyes relaxed. "Of course you're right. I thought I should apologize for disturbing you." He straightened, clearly relieved to have put the moment behind him. "I'm going for a run this afternoon. Want to join me?"

"You're doing a lot of running lately. I'd suggest you take a few laps around the library."

"You're great, Father. You don't ever miss a lick." He produced another grin. He seemed to have a ready-made, toothy stockpile. "Track meet's coming up. I'm running the relay and the 440. Hey, 440's your event, isn't it?"

"Distance," Father Murray said.

"I'm a little obsessed about that 440. Sometimes in practice I can get close to the conference record, so now it's my goal: I want to put St. Boniface in the record books."

Father Murray held his peace, but Adreson must have read his expression.

"I'll have plenty of time to be pastoral later. Right now, running's the best talent I've got." He winked. "I know what you're going to say: Not a very priestly talent, is it?"

"I wasn't going to say anything like that. You are the model of today's seminarian."

Father Murray waited for Adreson to leave the office before he swiveled to gaze at the maple outside his window. Hundreds of tender spring leaves unfurled like moist hands, a wealth of pointless beauty. Where, he wondered, was Quinn's father? Had he run off after the fifth child, or had he died, snatched away in midbreath or left to dwindle before the eyes of his many children? Cancer, heart attack, mugging. So many paths to tragedy. Now Quinn's mother was trapped inside a body that buckled and stumbled. Before long she would rely on others to cook for her, drive for her, hold a glass of water at her mouth.

"Too much," he muttered, his jaw so tight it trembled. He didn't blame Quinn for not wanting to talk to Adreson, who knew nothing about pain. He didn't have a clue of sorrow's true nature or purpose: to grind people down to faceless surfaces, unencrusted with desire or intent. Only upon a smooth surface could the hand of God write. Every priest used to know that. Father Murray knew it. Quinn was learning it.

Turning to the desk, Father Murray began to reach for the stale cookies in his drawer, then pushed back his chair. If an overdue visit to the track would make his legs hurt, so much the better. He couldn't take on any of Quinn's suffering, but at least he could join him in it.

Weeks had passed since Father Murray had last gone for a

run. His legs were wooden stumps, his breath a string of gasps. He flailed as if for a life preserver when he rounded the track the fourth time. Adreson, out practicing his 440, yelled, "Come on—pick 'em up, pick 'em up!" and Father Murray felt his dislike for the boy swell. After six laps, he stopped and bent over. Adreson sailed around twice more. Father Murray waited for his lungs to stop feeling as if they were turning themselves inside out. Then he straightened and began again.

At dinner he stood in line for a slice of pineapple cake. "Oho," said Father Bip. "You are coming down to earth to join us?"

"I should be earthbound after this, all right."

"Should you be eating cake?" Father Radziewicz asked. "Wouldn't a piece of fruit be better?"

"Of course it would be better, Patrick," Father Murray snapped. "Look, one piece of cake isn't going to make my feet fall off."

Father Radziewicz shrugged, and Father Murray stomped across the dining room to a table where Father Tinsdell, a sharp young number imported this year from Milwaukee to teach canon law, was holding forth. "You're all thinking too small. We can sell this as an apparition. Trot Alice out after Mass and get the weeping women claiming that their migraines have gone away and their rosaries have turned to gold. We'll have the true believers streaming in. Pass the collection basket twice a day; next thing you know, we're all driving new cars. We'll buy one for the bishop, too."

Father Antonin leaned toward Father Murray. "He found the mannequin in his office. Hasn't shut up since."

"The women are always grousing about how there isn't enough of a feminine presence in the church," Father Tinsdell said. "Well, here they go. Five feet, six inches of miracle-working doll. We can put her in the fountain outside. Stack some rocks around her feet: Voila! Lourdes West. Bring us your lame, your halt. If enough people come, somebody's bound to get cured. That should keep us rolling for the next century."

"You know," Father Murray said, setting his fork beside his cleaned plate, "Rome does recognize the existence of miracles."

"Somebody always stiffens up when you start talking marketing." The man's face was a series of points: the point of his needly nose, the point of his chin, the point of his frown set neatly above the point of his cool smile, directed at Father Murray. "Don't get in a twist. I'm up to date on church doctrine."

"People have been cured at Lourdes."

"I know it." Father Tinsdell leaned forward. "Have you ever seen a miracle?"

"No," said Father Murray.

"There are all kinds of miracles," Father Antonin broke in.

Without even glancing at the man, Father Murray knew what was coming: the miracle of birth, the miracle of sunrise, those reliable dodges. He looked at Father Tinsdell. Father Point. "Never. Not once. You?"

"Yup. Saw a fifteen-year-old girl pull out of renal failure. She was gone, kidneys totally shot. Her eyeballs were yellow. Even dialysis couldn't do much. For days her grandmother was in the hospital room saying rosaries till her fingers bled. She got the whole family in on it. And then the girl turned around. Her eyes cleared. Her kidneys started to work again."

Father Murray stared at the other man. "That can't happen."

"I know. But I was there. I saw it."

Father Murray pondered Tinsdell's mocking gaze. How could

a man see a miracle, a girl pulled from the lip of the grave, and still remain such a horse's rear? "I envy you," Father Murray said.

"Keep your eyes open. No telling what you might see." Father Tinsdell stood. He was thin as a ruler. "I'm getting coffee. Do you want more cake?"

"Yes," said Father Murray, though he did not, and would ignore the piece when it appeared.

Several times in the next week Father Murray paused outside of Quinn's door, his mouth already filled with words of compassion. But Quinn's door remained closed, separate from the easy coming and going between the other men's rooms. Father Murray respected a desire for solitude, the need for some kind of barrier from the relentless high jinks of the Adresons. He pressed his hand against the door frame, made ardent prayers for Quinn's mother, and left without knocking.

He should, he knew, have saved at least one of those heartfelt prayers for himself. His hunger was becoming a kind of insanity. Food never left his mind; when he taught he fingered the soft chocolates in his pocket, and at meals he planned his next meal. Nightly he ate directly from the refrigerator, shoveling fingerfuls of leftover casserole into his mouth, wolfing slice after slice of white bread. He dunked cold potatoes through the gravy's mantle of congealed fat, scooped up leathery cheese sauce. He ate as if he meant to disgust himself, but his disgust wasn't enough to stop him. Instead, he awakened deep in the night, his stomach blazing with indigestion, and padded back to the kitchen for more food.

With the other priests in the dining room he carried on the pretense of lettuce and lean meat; his plate held mingy portions of baked fish and chopped spinach unlightened by even a sliver of butter. He ate as if the act were a grim penance. For a week now he hadn't been able to button the waist of his trousers.

One night after dry chicken and half of a dry potato he made his ritual pause outside of Quinn's door, then continued down the hall to his own room. Fourteen papers on the autonomy of will were waiting, and promised to provide ugly entertainment. But when he opened his door he jumped back: Propped against the frame stood the mannequin, wearing his running shoes, his singlet and jacket, and his shorts, stuffed with towels to hold them up. From down the hall came a spurt of nervous laughter, like a cough.

Father Murray waited for the laughter to die down, which didn't take long. Adreson and three other men edged out of the room where they'd positioned themselves. They looked as if they expected to be thrashed.

"My turn, I see," Father Murray said.

"We didn't want you to feel left out," said Adreson.

"Well, heavens to Betsy. *Thank* you."

"We thought you'd like the athletic motif. It was a natural."

"An inspiration, you might say."

"I was the one who thought of having Alice running," Adreson said. "Some of the other men suggested your clothes. Hope you don't mind." He leaned against the wall, hands plunged into the pockets of his jeans. Relaxed now, the others ringed loosely around him.

"Did Quinn have suggestions for this installation?" Father

Murray looked at the mannequin's narrow plastic heels rising from his dirty running shoes, the wig caught back in his dark blue sweatband, the face, of course, unperturbed.

"Didn't you know? He's gone home to help out." His voice shifted, taking on a confiding, talk-show-host smoothness. "I don't think it was a good idea. His mom may be getting around now, but over the long run, he needs to make arrangements. Immersing himself in the situation will give him the sense that he's doing something, but he isn't addressing the real problems."

"Maybe he wants to be there."

"Not exactly a healthy desire, Father. Multiple sclerosis, for Pete's sake. I don't want to be brutal, but she isn't going to get better."

"No," Father Murray said.

"But you know Brian. He said he had to go where he's needed. I told him that he has to weigh needs. He needs to ask, 'Where can I do the most good?' He can't fix everything in the world."

"You weren't listening to him. Every need is a need," Father Murray said, chipping the words free from his mouth. "If you're hungry and you remember that children in Colombia are starving, do you feel any less hungry?"

"Sure. When I'm on vacation I always skip lunch and put that money in the box. And you know, I never feel hungry. Never."

"One of these days," Father Murray began, then paused. His voice trembled, which surprised him. He felt quite calm. "One of these days you'll find that your path isn't clear. Choices won't be obvious. Sacrifices won't be ranked. Needs will be like beads on a necklace, each one the same size and weight. It won't matter what you do in the world—there will still be more undone."

"My dark night of the soul." Adreson nodded.

"Your first experience of holiness," Father Murray corrected him.

Adreson flattened his lips, and his friends looked at their shoes. "Zing," Adreson said.

"Pay attention. I'm trying to get you to see. If you could take on Quinn's mother's disease tomorrow, if you could take it for her, would you do that?"

"We each have our own role to play, Father. That's not mine."

"I know that. Would you reach for this other role?"

Angry, mute, Adreson stared at the carpet. Father Murray understood that the young man was exercising a good deal of willpower to keep from asking, *Would you? Would you?*, and he meant to ensure that Adreson remained silent. If the young man asked, Father Murray would be forced to confess *Yes. Yes, I would*, his desire to save just one human life caustic and bottomless.

"I'll go ahead and get Alice out of your room, Father," Adreson was saying.

"Leave her for now," he said wearily.

"I'm sorry. It was just supposed to be a joke."

"I know that. I'm not trying to punish you." Father Murray watched the ring of young men shrink back. He was sorry they were afraid of him, but it couldn't be helped. "She's something new in my life. I'll bring her down to your room tomorrow. Besides, I need to get my clothes back."

The men retreated toward the student lounge, where they would drink Cokes and discuss Father Murray's bitterness, such a sad thing to see in a priest. None of them, Adreson least of all, would imagine himself capable of becoming like Father Murray, and in fact, none of them would become like Father Murray. Only Quinn, and he was gone.

Father Murray turned and studied the mannequin, which looked awkward, its angles all wrong. When he adjusted one of the arms, the mannequin started to tip; its center of balance was specific and meant for high-heeled shoes. Quickly he tried to straighten it, but it inclined to the right. In the end, the best he could do was prop the plastic doll against the bureau and berate his painfully literal imagination, which had flown to Quinn. He wondered how often the young man had already steadied his mother on her way to the bathroom or the kitchen. Father Murray's singlet had slipped over the mannequin's shoulder. He pulled the garment up again.

Adreson and the others must have gotten a passkey and skipped dinner so they could sneak in and rifle his bureau drawers. Father Murray didn't care about that—he kept no secret magazines that could be discovered, no letters or photographs. Then he remembered the nest of candy wrappers, the thick dust of cake crumbs. And he himself, talking to Adreson about hunger.

"Mother of God." He paced the room in three familiar steps, turned, paced back. The mannequin's head was tilted so that the face gazed toward the flat ceiling light, its expressionlessness not unlike serenity. A bit of paper lingered where a cigarette was usually taped, and Father Murray leaned forward to scrape it off. But the paper didn't come from a cigarette. Carefully folded and tucked above the mannequin's mouth, as precise as a beauty mark, was placed a streamer from a chocolate kiss. When Father Murray touched it, the paper unfurled and dangled over the corner of the mannequin's mouth like a strand of drool, and the doll pitched forward into his arms.

He thrust it back, resisting the impulse to curse. The mannequin's balance, he finally saw, was thrown off by extra weight in the pockets of the jacket. They were distended, stuffed like chipmunk cheeks. How had he not noticed this? Father Murray stabilized the mannequin with one hand and rifled the pockets with the other, his heart thundering.

He knew upon the first touch. Handfuls of dainty chocolate kisses, fresh-smelling, the silver wrappers still crisp. He dropped them on the bureau and let them shower, glittering, around his feet. The air in the room thickened with the smell of chocolate; he imagined it sealing his lungs. A full minute might have passed before he fished out the last piece and sank to the floor beside the pool of candy.

He thought of Adreson: grinning, amiable, dumb. Seminary record-holder in the 440, possessor of a young, strong body. He didn't look capable of true malice. He didn't look capable of spelling it. But above Adreson's constant, supplicating smile sat tiny eyes that never showed pleasure. They were busy eyes, the eyes of a bully or a thug. Eyes like Adreson's missed nothing, and Father Murray had been a fool to think otherwise. He had attributed the nervous gaze to self-consciousness, even to a boyish desire to make good, a miscalculation that might have been Christlike if it weren't so idiotic. Like mistaking acid for milk, a snake for a puppy.

Pressing his fist against his forehead, he saw himself illuminated in the silent midnight kitchen, the overhead light blazing as he shoveled food into his mouth: a fat man making believe he had dignity, and the community of men around him charitably indulging his fantasy. Only Adreson withheld charity.

He fingered the candies on the floor. Unwrapping one, he placed it on his tongue, the taste waxy. He unwrapped a second and held it in his hand until it softened.

The next day, Father Murray waited in Adreson's room, hunger making his mood savage. Before him on the desk sat two text-books and a dictionary that Father Murray found in the farthest corner of Adreson's single bookshelf. Father Murray's legs, clad only in running shorts, spread pallidly on the hard wooden chair. He had propped the mannequin against Adreson's closet, draped in a sheet for modesty's sake.

"Whoa! Father, you don't get it. The whole point is not to be caught in somebody else's room." Adreson's smile lacked anything like mirth, as Father Murray supposed his own did.

"I read your paper," he said. "I'm here to save you."

"I'm doing fine in all my other classes," Adreson said.

"That's hard to imagine," Father Murray said. He gestured toward the desk chair, but Adreson did not sit down.

"You're not dressed for teaching, Father."

"I thought we might have an exchange. I'll help you, then you can coach me at the track. I need some coaching."

Adreson needed a moment to process this. Once he did, the expression that crossed his face made Father Murray shiver.

"Don't look to me to cut you any slack," Adreson said. "I take running seriously."

"It's your great gift," Father Murray said.

"I just want to make sure you know what you're getting into."

"I know," Father Murray said. He hoped that Adreson could not hear the light edge of fear in his voice, but even if he could, it would change nothing. Father Murray was committed. "But I'm going to help you first."

ERIN MCGRAW is the author of four books, most recently *The Good Life* (Houghton-Mifflin, 2004). Her stories and essays have appeared in *The Atlantic Monthly, Good Housekeeping, The Southern Review, The Kenyon Review,* and other magazines and journals. She teaches at the Ohio State University.

RESOLVED

MARSENA KONKLE

"RESOLVED" FACES THE HARD TRUTH OF THE FACT OUR LIVES are inextricably entwined with the lives of others, and that even in the death of a loved one, we are still left to live our days alongside people for whom we cannot see a way to love. Though Christ's instruction to turn the other cheek might seem a possible answer in theory, it is only when we are at our darkest moments of the soul and are called to do so that our faith is truly put into action.

—BRET LOTT

RESOLVED
Marsena Konkle

W hen Theresa looked Miriam up and down with her lips pursed in disapproval, Miriam thought with a sinking feeling, *So this is how today's going to go.*

"Bad idea?" Miriam asked, plucking at one of the fuzzy yellow sleeves of her sweater, which she had chosen in lieu of a black blazer, feeling the rightness of this decision as the soft material caressed her arms. It had been her husband's favorite, buttery yellow, like a shag carpet made of chenille, and she had meant to honor him at his funeral by wearing it.

"Not if you're starring in a parade."

Shame flushed Miriam's cheeks. She left the sweater with her coat, regretting now the sleeveless dress she wore underneath. She rubbed her chilly arms, waiting for Mr. Larkin, the tall funeral director whose gangly body and high-pitched voice appeared to be stuck in adolescence, to finish showing the stragglers to the remaining open seats. Miriam thought to approach Martha and Henry, her mother- and father-in-law, to hug them or murmur something comforting on the loss of their only son, but was discouraged by their closed expressions, by the way they stood apart from the rest of the group, feet planted solidly, arms crossed, not even speaking to each other. She was saved from her indecision by Mr. Larkin motioning that it was time to begin.

Her brother, Steven, offered his arm and as they moved down the narrow aisle with the rest of the family following, silence spread outward like the waves from a stone dropped in a pond. She was aware of the suspended sentences, the heads turning her way, the eyes trying to gauge how the young widow was doing.

Her husband's best friend stepped to the podium, faltering over his first few words, but gaining control. He talked awhile and then invited others to share as well. Henry had been pleased with this idea, of turning the funeral into little more than a memorial service where people could tell humorous or touching anecdotes about Paul. In another setting, Miriam would covet every story, over a cold beer, perhaps, in a dark restaurant or on someone's back porch after the sun had gone down, but here? It felt sacrilegious. The talk should be of Paul's soul, not the funny thing he did in fourth grade.

Henry sat forward in his seat, hyper alert, eyes glued to whoever was bending earnestly into the microphone. Martha was weeping into a wad of tissue, but nodded her head gratefully every time someone tried to explain how much they had loved and would miss her son.

Miriam's phone call to Henry and Martha several days before to tell them of Paul's unexpected death had been typical (aside from the topic), as fraught with missteps and peril as petting a porcupine.

Over the course of her marriage, she had so rarely called her in-laws that when the need arose, she had to consult her address book for the number, dialing with shaking fingers, pushing the wrong buttons several times and having to start over again. The holes in the receiver bit into her ear and there was an eternity of echoing silence between rings. When Henry answered, she had the phone pressed so hard against her head that his voice exploded in her ear. Momentarily, she was unable to speak.

"I said hello," he repeated. "Who is this?"

"Dad," she said, the word sticking slightly, as it always did. "It's me."

"Miriam. You wouldn't believe the crank calls we've been getting this week. I can't prove it yet, but I know it's those damn teenagers next door, you know, the ones who—"

"Is Mom there?" Miriam interrupted. "I've got news that I don't—"

"Martha," Henry yelled without covering the phone. "Get on the other line, Miriam's got news!"

Oh, God, Miriam thought, her heart beating somewhere in the vicinity of her toes. *He thinks I'm pregnant.*

There was a click and the fumbling of a second extension.

"Son?" Henry inquired, expecting Paul to be on the phone, too, which was a fair assumption. Often all four of them talked together so nothing had to be repeated. "Is Paul on the line?"

"No," Miriam said. "Actually, it's about him."

There was a silence in which Miriam half-expected them to guess or ask questions, but when they did neither, she continued. "We had a snowstorm last night, about nine inches, and he was out shoveling. Actually, he went running this morning before he shoveled, which makes it even harder to understand because he was in such great shape—"

"What the hell are you babbling about?" Henry demanded.

"He's gone."

"Gone? What do you mean, gone?" Their minds did not transition quickly from pregnancy to death.

"Gone," she repeated.

"He left you." It was not a question.

And there it was. The ridiculously unexpected remark for which she was wholly unprepared, no matter how she tried to imagine and anticipate ahead of time the hostile labyrinth of Henry's mind.

Laughter burst from Henry in response to something one of Paul's coworkers had just shared, and Miriam realized her mind had wandered. She drew her tongue across her front teeth to check for lipstick, then felt appalled for caring about such things. She squinted at the sculpted spray of flowers draped over the foot of the casket, as if that would help her focus.

Earlier that morning, as Miriam's best friend, Esther, used a hundred pins to pull Miriam's hair into a French twist, they had talked about how many funerals they had been to. Esther's grandfather died when she was a child, but most of her relatives were either healthy or still living and dying in China. She had never even been to the funeral of an acquaintance. This was Miriam's fourth, counting both her parents and Steven's lover who had died of cancer when she was in high school. Two of her other brothers had died, too, and although she hadn't been present at either of their funerals, they were so much a part of her consciousness that sometimes she thought she must've been. Miriam couldn't fathom life without the occasional burial and trips to the cemetery every Memorial Day to tend the graves.

When her father was buried, Miriam was only twenty-five and she had squeezed out a few tears, not because she would miss him, although she would in theory, but because she had already learned that's what one did at funerals. Her tears had ceased, however, the moment she saw Steven crying silently, both hands covering his face, his fingers pushing his glasses onto his forehead. Loneliness had pierced her, watching him struggle to contain himself, because she couldn't comprehend—hadn't anticipated—his grief. Despite their closeness, she might as well have been in a different country, so little did she understand what was taking place within him. She never did ask what their father's death meant to him, why it had hit him so hard. She was afraid she might not be strong enough to handle her older brother's pain.

And here Steven was, slipping his arm beneath hers and giving her hand a squeeze. She shifted in her chair, returned the pressure, gave herself a mental shake. *Pay attention*, she commanded, too late, for now she was having to haul herself to her feet so she could follow the casket up the aisle and out into the cold day.

Pulling into the winding road of the cemetery, Miriam watched the rows of gravestones go by, struck by how unfamiliar they looked. She hadn't realized how much she had come to know her family's cemetery, not only their actual graves, but the names and shapes of the markers of all the others buried there, too. She wondered again at her decision to do as Henry wished and exclude her priest from the service, which meant burying Paul here among all these strangers rather than with the rest of her family in the Catholic cemetery.

When she stepped out of the car, she looked down the long

procession of vehicles, each with a flag on its roof, snaking all the way back to the entrance and onto the main road. People began making their way slowly toward her, the sound of their car doors a soft staccato in the chill air.

Mr. Larkin helped the pallbearers move the casket into place, and one of his assistants directed Miriam to a canvas chair where he draped a blanket over her knees. It was dark avocado, coarse and heavy. Martha squeezed into the chair next to her, and Theresa took the last one. The men would stand behind.

Despite the biting wind, people gathered in loose clusters wherever snow had been adequately cleared rather than pressing close together for warmth. Miriam craned her neck. She spotted Esther, her hair pulled back in a matching French twist, staring into space, cradling her four-year-old daughter in her arms and swaying back and forth. The little girl was sucking her thumb, cheek pressed against her mother's shoulder.

Over there was one of Paul's childhood friends. A few of her coworkers. His baseball teammates. As Miriam's glance traveled past groups of people, she caught numerous eyes shifting away from hers.

She saw near the hearse a glimpse of white and, thinking it was Father Jake in one of his ornately embroidered robes, heat sizzled along her nerves at the thought that Henry would see him, although this was precisely what she had been searching, hoping, for. But it was only a woman in a long white coat.

Paul's best friend took charge again, and while he read scripture and said a brief prayer—which was apparently acceptable to Henry, who reverently bowed his head—it didn't carry the weight or comforting authority it would have if Father Jake had been the one using the exact same words.

Miriam tried to imagine what would have happened if she had defied Henry's demand for a non-religious funeral. Although her father-in-law was generally on his best behavior around her, twice now she had seen a latent fire beneath the surface, a hard core of anger, a cruelty she could not fathom.

The first time was at her wedding, when she had turned to meet her father-in-law's gaze and in the reflection of his chiseled jaw, the calculating glint of his eyes, she saw herself as something to be wiped off the bottom of his shoe. It wasn't just that he disagreed with her faith. It was personal.

The second time had been a few days before, in the showroom of the funeral home, over a rush of forced air, where fluorescent lights buzzed.

Caskets lined the room, each partly open to display fluffs of material and small pillows. Each model gleamed, whether red, metallic, or plain wood. Miriam felt suddenly hot and shrugged off her coat, holding it tightly against her chest.

Martha gripped Miriam's arm. They made eye contact and Martha's lips twitched upward, not an expression to cheer or even to encourage, but one that took the other in, acknowledging the unique yet connected blow each had received. Her mother-in-law's grip was fierce, belying her unremarkable eyes that rarely seemed to have life in them. She was a large woman, bent under layers of extra flesh, which had also led Miriam to judge her as soft and ineffectual. Miriam felt surprise and shame for not believing all along that Martha possessed reserves of hidden strength.

Mr. Larkin seemed ill at ease. Rather than leaving them to look at the caskets on their own, he talked about each one in nervous detail, pointing to the durability of steel, the timeless beauty of mahogany, the fold-away handles for pallbearers.

Martha moved to a casket the color of honey and ran both hands back and forth along the smooth top.

"You'll also notice that in each casket are displayed the different linings. You can choose the fabric as well as style. Satin, for instance, or linen . . ."

Steven stood close to Miriam, arms crossed over his slightly protruding belly, watchful and listening.

" . . . velvet, tucked, shirred, fitted . . ."

Henry interacted with each casket, examining finishes, jiggling handles, pressing one or both hands into the depths of the box as if to test his weight against the comfort of the various cushions, unaware of the way his movements made Mr. Larkin's hands flutter.

"How do people decide?" Miriam asked no one in particular.

"Whatever seems most important to you," answered Mr. Larkin. "Some people like one wood better than another, others like stainless steel. Some decide based on the color of their spouse's hair—"

"Are you kidding me?" she said.

He shrugged as if to say he had nothing to do with it.

"Finances," Steven said. "Money is a factor, too."

Henry looked up from his examination of bronze fixtures. "Price is not important."

"Actually, it's a serious and valid consideration for Miriam," Steven contradicted.

"I'll pay for it. Price will not be a factor for my son."

"What?" Miriam was taken aback. "Why would you pay? I can't let you do that."

"No arguments." He glared at her, then turned back to examine a little treasure drawer, where loved ones could stash jewelry or ball caps or notes or whatever else they could think of.

She looked helplessly at Martha, who was no longer rubbing her hands back and forth, but stood with her palms flat against the coffin lid. Steven merely raised his eyebrows and shoulders ever so slightly.

"Which one do *you* like?" Mr. Larkin asked her.

"None of them."

His hands rose like sparrows, alighting on the knot in his tie.

"Here," Henry proclaimed. "This one's good. Solid." His knuckle thumped the side twice. "But I don't like the gold hinges and designs. Silver would be better." The lid had a rope-like molding, the sides heavy with gold appliqué. The wood was dark walnut, the color of their kitchen cabinets.

A noise escaped from Miriam, which she tried to turn into a convincing cough.

"This is the one." Martha's voice, unheard until this moment, was barely more than a murmur, but every head swiveled as if she had used a megaphone.

"This is the one," she repeated, her hands once again caressing the plain, honey-colored casket. "And Henry will pay for it." Her voice assumed such authority that even he didn't protest.

"Okay," he said, hooking his thumbs into his belt loops and going back on his heels. He nodded in Mr. Larkin's direction. "That one. And I'll pay."

Back in his office, it didn't take long for Mr. Larkin to gather the rest of the information he needed. Behind him, a window revealed an expanse of dull clouds, yet his mahogany desk, lacquered like one of his coffins, managed to capture enough light to glint painfully against Miriam's eyes. She was glad to finally thank him and shake his hand, but when she stood to go, Henry leaned back in his chair, extending his legs and blocking the doorway.

"Now let's talk about the funeral," he said.

"Yeah, we'll do that now," Miriam said. "We've got an appointment with Father Jake—"

"How about you sit down and we deal with it here. There's a nice room here that I'm sure Ted—can I call you Ted?—would let us use for the funeral." He turned to the director, who paled. "Isn't that right?"

Again, Miriam looked to Martha for help, but she was sitting with eyes focused on the floor, not listening, or simply incapable of taking part. Had her mother-in-law's earlier decree been a fluke? Miriam swayed slightly and touched the edge of Mr. Larkin's desk for balance. Had Henry really said this was costing him too much to not have a say in where the funeral was held? Surely not. She dropped back into her chair.

"Paul wanted a Catholic funeral," Steven said.

"What do you know about it?" Henry demanded.

"He and Miriam talked about it. Specifically."

Miriam nodded. "We did. We both wanted our funerals at Immaculate Heart."

"I didn't raise my son to be a holy roller. Now that he's dead," he paused for effect, "it's time for you to show me and my family some respect."

Martha closed her eyes and dropped her chin to her chest.

"Just because you don't share the same faith as your son

doesn't mean you have the right to say that," Steven said, standing, as if ready for a fight.

Miriam had never heard this tone of voice from her brother. Her father-in-law's face had gone white, his thin mouth a slice of red above a thick chin. He shifted to get out of his seat, and Miriam popped out of her chair.

"You know what?" she said, "I don't think Paul would want us to fight over this. Let's just have the funeral here. I think that would probably be best." She reached for Steven's hand and pushed at him, gently, until he sat down. "Would that be okay, Mr. Larkin? Do you have a room we could use?"

He nodded and she sat back down, pressing her palms flat against her knees to hide their trembling. She could feel Steven staring at her in disbelief.

Yes, she thought, with hard-earned fortitude, as she listened to the simple prayer being said over Paul's grave. *It's better this way.*

When the casket was lowered, Miriam stood to drop the first handful of cold dirt on top. This was one of the only things she had insisted on. Her family had always witnessed the lowering of the casket, and she could not be swayed, even by Mr. Larkin, who felt the newer tradition of walking away before that happened was for the best.

She had expected the dirt to be frozen hard, but it felt strangely warm and damp. Just this side of mud. She looked at her hand in surprise and before she knew what she was doing, brushed a finger across her right cheek. Theresa, after dropping a rose and crossing herself, dug a tissue out of her purse and handed it to Miriam, who looked at it blankly. Theresa took it back and used it to wipe Miriam's face. Miriam closed her eyes at the unexpected tenderness with which Theresa touched her.

A gust of wind blew her coat open and she felt her bare arms cold against the slippery lining of her coat. Her yellow sweater was lying in the trunk of the car.

Across the open grave she could sense Henry watching her and was careful to avoid looking directly his way.

Turning away from Theresa, Miriam wondered how she would get through the rest of the day. Perhaps, she thought, it would be enough to simply put on the sweater as soon as she got back to the car. Parade or no.

MARSENA KONKLE is the author of the novel *A Dark Oval Stone*, from which the story "Resolved" is taken. She was a finalist in the 2004 Paraclete Fiction Contest and has an MFA in Creative Writing from Vermont College. She lives in the Chicago area with her husband and great aunt.

AN EVENING ON THE CUSP OF THE APOCALYPSE

BRET LOTT

"An Evening on the Cusp of the Apocalypse" is a comic parable of our end times, when it seems so many of us live perched on the edge of a knife, but believe ourselves to be standing on solid ground. The prophet Amos wrote, "'The days are coming,' declares the Sovereign Lord, 'when I will send a famine through the land—not a famine of food or a thirst for water, but a famine of hearing the words of the Lord,'" and it is the hope of the author that this story of the folly of believing we're all okay will illuminate the need for the bedrock wisdom God's Word has to offer.

—Bret Lott

AN EVENING ON THE CUSP
OF THE APOCALYPSE

Bret Lott

T he mail hadn't come.

Larry'd put the bills—the electric, water, Citibank, the mortgage—in the mailbox when he left this morning, then pushed up the red flag, and headed for downtown, confident in the way things worked: he would offer up these sacrifices, these slabs off his paycheck, in order to live as he and his family did, content in the good knowledge the lights were sure to come on when he flipped the switch, the water to flow when he turned on the faucet. Soon, he'd thought as he placed the bills in the box, a representative from the United States Postal Service would arrive, take up these obligations, and send them on their way, route them as they ought to be routed, deliver them as they ought to be delivered. The way things worked.

But the flag was still up, he saw in his headlights, this day over, the sun already down, dusk making way for dark, and he only shook his head at the sad truth of how seldom, in fact, things actually worked as they were meant to work. He pulled up the driveway.

Take, for example, the library bid. He'd had this one in the bag, he'd believed, had done his homework, followed the paper trail first to the federal building, then to county, then to city, all in an effort to find exactly who it was could authorize the wiring bid. Routine, certainly: be pleasant to Laqueesha, the black woman who worked the archives at federal, offer to buy her a cup of coffee and a jelly-filled, let her turn him down twice before trying one more time, when she always took him up on it; offer Dorinda at county a Snapple Raspberry Iced Tea, who would take it on the first go-round; make certain not to make eye contact with Benny O'Hearn, the jerk, down at city hall.

It'd paid off too. The bid on the new library, he'd finally figured out, had to go through county, but not before approval by federal and by city.

Routine.

But then he'd gotten the flat tire, then the ticket for speeding, then, once he'd finally made it back to the office a little after five, he'd watched from his desk while a uniformed officer served papers to the boss, who turned, papers in hand, and went into his own office, closed the door gently behind him. A few moments later he emerged, briefcase in one hand, softball trophy in the other, and headed for the door.

Of course this would be about the death of that janitor at Whitesides Elementary last week, the one who'd touched wires he *should* have been able to touch.

They watched their boss go, no one saying anything, all nine of them at the offices of Hemley Electric, Inc., only staring as the door closed behind Mr. Hemley.

Then, one by one, they left, no words between them.

So much for the library bid.

Now he was home, the red flag still up, the bills not mailed. *What next?* he thought, and reached to the visor, pushed the button on the garage door opener.

Nothing happened.

He saw, too, there were no lights on in any of the windows, and his home, here in the failing twilight of a day gone bad, seemed somehow not his home at all, but a hulking shadow, big and anonymous, nothing he knew as his own. It was a house, he saw, dark and vaguely empty for the lack of lights and a garage door shut tight, no matter how many times he mashed the button on the visor.

Is this my house? he wondered. Had he mistaken this one for his own, where each evening warm light through windows spilled softly onto the sidewalk and lawn and driveway? *Maybe*, he thought, he'd simply skipped a street, too preoccupied with the ramifications of that janitor's death and the ensuing fire that'd razed the entire elementary school the day before classes started, all of it simply cutting too close. It had been his schematic, after all, that'd been used for the layout and hookup, though his boss had given him the final verbal okay. He'd approached Mr. Hemley with the layout, sketched out on a Burger King napkin, between the top and bottom of the ninth inning of the last game of the season. Mr. Hemley'd just finished off his sixth beer and was headed for the on-deck circle when Larry'd made the presentation; Mr. Hemley'd smiled, nodded, then gone to bat, knocked a solid line drive down the first base line, drove in the winning two runs. Game over, schematic okayed. The world a wonderful place, Larry recalled. The way things worked.

But then had come that janitor, that fire. Maybe, Larry figured, he'd just made a left turn one street too early, or one street too late, in this tract of homes. Maybe this house was just somebody else's, a simple mistake.

Then the garage door opened, not from the button—he'd finally given up, had in fact placed the car in reverse, so convinced he was of his error—to reveal to him his son, Lawrence, there in his headlights.

He was pushing up the garage door from the inside, his thirteen-year-old grimacing with the effort, the red emergency release handle from the opening device dangling above him once he'd gotten the door all the way up.

"Hey Dad!" he said, and waved, then stood to one side, made a sweeping gesture to usher him into the garage.

Larry smiled, pulled in, parked.

"How goes it?" Larry said, and climbed out. "What's with the garage door opener?" he said. "And the lights?"

The boy was a black shadow now that his headlights were off, weak evening light in from the open garage door useless. He believed Lawrence shrugged at the question. "I don't know," Lawrence said, then, "Promise you won't be mad."

"Mad about what?" Larry said. "About the lights?" He came around the car, stood before his son. "Mad about what?"

"Just promise," the shadow said, then, "It's no big deal, really. But you have to promise."

"All right," he said, and wondered what this might all be about. "I promise."

Lawrence said, "I got a tattoo."

"You *what*?" He tried to focus on the figure before him. "You got a *what*?"

"A tattoo," he said, and now he saw his son moving, turning toward him, pushing up, he believed, his T-shirt sleeve. "A couple days ago. I saved up for it." He paused, as though Larry might be able to see his arm in the dark.

"You *what*?" Larry said again. "You're thirteen years old!"

"Dad," his son said, "you promised. You promised me you wouldn't get mad."

"Where is your mother?" he said, and brushed past his son,

took the three steps up to the kitchen door, pushed it open, his son silent behind him, his moves, he knew, too quick and hard even to allow an answer. He would find her, see what she had to say about this.

The kitchen was dark, the only light the pale purple in from the windows, so that it seemed he might be walking in a dream, the things around him—the refrigerator, the breakfast nook table, the sofa and chairs in the family room, the hall table, even the individual rungs of the banister as he mounted the stairs—as pale and meaningless as the empty sky out there.

What was with these lights?

He found Debbie in their bedroom, and in the instant he pushed open the door he saw her throw something from where she stood at her dresser to something big and dark lying on their bed.

It was a suitcase, he made out, open.

"This is it," she said, "this is it, this is it."

"What are you doing?" Larry said, and came to the bed, saw sail from the dresser to the suitcase before him a wad of something. Clothing, he believed. Hers.

"This is it," she said, and slammed shut a drawer. He saw her figure bend at the waist, heard a drawer scrape open, saw more wads of clothing fly.

"Honey," he said. "Debbie," he said, "what's going on?"

She stood then, and he heard her breathing, sharp and hard in the growing dark of their bedroom.

"I'm having an affair," she said, and then it seemed she burst, those sharp and hard breaths gone in an instant, replaced with sobs as open and clear as the day had seemed when he'd backed out of the driveway this morning, as open and clear as when he'd put that red flag up to signal the mailman.

Have I known this was coming? he wondered. Were there signs? What had he missed?

He turned, sat on the edge of the bed, his back to his sobbing wife. She sobbed, still at the dresser, and he wondered what words there were for this, for something he hadn't foreseen.

What might he say, now that everything had been lost? And did that job even matter now, that death of a janitor and all those schoolchildren forced to hold class in camp tents that families in town had donated nothing more than an odd item in the newspaper, a funny photograph he and Mr. Hemley had laughed over just yesterday morning, when the world lay before them, untainted and pure?

What about his son's tattoo?

And what was with these lights?

He looked up, saw the switchplate by the door, the one that controlled the ceiling fan in here, and the lights.

He'd laid out the wiring schematic on this house himself. He'd done that work, and had for the last seven years rested each night with the good knowledge he'd done his work well, all the lights working, and that ceiling fan, even the garage door opener.

But what would happen were he now to flip on the lights in here at that switchplate? Would he, too, fry as had the janitor? Would his wife sob even louder were he to die here, his own house razed by his own inept schematics?

Was this how his life would end? he wondered, and believed, perhaps, it already had: His wife was having an affair, his thirteen-year-old had a tattoo, his boss had left with the softball trophy.

Why not try? he wondered.

He stood, went to the switchplate. Still Debbie sobbed, there at the dresser, and it seemed the few feet to that switchplate had suddenly become a maze a mile long, as much an ordeal as a day courting Laqueesha and Dorinda and avoiding the eyes of Benny O'Hearn, the jerk.

He reached the wall, put his hand to the switchplate. He swallowed, closed his eyes, and here came a picture of that janitor in the moment before he touched those wires, beside him a galvanized bucket of clouded and antiseptic water, a mop in the other hand, his feet planted square in the patch of wet linoleum he'd just finished with.

He opened his eyes then, blinked away that image. He'd done a good job on the wiring here. Yet he'd believed he'd done a good job on that Burger King napkin as well. Still, that school had burned down.

And it came to him: Things happened, he only now knew, took strange twists away from you, and in a single second headed straight for hell in a handbasket with no input from you whatsoever.

That, he finally realized, was the way things worked.

He flipped up the switch.

Nothing happened.

"That's nothing," Debbie managed to say then, her voice winded, empty, relieved of itself for how openly and clearly she had sobbed. "That's nothing," she said again, and turned from the dresser, headed for the master bath. "Listen to this," she said, and he followed her, saw her in the near-black of the bathroom twist at the faucets of their double sinks. Immediately the room filled with sound, rapid-fire thuds from air-filled pipes.

"No water," she said. "No water, and no electricity." She paused, and here were the sharp and hard breaths again. "I'm having an affair," she said, and the sobbing started.

He'd had nothing to do with the plumbing in here, and for a moment felt relief, felt himself almost smile. He had nothing to do with the plumbing.

But then his life came back to him, and he lost the smile.

He turned, left her there in the bathroom, left the rapid-fire thuds and her sobbing, and went to the window across the dark room to see what this day's last moments of light might bring.

He saw out there a blue sky so dark and heavy he knew it would be only a moment or two before the black would take over completely, and stars would emerge like celestial master electricians come to jeer at him, his life out of his hands.

"Citibank called today," his wife sobbed from the bathroom. "They canceled the cards. They said they called TRW, too, and told them to put our name on their list," she sobbed, and took in several quick breaths.

And he noticed then that no other lights were on in any of the houses he could see. Not in the Tolman's across the street, or the Neezak's to their right, the Doherty's to their left. He saw no street lamps, either, saw only darkened streets and a deep blue sky empty of stars, as though perhaps this were the end of the world, and civilization as he knew it—a garage door opener that worked, a faithful wife, the United States Postal Service picking up his mail—was finished. Done and done.

"They put a lien on the house too," she sobbed. "The bank." She took in more quick breaths, then sobbed. "And Ed Hemley," she sobbed, "is great in bed."

His life, done and done.

Then, out there in this evening he believed to be on the cusp of the Apocalypse, he saw the headlights of a car down on the street, moving slowly, stopping, moving slowly again, stopping before each house a moment, as though in search of an address, and he imagined it might very well be the same officer as had served papers on Mr. Hemley—Ed, now—come to get him, and he crossed his arms, held himself, waited for whatever might come next.

It stopped at his next door neighbor's house a moment, then pulled to his own.

A white jeep, there at his mailbox.

The mailman.

He saw the mailman lean out, flip open the door on his mailbox, saw him extract small slips of paper, saw him insert some of his own. He saw this all beneath a sky as close to black as a sky might ever be and still hold no stars, and thought it a miracle somehow, so dark out there, and yet light enough for him to see the quick flick of the mailman's wrist, a practiced move as professional and smooth and confident in itself as anything he had ever seen. Then he saw the mailman look up to him, here in this darkened window, and saw, he believed, the mailman smile, saw him wink, then wave, a brief gesture filled with possibility and courage.

Larry felt his own hand move of its own accord, and he, too, waved, the same gesture a passing on of something: courage, he thought. Courage, and possibility.

And one by one, throughout his neighborhood, he saw lights come on. Here, there, the next blocks over, then the Tolmans, and the Neezaks, and the Dohertys, until his hometown seemed a spray of celestial gifts, myriad constellations, a map of the galaxy, untainted and pure. *Who needs stars?* he thought.

Then his own lights came on, first downstairs, and he saw that light he knew from every other night spill softly onto the sidewalk and lawn and driveway; next came upstairs, this room in which he stood with his wife, and all view of the night outside was suddenly gone, replaced by his own reflection in the glass, the lights on behind him, so that what he saw was a man, himself, with his arm up in a kind of snappy salute, confident in himself.

Debbie had stopped sobbing, and he turned, saw her where he'd been on the edge of the bed. She was weeping now, carefully, gently, and he went to her, put his arm around her, held her.

He heard water flowing now, saw from where they sat on the bed into the bathroom clear water stream from the faucets, the water back on.

"I was lying," she wept. "I'm not having an affair," she wept. "I would never do that to you. I just want you to cherish me," she wept. "That's all."

He held her, held her closer, watched the water flow, smelled his wife, her hair, that same shampoo she always used, and the phone rang.

He would not answer it, he decided, chose instead to cherish her in this moment. But it rang only once anyway, and he held Debbie close, smelled her hair.

Then it rang again, and though this time he thought perhaps he ought to answer—maybe this was Mr. Hemley calling, begging Larry to come bail him out—the phone again rang only that once, and no more.

"There," he whispered to Debbie. "I cherish you," he whispered, "you know I cherish you," and thought of the mailman's wave, his own perfect copy in the glass reflection, and thought, too, of how he might get the library bid on his own. *Hemley Electric, Inc., was ripe for a takeover*, he thought. And the wiring wasn't, finally, his own fault; Mr. Hemley had in fact given him the okay; no way was he liable for it. No way.

He heard a small and tentative knock on the doorjamb, and turned, saw standing in the doorway Lawrence, who smiled, gave a small, tentative wave. "Can I come in?" he said.

Debbie sniffed, sat up straight, dabbed at her eyes. She gave Larry a nod, a broken smile.

"Come on in," Larry said.

He took a step into the room, and another. He said, "I answered the phone." He shrugged. "The first one was somebody from Citibank." He shrugged again, smiled. "The guy said they made a mistake, and they had you down as paid up. The guy said he was sorry, and that he'd called TRW, whoever that is." He shrugged yet again, still smiled. "He said this TRW was wiping clean your life. That was what he said, 'TRW is wiping clean your life.' And that they upped your credit limit too."

Larry looked at Debbie, whose smile was no longer broken, but strong and healthy.

"Who's TRW?" Lawrence said, then, "And what's a lien? Because that was what the second one was about. Some lady from NationsBank said the lien was off, and it was a big mistake, the mortgage was in."

"When you're older," Larry said, and felt himself smile, "you'll understand about all this." He patted the bed next to him, said, "Come sit down. It's been a long day."

Lawrence came to the bed, sat beside him, his hands in his lap. He shrugged.

Still Larry smiled, smiled at this faithful wife, a loving son, lights and water. He smiled at Citibank, and the mortgage, and the miracle of the mailman, the graceful bestowal of fortune he'd signaled was on its way with a smile and wave of his hand. All this, in just the smallest of gestures.

"Can I show it to you now?" Lawrence said. "In the light?"

"What?" Larry said, his smile grown to beaming now, the way the world worked no surprise at all, finally: a representative from the United States Postal Service had arrived, taken up those obligations, and sent them on their way, the world a wonderful place, full of possibility and courage. The way things worked.

"My tattoo," Lawrence said.

"You're just kidding, right?" Larry said, still beaming.

"No," Lawrence said, his own smile grown into its own beam, and he looked to Debbie, beaming all of her own. They beamed.

Lawrence rolled up his T-shirt sleeve. He said, "I saved up for this for five months."

There at the top of his son's shoulder was a tattoo, a jagged bolt of red lightning six inches long, its edges crisp and keen, beneath it a scroll, the word *Dad* stitched into the skin of his thirteen-year-old son's arm.

It was beautiful.

"This isn't one of those wash-off kid's things, is it?" Larry asked.

"Nope," Lawrence said. "Permanent," he said, and nodded.

"Good," Larry said. "Young people these days need something they can depend on," he said, and put his free arm around him. He held his wife, held his son, and decided he would give his son a raise in his allowance, give him a boost toward the next tattoo, one for Debbie, and imagined a heart, pink and plump, on his other shoulder, *Mom* stitched there.

Ed Hemley served with papers. That was something. And the janitor's family would come out all right after this, once they'd settled out of court.

Water flowed, light fell.

What more could he ask?

BRET LOTT is the author of eleven books, including the best-selling novels *Jewel* and *A Song I Knew by Heart.* His work has appeared in numerous journals, anthologies, and textbooks, and has been translated into five languages. For eighteen years, he was writer-in-residence and professor of English at the College of Charleston, but in 2004 he and his wife, Melanie, moved to Baton Rouge, Louisiana, where he is now editor of *The Southern Review* and a professor of English at LSU.

FIRSTBORN

LARRY WOIWODE

In this classic short story, a young married couple must face—both together and alone—the life-and-death struggle of childbirth, a struggle that reveals the tenuous nature of their marriage itself, as well as their own confessed and hidden sins, and the confrontation with the self that a believer must face boldly and humbly in order to know the true forgiveness only God can give us. This emotionally and psychologically and physically intense story is a portrait of the battle with the sinful nature of our fallen selves, and the free but hard-wrought gift of freedom from ourselves that we can know only in Christ.

—Bret Lott

FIRSTBORN
Larry Woiwode

harles tried to settle himself where he sat on the edge of the bed. It was a bed they had bought from the couple who had lived in the apartment before them, and consisted of a mattress on a metal frame equipped with casters (concealed by a dust ruffle Katherine had sewn), with a loose headboard that had to be wedged against one wall in order to stand upright, and a footboard that kept falling off—too capricious an affair to sit comfortably upon. *But comfort has never been an asset to me in any crisis*, he thought. Actually, the opposite. Lack of it kept you alert.

He looked up from the book between his knees, keeping his place in it with his index finger, to the clock on the top of her oak secretary: 5:15.

The clock was rectangular, white plastic, a remnant of Katherine's single life, with a crack down its face and her maiden name written across its back in slanting exuberance, with a marking pen, as if the hand that didn't bear his ring would always dash away on its own under that other name, denying that marriage had made them one, proving her to be as divided on this as he was. He looked over his shoulder at her. She was still on her side, turned away, the covers over her hair, her knees drawn up; one arm flung over the other edge of the bed, her hand hanging limp from its swollen wrist. As far as they were able to tell, she was in labor. Their first child.

Faint beginnings of morning light appeared as milky blueness at the windows in the turret off their bedroom—one window oblong, one circular, one square, with a balanced shapeliness to them he hadn't noticed until now. He was seldom up at this hour. Drapes that matched the mahogany of the dust ruffle, drawn back in eloquent swags from the ceiling, framed the alcove of the turret, where an ivory telephone sat on a steamer trunk below the windows. It was September. The crown of the pin oak outside, which he could begin to see in outline, was straggly and insubstantial from shedding its leaves.

He'd been reading to her from *War and Peace,* a last straw in the whorl, or a raft in it, and she'd fallen asleep. That quick. But he'd gone on to the end of the section, after Andrei has learned of Natasha's attempt to elope with Anatole Kuragin and, like anybody afraid of his anger, has sent a go-between, Pierre, to return to Natasha her portrait and her letters, signifying the end of their betrothal, and Pierre, who can't think that this is final, plans to lecture her for falling prey to his frivolous brother-in-law, but finds himself so moved by her and her state that he says if he were not Pierre but the handsomest, dearest, best man in the world, and free, then he'd be down on his knees asking her to marry him (the first intimation of what is to come), and then goes out in "twenty-two degrees of frost" and sees from his sledge the comet of 1812 arrayed among the stars above Moscow—a comet that is supposed to portend a multitude of disasters but, for him, speaks to "his own softened and uplifted soul, now blossoming into a new life."

A residue of the moment and Pierre's emotion still troubled the room; the shapes of the three windows sparkled as if out of that night's moment of change. Which came at the middle of

the book, indicating the swing the story would take in the opposite direction from that point, as if pulled by celestial powers.
Charles looked down at the parted pages, as if to measure their
ability to affect him in this way. He'd begun the book the month
they were married, when they first moved into the apartment,
and she had picked it up; she'd completed a major in Russian
but had never read *War and Peace*.

They dropped everything and let the apartment lie in dis-
order around them during three days of immersion in this
Russia that bore the dimensional stability of Tolstoy's moral
stamp. And just as they looked up from the end of the book,
blinking still, or so it seemed now, the Soviet film of it appeared,
and they sat through the eight-hour extravaganza of that. (Just
as when they'd met, two years ago, he'd finished *Doctor Zhivago*
to appease her, and then the movie of that appeared.) He was
appalled at the paucity of his imagination within Tolstoy's
world, or at the timidity of it, so far as it went, since it was
leagues removed from the actual opulence of that life as it was
lived on the grand scale, according to the movie's depiction of
it—or was this Soviet propaganda?—and she was furious that it
was dubbed. She kept shifting in her seat, as fitful as the images
reflected over her, he noticed, uneasy, and when they went out
for dinner during the break that was provided, to an expensive
restaurant he'd chosen with her in mind, she said, "I wish this
place were old-style Roman, so we could lie down and eat, I'm
so sick of sitting through those ugly Britishy accents. *Ugh!*"

"Vomitorium?" he asked. It was at about this time that
they'd become a kind of comedy team, with him responding to
her puzzling pronouncements in these quirky, semisequitur
twitches.

His reading was meant to recall those days to her—a form of reconciliation, and the closest he could come to being straightforward with her, now. She was pregnant when they were married, four months ago. He assumed the child was his, since they'd been planning to "legalize their status" whenever circumstances were right for them both, and she assured him it was. And then recently, in the center of this same bed, hysterical, her hair down over her newly ample nakedness, she had confessed to another liaison while "finishing" the relationship she was involved in when he met her, meanwhile insisting that the child had to be his, or she wouldn't have married him. As if she'd reached the ultimate in logic at last.

He had started for the telephone, to call a lawyer about a divorce, but since he hadn't carried through on the impulse, he could never mention the possibility to her, though he still considered it. Then, as they were leaving a neighborhood party a couple of weeks ago, and he was stepping down the stairs with that practiced carefulness that too many drinks can bring on, her provocative backside suddenly seemed packed with such shifting and separated willfulness he kicked at it, and when he could next see, he saw her thumping like a child down the bottom stairs of the flight. He'd been in a remorse that gripped under his ribs like talons ever since: for the danger to the child, the bruises she still bore, and his lengthening vision of the sick fits that any marriage, even theirs, which he'd presumed to be one of the best, could find itself thrashing within as if for life.

They'd had arguments, loud shouting ones that had caused the neighbors below to pound on the ceiling with the handle of a mop or a broom—and these got worse, until his senses felt worn raw with an endless colloquy of his rights and wrongs, as if even the halves of his brain were in conflict. He'd always thought that one of the most fatuous statements he used to hear was "I don't see how she puts up with it," meaning injustice in a marriage, since it never considered a woman's ability to turn around and walk off, but now he saw how it applied to them, and he was grateful that she hadn't left yet.

He stared at the clock and then through it, in the outpouring of his impulse still to crush and break, and was retrieved by the thought that it was up to him to time the intervals. 5:17. She'd seen the secretary in an antique shop on Montague, the Madison or Third Avenue of Brooklyn Heights, depending upon which side of the street you were on, and he'd walked over one Saturday afternoon and talked to the dealer until they'd arrived at a price he considered bearable; and then, after he'd paid, in cash (the only medium that satisfied his sense of anonymity in the city), the dealer said that the price of course didn't include delivery. So he came back the five blocks to their apartment, got one of the burlap carrying straps the movers had left behind when they'd brought up the heaviest pieces, returned to the shop, and carried the secretary all the way home on his back, in the bent-over shuffle he'd watched the black movers adopt, and had been so invigorated by the look on the dealer's face, and the flex of strength returning to muscles he'd hardly used for years, he hadn't once set it down. He'd been a high-school athlete, a quarterback of the sort who would spend so much time trying to outthink the opposition, from the coach on the sidelines to the tackle hurtling toward him, that he'd have insights he never should have had in the middle of a pass, or become impulsive, led by his imagination, "like a girl," his coach would growl—unpredictable.

The secretary was solid oak. He had scraped and sanded and worked it, from its squat turned legs to the fragile basswood of its pigeonholes, and now yellow-gold striations rose in relief from the broad hashmarks of black grain in the growing light. It had become her niche, or nest. Her nature was to be in control, to the penny, to the framing of the proper response in writing at the proper moment, and she worked on their accounts here, running down his cash outlays; and sometimes sat for hours composing letters to her family or to friends, many of which she never sent. Or, when she did send them, most remained unanswered. None of her family knew that she was pregnant. Nobody in his family did.

They had both come to the city separately, far from those connections, largely to sever them, for their own complicated reasons and to their own satisfaction. He was from the Western Upper Plains, she was from the Northwest (two unrelated regions that in New York came under the category of "the Midwest")—Wests they wanted for the moment to be free of, and here be *Eastern*, as was true of most of the disenfranchised people their age that they met in the city. He had worked before as a performer and an announcer—"live talent," in the creeping jargon of the medium—and could do that again, but for now preferred a shadowy role. He sold time for an FM station, his hours his own.

"Katherine," he said, sure that she'd moved, and turned and put a hand on the covers, over the thigh he'd bruised, he realized, and drew it away. He thought he'd felt a revelatory swelling, but there were so many unpredictable areas to her now, extra padding in unexpected spots and new curves over the familiar ones, it was as if the body he'd charted so many times were being withdrawn inside this other. "Katherine, did you fall asleep?"

There was no answer; then a wash of the covers as she moved. A contraction, as she and her OB, Harner, called it? He'd begun to shy from their technical vocabulary at about the time she came home from a visit to Harner and stripped and lay down on the bed to demonstrate her "Braxton-Hicks contractions." 5:22.

He turned. "Are you awake?"

No answer.

"Are you"—he couldn't quite get out "contraction" but didn't want to say, "labor pain"—"feeling another—?"

Nothing.

"Would you like something to eat?"

"No! I'd puke it all up!"

"Do you want me to go on with the chapter?"

"No!"

It was as well. Her attitude had eroded any equilibrium left in him, and the events of the last day had worn his nerves to visionary frailty. She'd hear that in his reading voice. She was stronger than he would have suspected—it was all he could do to keep her nails from his face during some of their arguments, as they rolled over the bed or the floor—and stoic, usually, shifting without a hitch into the next situation and moving through it at her own speed, her eyes ahead, as if she'd been raised in the absence of any expectations and whatever arrived, no matter how troublesome or perverse, was a gift to get open and onto her desk and put into place. She was able to shake off circumstances the way she shook off her umbrella, entirely, so that she didn't have to leave it open in the apartment to dry, and after she'd recovered at the bottom of those stairs, wiping a hand under her eyes, smearing her running mascara, she looked up at him and said, "I deserved that."

But through yesterday and the night, into this morning, she'd been absent from the level of the commerce of life, as if the child in her had taken hold and was drawing her under. He'd never pretended to be able to enter her inner state, but he was usually able to reach her. Or she was able to reach to him out of her concentration that became so pure she could take on the aspect of stone. Artists and photographers came up to her and asked her to pose. She gathered her intellect like an essence in her, unreachable, and its concentrated power drew your eye over a harmony of lines of resolved womanhood, or that was her impact, at any rate, and she'd begun to get work as a model, which was her work now. In the last months, she'd withdrawn to even deeper recesses of solitary silence, into an intensity of beauty that left its mark on every eye (or negative; she continued to work), until he feared she'd be refined away into oblivion. As now. As it seemed to him.

They had gone to the city the day before to look at a lamp she liked, which might well have been a chromium sculpture, it was so expensive, and on the way back, on the subway, as he rocked in a semitrance on the seat beside her, as content as he'd been, in spite of her recent revelation, she took his hand and said into his ear in a breathy moistness, "You'll never believe this. I think I've lost control of an essential function."

"Faction?"

He tried to study her, as full of interior upheaval as the car shaking over its rails; lately, any reference to her body took on this evasive, almost clinical cast. There was a sunken expression of fear in her eyes, which had widened so much over the last few weeks he felt he was looking into a diminished face overtaken by their enlarging, liquid presence. But her face was broader, too, and her nose and nostrils were, as if every cell in her were making accommodation for the child; the arch, even, of each nostril had heightened, along with an accompanying looseness he could feel in her limbs (present now in her hand), which made him wonder with uneasiness whether the cartilaginous parts of her weren't being consumed.

She drew him closer, so he couldn't stare, and, in the pretext of putting her head on his shoulder, whispered, "It seems to have really given out this time—ah, I mean, you know, my bladder."

"You're joking."

"You know how improvident I've become."

"Incontinent?" he asked, somehow in time and tune to the train, so that the syllables seemed shaken from him, not voiced, and once out of him not spoken.

"Well, neither, literally," she said, and settled against him as if to sleep. "Neither, but both. Sometimes it's an affront to reason to be at the mercy of a body you don't know." Then it was their stop. "Get up before I do," she whispered. "Walk one step behind."

He obeyed and noticed only what might be a spot of rain at the back of her trench coat. He maintained his position across the platform and up the ramp to the elevators. Outside the hotel, in the September sun extending a rich spill of copper over car tops and bricks, he felt a rush of renewed hope for their marriage, as if it had just begun. He looked across the street and up the block to their corner, at the ornamental iron fence whose scrolled yet jagged lines were like his impatience for this newly perceived future, and was about to say, Let's get home.

"How do I look?" she asked.

"Great!"

"No, I mean"—she tipped her head as if glancing into a mirror, and her hair swung wide in a whitish shine—"there."

"Oh, fine. Wonderful. Nothing."

"Good, then let's go to the store." She took his arm. "We haven't shopped for days. It's time to. What a weakling I've become!"

"And me?" he said, and saw that she didn't catch this, and was relieved. When she planned to do anything, she carried it through, shifting the expected order of things into an altered state resonant of her, until the doing itself took on her distinctiveness—a new aspect he kept trying to compare with what once had been, but never could, since it was gone. That quick. It was a pleasure for him merely to witness her effects.

But at the supermarket, as she lingered over every item in her new, slow, considering inwardness, which he'd forgotten about, as if she were agonizing over the details on each label, he wandered off. His impulses had become as unpredictable as hers, and when the fatherly internist who saw them both suggested that this younger crop of American husbands had a tendency to enter into couvade at the onset of pregnancy, long before birth, and they'd returned home holding the word like a sweet on their tongues, and had looked it up in the dictionary, and then looked at one another, they both had to nod.

The man's name was Weston, and he was a forensic expert and a collector of first editions of nineteenth-century philosophy, and a dispenser of it—one of their few real friends in the city, in their consideration, even though they had to pay to see him. He was a willing participant in the tragedy (as they saw it) of their daily, domestic unease within the dedicated depths of their love. As they saw it. How were they to go on, given that imbalance? There were some good discussions, they felt, or dialogues, as Weston called them; he was well enough read in current literature so that his apparent mintings of this month were next season's jargon.

He kept careful records, and whenever they stepped into his inner office after an exam, into the sunlight from French windows that looked out on a balcony with a stone balustrade, and found Weston at his desk in a suit jacket already exchanged for his smock, every hair in place, jotting down notes, they couldn't help smiling. The thickness of his file folders on each of them was that reassuring. *Home,* Charles almost sighed, feeling as particular as family under the care of this scrupulous man, who knew absolutely what he was up to, and who, with his Century Club manner and Manhattan dapperness, was valued highly, Charles realized, among people in the places that matter most.

When they had got their apartment decorated to the degree that suggested a newly married couple on their own in the city and making it, they had a party, and the first person they invited was Weston, who of course didn't come. They invited all the tenants in their building, but only the couple from the apartment below showed up, as if to observe firsthand what sort of degenerates were able to cause such resounding bedlam. On their way out, after a quick drink, the husband of this couple suggested putting padding and carpet down in all of the rooms. "Bathroom?" Charles asked, as they started down the hall. "Let me know with a bang of the mop if the thickness isn't suitable to you, okay?"

"Yardstick," the man said, and turned on him in a sudden, reddening fury. "I use a yardstick!"

A can of imported corned beef caught at an urge, and Charles looked around to ask her about it. She was at a freezer case with her back to him, her head held as if listening, and he saw her, with a shock, as separate from him, an abstract, pregnant woman, and then felt a chill as if from the case where she stood. A clear liquid, like the pure line of a song, was pulsing in a threadlike stream down her inner calf. The top of her tennis shoe was wet. He hurried over and saw a wet track on the floor behind her, where she'd taken a step. He put a hand on her shoulder.

"We better go," she said, without looking at him. "Get what you want."

At the apartment she dropped her coat and pulled off her dress—a lime-colored shift imprinted with miniature flowers, which she'd removed the belt loops from and wore wherever they went, drawing the line at maternity outfits, or "advertising costumes," as she called them—and got into the shower. He picked up her coat and hung it in their closet and paced around as if pursued and then went into the bathroom and drew the shower curtain aside. She was soaped, soaping, and when she shifted her weight he could see the liquid dart in a pulse down her leg through the suds. "Kath!" he cried. "That's not—" And didn't know whether to use "urine" or a commoner term.

"What are you doing in here!" she cried, the sunken fear again in her face, and covered her stomach with her hands.

They called Harner, her obstetrician. He'd been recommended by Weston, who said that a woman's response to her obstetrician was apt to be "chemical." So Katherine might like this man, he said, and might not. If she didn't, she was to ask him to recommend another. Harner was his wife's OB, Weston said, but his daughter couldn't stand him. "He's fairly brilliant, I believe, but a bit impulsive." Katherine was vague about Harner, as she recently was about so much, and seemed to stay on with him mostly to keep from calling the taste of Weston's wife into question.

Charles had met Harner at her first interview, and he had appeared to Charles too ready to pass off their questions with a humor that didn't seem natural, as if he'd learned it from somebody else, or with his authority, which didn't rest lightly on him. He was young, portly, going bald on top, and his remaining hair looked combed back in haste with heavy oil, which offended Katherine; she'd mentioned that much. He promised them that Charles could be with her all the way through labor, right up to delivery, which was what they wanted, and then he went off with Katherine to perform an examination.

Over the phone, as Charles sat on the steamer trunk and stared at her on the bed, with a towel around her after her shower, Harner said, "Well, we'll soon know whether it's the amniotic fluid or not."

"How's that?" *Herr Harner*, as Charles thought of him, because of his smiling Germanic demeanor, which Charles could picture over the phone.

"She'll go into labor. If she does, call me right back."

"But this is only her seventh month."

"I'm quite aware of that, you can rest assured. We'll have to handle the situation as it develops."

"Isn't there anything I can do? I mean, wouldn't it be better if we went to the hospital now, and—"

"Oh, no, I don't think that will be necessary—not till we see where this is headed. Unless you're afraid. Give her some hard liquor, if you like—it's marvelous for premature or false labor—and keep her in bed, on her back. If things stabilize, I'll have her in in a day or two for a checkup. These things happen. Give me a call otherwise, okay?"

He hung up.

She'd been in bed ever since, and when it seemed to them that labor had begun, in the middle of the night, Harner said, "You might be getting a reaction to losing some of the fluid. Don't call me again unless the contractions get real hard—it's unmistakable—and about ten minutes or less apart, okay? Time them." He hung up.

Charles had gone over to the St. George and persuaded a bartender to sell him a bottle of Old Bushmills, her favorite whiskey, but after a couple of sips she set it aside, as if it were a placebo she wasn't about to be taken in by. He had poured it straight over ice cubes, and its pale remains now sat on a wooden chair beside the bed where her arm was outstretched. He hesitated to touch her, and then did.

"Kath, do you want to leave for the hospital now?"

"I can't believe this is happening to me! I'm worn out just from the movement inside! My stomach's like a rock!"

He tried to modulate calm into his voice. "Well, Harner said if—"

An arm struck him as she rolled and drew up with the force of another struggle, starting to pant. He knew why this was called labor—for the effort it was—and why travail; he was sure he'd never be the same as he watched her features flatten as if by extragravitational force into a face that wasn't hers. Then she began going "*Gur, gur, gurr,*" as every shade of color emptied from her.

"Katherine! We have to go!"

"Ah! All right!" she got out, and her tight-shut eyes fluttered open on unfocused depths. "Just—stay with me *through* this!"

He took her hand, icy, its veins going vivid in wheyey paleness, and held on tight. Her fine blond hair was whitened from bleach and afternoons spent sunbathing on their roof (*ghostly* came to him, as he stared·down on its snowy disarray), except for an area over her crown in the shape of a skullcap, coming in in her natural blond shade—an effect he'd noticed from their windows one day when she'd gone shopping. Now it seemed the place where the power of her will was concentrated, vulnerable. He placed his other hand over it, wondering how he'd let her go off on her own that day, and she said, "Thanks. Thanks. Oh, thank you a lot."

All he wanted was to have this over, so she would be herself again. But it was clear she couldn't admit that it was already beyond her control. He didn't even care about the child anymore, for her sake. The child seemed the cause, and he was well aware that women died in childbirth.

"Put your hand here!" she said, still fighting for air, and pulled it with both of hers over her stomach. Her skin was extraordinarily sensitive, delicate as a baby's neck over her entire body, but here so much more so it was nearly a profanation to touch, and now it rose tented over a hump like a stone. An elbowish bulge revolved under his palm from beneath, and he started to pull his hand away, then felt a sensation spread from there and concentrate in an unsettling tickling under his chin.

"Must be his *head*," she got out. "Currents from it."

What? He didn't dare ask. They were so convinced it was a boy they'd named it Nathaniel.

Then her eyelids, shiny and purplish, closed down, and her lashes went flickering over crescents of white. And then it was over, as if a wave had passed.

"All right," he said. "That's it. Get ready. We're going."

Once something like this gets off the tracks, he thought as he ran down the street, his throat still tickling, it keeps plowing into places that get worse. There wasn't a cab in sight in the early-morning quiet of the streets. There weren't any at any of the hotels he ran to. He took off for Fulton Street, and the rattle of being winded brought up a picture of her alone and fighting for breath, which sent a shock through him he couldn't contain, and then he was on the curb at Fulton, beside a chain-link fence clogged along its weedy bottom with paper and wrappings like leavings of the bulldozed lot it enclosed. He was aware now of the cold and of being in shirt-sleeves, probably the picture of a burnt-out derelict suffering his ultimate vision of absolute destruction—the worst sort of prospect to pull over a cab at this hour—and he couldn't keep from jumping off the curb, and then wading out into the street, as if to bodily stop one. Finally, an old Checker swerved over, and he was in the back, spilling his situation to the driver, who seemed incredulous, already enmeshed in it all.

He was an older man, with twists of gray in his tangled curls, which he pulled at, wide-eyed, as if to pull them out, and his rumpled clothes were aromatic of the nervous hours, or days, spent in them. Charles directed him down the narrow streets to theirs, lined with cars on both sides under the slim oaks and maples (too early for the alternate-side-of-the-street parkers to have started their morning shuffle) and barely wide enough for the bulky Checker cab to squeeze its way down. Charles had hoped she would be outside their building, waiting, but she wasn't. "Here," he said, and hopped out before they were stopped. "It'll just be a second."

"Hey, you haven't paid—"

Which the door clopped off. But he was reminded to get money as he went up the steps to the vestibule in two bounds, and was inside. He'd forgotten his keys.

He rang the buzzer. No response. Then he remembered their signal and repeated it several times. There was another mind-dimming shock he couldn't contain, and then the lock went into its rattly vibrations, and he took the steps in leaps and swung around on their landing to see the door ajar. He hit it with his shoulder and felt it thud against something inside. Her tennis shoes. Their soles were facing him, their laces loose, and she was on her elbows and knees, her head down, hair splashed over the carpet, her spilled makeup and compact beside her, its mirror shining up at him, rocking on her haunches and crying, "*Ahh! Oh, ggaaah!*"

He tried to lift her up.

"No!" she screamed, then got control of her voice. "No, wait—*till* this is over. Can't *talk* when—"

He hurdled her and was in the spare room, which was to be the child's but wasn't fixed up yet, and where a plain door was laid across stacked milk cases filled with ring binders and station logs. His desk. Under this he jerked open the drawer of a file and fumbled out his manila folder of cash, and noticed at a glance, as he stuffed the bills into his pocket, over two hundred dollars. He sprang into the bedroom to their closet and jerked on a suit jacket, coat hangers clashing, and with an emerging hand swept up the watery whiskey from the chair and knocked it back (seeing an image from somewhere of a well-dressed man down on his knees, head thrown back, draining a bubbling bottle)—a mistake. He would need every ounce of clearheadedness and nerve he could summon, the convulsion of his stomach suggested. And from the altered angle it took to drain the dregs his eyes rolled toward the bed: it was disordered, gray with damp over one half, and across its center were streaks of blood.

She was at the table, her hands pressed on its top, leaning so far forward her hair hid her face in a whitish cloud. Her lime dress looked stained. He put his hands around her from behind.

"Do you think you should wear this?"

"It was all I could do to get it on, and it's all I've got on and I mean all!"

He went down on his knees and started tying her shoes from behind and realized what a blur his haste had built to, and forced himself to slow down by watching his trembling hands attempt this simple task, with its folding intricacy and—

"Oh, this is absurd!" she cried, identifying for him the feathery ascension troubling his throat, and then they were gripping one another for support at the laughter that broke from them in diabolical barks.

The cab was gone. No. The man had parked at the hydrant a few buildings down. Charles helped her into the back with the premonition that they'd never make it and felt this undercut by the realization that the cab needed new shocks. They pulled away, and she closed her eyes against the lurching and un-cushioned impacts. Her mouth drew down at its corners. He put an arm around her but felt at such a distance he wanted to lift her into his lap.

"Move over," she said, and as he slid to the other side she lay down, dropping her head into his lap so hard it hurt, as though she'd read his thought at least in part. He drew away filaments of hair caught in her eyelashes and stuck to her lips, and smoothed them back. Her forehead, with bits of perspiration glittering in its pores, was as icy as her hands, and as the cab yawed around a corner and she groaned, he yelled, "Can't you speed it up?"

"Who'll pay the tickets?"

"I will."

There was a surge of acceleration, and then the purling of the bridge's grid beneath their adhering tires, and he experi-enced their rising suspension over water as a chasm opening under him, seeing the idiot uprights of gray-black stone ahead, with their paired, churchlike arches, apparently in the process of sinking, both still to be passed through, while the swoop and stutterings of the cables out the windows were like projections of his nerves in strumming onslaughts across the city below. Then he pictured his keys on the grain of the table, next to her outspread hands, forgotten again, and felt his focus narrow in on them as on a vision: he had held the keys that would have opened up an easy passage for her through this, and had let them slip. Every lie he'd told and every person he'd hurt had led to this, he saw, and started pulling at his hair, like the driver, as if to tear his thoughts loose from the tangle this implied.

"Take it easy," she said, and smiled crosswise below. "It'll be all right. Can you move over more?"

"I'm against the side."

This time she chewed at her lips in her attempt not to cry out, as her body went into its arch, sending her darkening crown in a crush against his privates, like an assault on the cause. Then she raised her knees, gripped them, and pressed down on him with her entire force. "Ow!" he cried as they slid underneath a red light somewhere, and he had to grapple with her and an armrest to keep them from striking the seat ahead. There were cars with people in them on all sides and horns were going off.

A man at a wheel an arm's length away, out her window, looked over and did a take, eyes widening, and Charles wished he had a pistol to blow the pervert away, for taking advantage of her in her helplessness. He gave the fellow the finger as they squalled off, and then reached up and dropped a twenty-dollar bill on the driver's seat.

Inside the emergency entrance, he was told he'd have to check her in before they could go up to the maternity ward. "But she's fainting!" he said, because she appeared to be. He had to support her; her legs were giving way. The nurse was young, with blonde hair up in a French roll—exactly as Katherine wore hers whenever they went out, to look older—and now she touched an arranging hand to some wisps at her neck at his attention. She'd been summoned by phone and had appeared pushing a wheelchair. "I'm sorry," she said, and looked appealing and flustered. "It's procedure here." But Katherine grew worse, so that he had to lock his arms above her breasts to hold her up, and the nurse said, "All right, I'll take her up and go ahead and prep her, if you'll admit her right away. Then come right up with her papers. Okay?"

The procedure took a half hour, carrying him to the opposite end of the building, where he had to fill in a four-page form in the forgotten cramp of a student's writing chair. A woman behind a counter, at a teller's window he was directed to, wondered if it could be true that they actually didn't have hospitalization insurance. "We pay for everything by bank draft or cash," he said, and pulled out what he had in his pocket.

"Oh," she said, and stared at the bills as if in distaste, while covertly trying to tally them, it seemed. Then she paged through a floppy book of computer printouts, turned her back and made a phone call, and finally said, "We require a three-hundred-dollar deposit for maternity."

He counted out a hundred and fifty and said he'd bring the rest later.

"We'll have to have it before three this afternoon."

"What will you do if you don't?" he asked. "Kick her out?"

It took him some time to get to the seventh floor and find the correct "suite." A graying nurse in half-glasses, at a desk inside the swinging doors, accepted the papers and said he'd have to wait. Katherine was being prepped, she said—whatever that was. He felt a cold caul of air-conditioning over his scalp; a fluorescent-lit anteroom swung off behind the nurse in lines that verged on circularity, with doors leading off it all around, as in a maze. A huge column at its center was encircled by a desk partitioned into pie shapes with slabs of glass. Nobody was at the desk. Heads of bolts showed in uprights and ceiling beams and in the metal panels of the walls, as if he were in the interior of a ship, and horizontal strips of chromium reflected the unsettling curves of the place upon itself.

A stretcher banged through a pair of metal doors and went wheeling along the opposite wall, the young blonde nurse pushing, and he saw by the swinging drape of hair and profile that the sheet-covered figure on it was Katherine. The nurse at the desk cried, "Sir, sir" as he took off, but the blonde one beckoned. An overweight Latin attendant in a white suit who had come through the doors behind the nurse and was forced by her pace into a tripping step that had him out of breath, while a stethoscope jogged in wild loops from one ear, gave Charles an okay sign, so he joined the entourage as it went banging through a single door.

Into a tiny room, a cubicle really, hardly large enough for them all and the stretcher, on the other side of an elevated bed, which had bars up on both sides—the whole place also fashioned of metal, trimmed with the same chromium, like a miniature hold within the ship; or, worse, like a quadrant at the outer perimeter of a centrifuge just starting to spin. Because now Katherine rose as if in protest, white as the smock she had on, then swayed to one side, the sheet flying up. Bars on her side of the bed banged down, and he reached across as if to pull her up from drowning but missed her grasping hand. She was reaching back at the attendant, who now had her under the arms, so that his big belly pressed her head forward, forcing a cry from her cramped throat.

"Hey!" Charles yelled. "What the hell—"

"Please, sir," the blonde said. "Or you'll have to leave. You may help with her feet, if you would."

He leaped around and took Katherine's ankles while the nurse, placing a hand below his shoulder blade, passed with a taut swish across his backside, and eased away the attendant, who acted so inept he must have been new. The fellow gestured apologetically at Charles and gave a dog's overacted gape of shame. Then sudden sweat seemed to strip his face to its essence, grainy fat, and ran in streaks around his eyebrows, dripping from them and the manicured band of his mustache. They got Katherine on the bed and Charles saw indentations left by his grip on her ankles. He hurried around to the other side, to be out of the way of the attendant, and reached over the bars and took Katherine's hand, and in the light from a window above he saw her closed eyes pouring tears.

"Where's Harner?" he asked, with a fear that collapsed his voice into breathlessness.

"He should be here any minute." The blonde. "He was almost in from the Hamptons when he responded to his beeper. They're vacationing there." An intimacy had been touched on; her eyes widened, then she blinked this away.

"We're paging him right now. Dr. Ramirez is our resident on duty. He'll fill in till then." She wheeled the stretcher out.

P. Ramirez, M.D., Charles saw on the plastic clip above the stethoscope pocket of the "attendant." The man now drew the sheet down from Katherine and then pulled up her smock, jerking at it, and Charles was shocked to see the clenched bulge slide across her shining abdomen. Then he realized she was shaved clean. He draped her there with the sheet and discovered himself caught in a kind of contest with the resident, who was trying with his stethoscope to keep up with the strumming sidewise roll of the bulge. The man's eyes bugged. He pressed his hearing piece so hard it became buried and left little red hoops, and Charles, as if from a deafening distance, watched her arch against it and cry out and saw the exposed swath of her as this man must, as meat.

The bulge revolved in reverse, and now a three-way struggle began as she pushed at the resident's hands, one of which Charles was trying to restrain while the other dug into the scoop of her hip as the man leaned close to listen. She cried and coughed to get her breath, and her lips, usually so blood-infused they didn't need makeup, blued, and then she went limp and her eyes rolled up.

"Holy God, she's passed out!" Charles cried. "Watch it!"

The man swung to the head of the bed and fumbled at the wall with equipment there, his hands shaking, got loose an oxygen mask and set it over her face, the strap awry and in the way, and then swung back and fiddled with some knobs. There was a hiss and he picked up the mask and listened to it, shook it, and then sniffed it. "Hole dis," he said, setting it over her face in the same way, and Charles lifted the strap free, onto her hair, and pressed the mask in place. "Say 'Breeze deep,'" Ramirez said.

"Kath, please, breathe."

An outside force seemed to seize her ribs and pull them up in shuddering bands, and he saw water pool over her lashes as her eyes squeezed. "Ahhhh!" she cried, so loud he had to gasp at the noise. "Hurts me!"

"Breeze deep," the man commanded, and then, beginning to pant himself, pointed and said to Charles, "You. Tell hor." And in quick squeaking strides he was out the door. In a frantic scrambling to reconstruct the moment, in order to make sense of it, Charles realized the man had pointed not at him but at a sign before he'd left: NO SMOKING. Did the fellow think they would here? Now? With what was in the balance?

She was awake and trying to focus on him. She shook her head and flung the water in her eye sockets free. "Oh, hurts," she said, under the mask, and her voice came to him as over the telephone, distantly metallic, with most of its overtones abstracted into a nasal, girlish version of her—a child with a cold. She took his hand that held the mask.

"Don't leave me," she said, in the same tinny girlishness, which he heard as through a disk at his ear.

"Don't worry, I won't."

"What happened?"

"You needed air."

"Am I in delivery now?"

"No."

"Everything exploded in slow motion, all blue. The Battle of Borodino."

The window above, oblong and blank, appeared to pulse, and he saw through to the moment she meant: choreographed columns of uniformed men going down to death through billowing smoke. Then Ramirez walked in with a thing like a trike horn strapped to his forehead, with the blonde nurse at his back, her face set, carrying something like ice tongs, as if to protect him. On their side of the bed they lifted the smock Charles had drawn back down, the nurse more sensitive in her attuning to abasement, and used the tongs, or calipers, to take a measurement, then covered Katherine except for the active bulge. Ramirez inserted listening tubes into his ears and bent down to force the trike horn into the now relaxing mass. Katherine pushed the thing away. "Not that," she said under the mask in her tiny voice. "Hurts!"

The man's shoulders went up and his hands out as if to say, "What can you do?" to the nurse, whose face had turned the naked red of a blonde. She slipped on her own stethoscope and moved it over the area of the bulge with a cold agility. "Try here," she said, and placed two fingers flat. Then she gripped the horn and guided it as the resident hunched over with his eyes rolled up in the swarthy polish of his face. He listened, and when she let go, he shoved the thing so deep that Katherine began to kick and arch, the sheet flapping, and again was unconscious, in spite of the mask.

"Stop that crap!" Charles said, grabbing the horn and lifting the man upright with it.

All three of them stilled, frozen in confrontation, and then as Charles bent to get the mask back in place he heard in his ears what he thought was his heartbeat, but it was footsteps, and Harner came through the door. "What?" he said, and stopped, startled, studying them with birdlike concern, in a trim tan summer suit, with a blush reddening his wrinkled head, as if locked in a conflict to establish his control. "What the—" This came out half-cocked. "What's going on here? Answer me at once."

"She's ten *sahn*-timeters dilated, Doctor," the nurse said, all professional, as if to obscure some complication with jargon.

"What!" he said. "Good God, why didn't somebody give me an idea of the problem?"

The blonde let this pass and in a swoop got the mask from Charles and over Katherine's blue-spotted face.

Harner pointed a finger, surprisingly small and delicate, at Charles's forehead, only inches away in the cramped room, and said, "What the hell is he doing here?"

"But you said I—"

"And where's his sterile gown and cap, for goodness sake?" Harner asked the nurse, ignoring Charles, so that the word *he* stung worse.

"Katherine specifically asked me—"

"This is an emergency. Get out!"

"But my wife asked me not to—"

"Get out! Do you understand English? Get the hell out!"

Charles turned, nearly colliding in the doorway with the resident, who apparently felt Harner meant him. In the anteroom Charles found himself fighting an anger so fierce it seemed brighter than the fluorescent tubes flashing overhead as he walked, as in the aftermath of a stunning concussion in football, when criticism from a coach, as much as the injury, could throw his body off balance. The nurse at the desk smiled as if she'd overheard the scene, and said, "Why don't you wait in the lounge, down the hall to your left?" And then plucked at his coat sleeve as he passed, so he had to turn to her. "I could never see the sense of those gowns in the labor rooms anyway," she confided. "Since we go in in what we've been wearing all day. But that's what I was trying to tell you when you ran off. And then Dr. Harner—well, he can be so touchy."

She wrinkled her nose at him.

The lounge was lined with chairs upholstered in primary colors, stilled in a compression of sunlight. Windows went from ceiling to knee level along the length of one wall. It was empty. To sit, to him, was to concede to the hierarchical unreality closing around Katherine, like the structure of the hospital itself, until it seemed she would disappear. So he went to the wall of plate glass and stood like a sentinel for her on the real world. His knees, at the level of the ledge below, had been magically unlocked, he felt, and would suddenly bend in the reverse direction. He was staring down at the river they'd crossed, in a muddied surge at this point against the city's sculpted edge, cut as fine as if by a razor. A growing sound like voices at the fringe of understanding was, he realized, from the traffic building into its morning patterns over the streets below—a tentative stir that reached him like the first billow of an unexpected, unpredictable wind.

The grayish cavern of a basement under construction—a further addition to the building—opened into the ground directly below, and he could make out reinforcing rods, like wires bent awry, rising out of the lines of future walls, until his exact place in relationship to them was brought home with such an impact everything in him blanked out except a central sexual core, growing in magnitude, so that he had to battle the perverse pull to throw himself down.

It was this silence. The still sheen of the glass with bands of gold sun resting in its thickness—He felt a spraylike dispersion within him, which seemed to spill outside his boundaries through the window, hesitating in the air beyond, and then he was blinking back tears as he tried to remember how it was that Pierre had—

He couldn't get his breath and felt afloat as he watched his own unfeeling hands slapping over his front for cigarettes. He finally got them out and lit one as if to anchor himself. Then he had to fight visions of the glitter and gore of an operating room where he had Harner strapped down and was hacking at him with every instrument he could get his hands on.

He had to talk to somebody.

He'd cut off his family, since none of them appeared to approve of Katherine to the degree he believed they ought to. What could his father or a brother say anyway if he called, not even knowing that she was pregnant? He'd talked to Katherine's father so little the man could hardly be considered an acquaintance. Maybe he could talk to Weston. Sure he could, certainly he could. He might even meet Weston in the halls; Weston taught here.

He caught a reflection coming toward him and turned. It was Harner, who halted at his look, taking on an air of also being afloat, in a ballooning green gown and a cap like a house-painter's cap but without the bill, which gave the grin he put on a sillier aspect. Harner came up and put a hand on his shoulder, and Charles felt a response there like the sparking at a battery's terminal; he didn't like to be touched.

"Say, I'm sorry," Harner said. "I guess I blew my top back there. Nobody likes to walk in on a situation like that."

Charles looked into his eyes and encountered only an evasive fear—as if Harner had had glimpses of his operating-room assault—and managed to say only, "How is she?"

"Well, it was a precipitate delivery, a classic case of it."

"Is that bad?"

"It's not so common that it didn't have us thrown a bit, you'll have to admit that." He tried to smile, and Charles felt that they were high-school enemies who'd met on a street corner and decided to be civil, and with that illumination Harner's smile came clear; it was the slack-lipped grin that cowards get, of having secretly eaten something tasty, just before they're socked. "It's not from anything either of you might have done, but unfortunate coming this early in her final trimester. Also, she's pretty badly edematous."

"What's that?"

"Gathered fluid. The swelling you see in her extremities. I wish you had told me about that."

"I did, over the phone."

"Oh, I guess you did, yes," he said, and looked down to recover himself, then up with a professional stare. "I want to reassure you that as far as we can tell it's doubtful that anything you or she might have done yesterday or the day before could have caused this. Certainly nothing that happened a week or more ago. Rest your mind on that. These things happen."

He'd seen the bruises.

That wiggly smile appeared again, and he said, "We'll want to keep a close eye on her, though, after this, and next time I might recommend some conjugal restraint over her last trimester." His eyebrows bobbed. "In certain cases, that seems to trigger the contractions."

"Precipitate delivery?"

"Yes, it's precipitated by God knows what and comes on like gangbusters. It takes a fraction of the time of usual labor and delivery, once it gets started, and there's no way of knowing what to expect. We'll have to watch that, too, the next time around."

"You mean Katherine—"

"Oh, she's great; you have a wonderful wife there! You're a lucky guy! She came through it like a pro, wide awake all the way. The sedative didn't even have time to take effect before it was over."

"It's over?"

"Well, yes—that is, the birth is, yes."

And now Charles had to wait while the enemy, who seemed to have been priming for this, underwent an alteration that appeared in his eyes, like awe, before disclosing his dirty secret. "You had a boy. We have one of our best pediatricians with him right now. There's no use falsely getting your hopes up. He's very small and weak, almost two months early, and this has been a terribly severe trauma for him. His respiratory system isn't responding as it should be. He's fighting for his life right now."

"What about an incubator, for crying out loud!"

They both flinched at the tone.

"We're giving him oxygen. We've done all we can, actually, medically."

"I want to see my wife." Needlelike intrusions started stitching at the corners of his eyes.

"She'll be in the recovery room soon. There are a few more things we'd like to check out, and then I have to tidy her up a bit."

He put a hand on Charles again, this time over his flexed arm muscle, as if to intercept any violence, and wrinkled his nose (had the nurse talked to him?) and said, "There are some restaurants and some little"—he waved his hand at the window—"some little *places* across the street. Why don't you make it an hour, say."

This seemed a command.

"I'll wait right here."

But a few minutes later, when Harner came back and told him their child had died, he walked out.

The bartender was scattering violet sweeping compound over the floor of one of the little places that had recently opened. Charles took his bottle of beer to a table, to be alone, although nobody was present but the bartender. Low morning light came through the open door at an angle that didn't quite reach to his shoes. The sprinkled boards beneath gave off cold and damp. The door faced the river, with the ascending stories of the hospital between, and half of the pedestrians wore white, as if to claim their affinity with the constant newness of the business they hurried toward.

He was too terrified to feel remorse. He had sensed that this would happen and was sure that when it did he would be off at a distance, apart from her, the expendable party. No recourse. No help. He'd had complete freedom most of his life, he realized now, or he'd taken it, even after they were married, but this he wouldn't be free of. This was on him, and he didn't know how he'd ever get out from under it. He would take the responsibility for it upon himself. He'd tell her that.

There was no possibility of divorce now, not for him. He couldn't live with this if he didn't have her side of it, or her portion of the experience, under him in support. She'd done all she could, given the circumstances. He was lucky to have her, as Harner said, and lucky she was alive. From this moment, their relationship would have to be as open as that door. He'd tell her that, and how the thought had come to him, like further sunlight through the door, but first he had to ask her forgiveness. The way had to be cleared with that, or they couldn't take the first step to begin anew. He'd do what he could to exist from day to day after that, for her sake. No promises. No—

A raying silence, like the silence that invades a house in a driving rain, spread through his consciousness. He would not sit and imagine what it would have been like to have had a son.

The door darkened, and an elderly woman with a stocking cap pulled over her ears came rocking into the place, carrying a shopping bag in each hand. She sat at the table next to his, talking to herself as she sorted through her bags and smoothed scraps of paper from them on the table as if they were dollar bills. Under a sweater, under a number of open coats, she appeared flat-chested above her pot belly, and her wide face was kept active by her licking at and worrying a single lower tooth. He thought with an impact that set him back in his chair how his mother would be this age if she were living.

He'd had enough; this was over; he wanted off; and he was about to move from the pall of irritation the woman spread, when he heard "Could you get me one of those, sonny?"

He set his face toward the light, in case she was referring to him.

"Hey! Sonny, could you—"

"Aggie," the bartender said from behind. "Leave the kid alone."

Charles put down a dollar. "It's all right," he said. "Get her one."

"You know the house rules," the voice said. "Not unless she walks in with you. You know, Aggie."

There was a silence of restructuring accommodation, as if they were contemplating the movielike beams within the broader band of light, with only the sound of traffic in its breezes of accompaniment outside and, as if in answer to that, the broom sweeping the floor behind. Then the woman's talk seemed to stir in a different direction. "You hurt?" she said. "It's my fault, it's all my fault. You think you're the only one who suffers? One-crack mind, one-crack mind. One of these days you're going to wake up with your voice changed and realize you was always queer."

Sensation gave like snowslides in him, and his joints ached from dread. There was something terribly wrong with him, he was convinced, that he kept attracting these grotesques. He must be more than monstrous himself (he had to fend off text-book images of abnormalities at birth), if he was already accli-mated to this death, or acting as if he were. Because what had been disturbing him under everything else these past months was that he'd had an affair at the same time Katherine had had hers, as if they'd been signaling one another of their need to break free at the thought of being bound, and he felt he got what he deserved when she confessed. But then he'd feared, first, that the child wasn't his and, next, that it wouldn't live.

"Like you lost your best friend," the woman said, and he turned and found her eyes on him, gray-gold in the light. She sucked at the tooth awhile as if to extract its essence. "Don't let it get you down. They're always at you. They never let up. You got an ounce of sympathy yourself? You got sympathy with me?"

"Yes."

"Yeah, you say you do, but they all do." Customers had come in, and she threw her head back as if to indicate them, then called in a loud voice, "Ain't that right, Jack?"

"Sure, Aggie," the bartender said.

"'Sure, Aggie,' he says, like he's my echo. They don't let up no matter what. I said to him, 'You want a mother, a wife and kids, you want a young girlie type, or you want a queer?'"

"What are you after?" Charles asked.

She leaned toward him and smiled a sweet-old-lady's smile, pegged at its corner by the tooth, and said, "A nice big jug of rosé wine. Maybe a hunk of you, Butch."

He took two dollars and dropped them and the other over the papers in front of her on his way out, feeling mistily benevolent; she'd never know the state in him this had risen from. Then out in the sunlight, blinking as if stunned, he felt he'd been lanced through the place near his ribs where the talons curled. He couldn't tell Katherine he'd come here. Not while she'd lain over there alone. How could he have listened to Harner? And then he sensed something further hurrying close and heard in a whisper at his ear, *Murderer. You'll never quit paying for this.*

The gray-haired nurse stood up from her desk as he stepped through the swinging doors; she, too, had her duty to see to now. He'd decided to talk to Katherine, and let everything take its turn from her. The nurse gripped him by his coat sleeve and said, "This time we won't forget," and led him to a line of lockers behind a wall of the curving anteroom—dim atmosphere of high school and the stripped-down purity of physical sports, with their innocence of the actual world, he now knew, in their unvarying perimeters and established rules, not to mention the false assumption that they were training grounds for life. From a shelf over the lockers she got a gown and shook it so it unrolled, unraveling its billowy length, and then held it out for him, and he stepped into it, over his jacket and all. With a hand on him as if to hold him there, exhaling something minty, she came around and started tying it at his back, and in the starchy chill of its cloth drawing close he felt he'd entered the hospital at last, and the hospital held Katherine and their dead son.

He gulped at the grief that went down his throat like brine and saw sudden dark spots traveling over the front of the gown as though its substance were eroding. "I understand," the nurse said, and set one of the caps on his head, then rested her hands on his shoulders. "It's terrible to lose the first. God comfort you." She shook him.

He recovered, but in the anteroom, seeing Harner at the column encircled by the desk, in his suit and tie once more, motioning him over, he felt his anger and grief collide. "We have some forms we'd like you to sign," Harner said, and put on his slack-lipped grin. Two minutes alone with him, Charles thought, just two minutes.

"It's merely a formality," Harner said, and his eyes swerved at the freezing cry of a newborn. "Then you can see your wife."

In heavy type on the top sheet on the desk Charles saw *Death Certificate*. Farther down, written in: *respiratory failure*.

"Why should I sign it?" he asked. "I haven't seen him."

"Oh, not that," Harner said, and shuffled the papers until he came up with two others, one of which read Waiver. Again Charles said, "I haven't seen him."

"Well, in effect what these say is there's been a birth, and then that you'll be making a gift of the case to the hospital. Our research is acknowledged across the United States, and this might be a way of helping out somebody in a similar situation. We would take care of all matters of disposal, so you wouldn't have to worry about that."

"It's no worry. I want to see him."

"I think perhaps it might be better if you didn't." That smile once more, which quivered now at its corners with Harner's authority.

And cut into Charles's own fears, so that he couldn't ask why it would be better if he didn't, while "disposal" brought to mind the whirring mechanism that can shake a whole sink. He pictured a miniature casket at the edge of an open grave, with Katherine down beside it, the air black around her, and wasn't sure he could take that. He was trapped. "I want to talk to Katherine first."

"I don't know if it's something she should have to handle now, seriously. Do you? I know it might feel like a tough decision, but it's pretty much routine, or procedure here, because of our research."

And then Charles saw, as down a corridor darker than the one where the lockers stood, a flaking fetus in a jar, on a set of shelves among hundreds of others, and heard the refrain from a folksinger's ballad, that for every child born another man must die. He felt an exchange of that sort, with deeper implications, taking place right now, while the tick and cluck and shuffle of doors and footsteps and equipment seemed to be those actual lives and deaths moving in and out in an endless passage. The only light of exit at the other end came shining from the promise of seeing Katherine.

He signed the papers.

Harner gave a nod, as if to confirm Charles in his manliness, and then led the way to one of the branches off the anteroom, down a hall, to a door. "She might be resting," he said in a rasping whisper, as if he'd injured his voice. "If she is, maybe you should let her. Just take a peek so you can say you were in. She's been terribly excited about this—maybe overly so. We'll give you five minutes, and then in a while get her to a room—you'll want a private one for her, I know—and you can spend as much time there with her as you like."

This place was still smaller, with monitoring equipment against one wall and only enough space to pass by the stretcher where it was parked. The blonde nurse stood facing him, at its foot.

"Done," she whispered, her eyes enlarging on him, and then there was only the door at her back flapping in its frame at her retreat. A hypodermic syringe, with a final crystalline drop depending from its needle, lay on a stainless-steel tray on the stainless-steel counter supporting the equipment.

Katherine's hair, curled from exertion or moisture, hung less low from the stretcher, and she was moving a hand under the smock, testing her stomach. He stepped around to where she could see him, taking her free hand, and was confronted by a glossy incandescence in her eyes.

"It's so flat!" she exclaimed. "It's hard to believe it's so flat! That that's me! I wish you could have been with me through it all. I was totally engulfed by it, by the birth—by him, I mean. I'm sorry I was so out of touch before. I got afraid. Once things were going all right, I kept saying, 'Nathaniel! Nathaniel! I'm here, I'm with you all the way!' I felt his head come out—it was wonderful!—and then I knew something was wrong. The rest was hardly there."

She looked away, toward the monitoring machines, and he knew he couldn't tell her what he had to until this, which must be the ecstasy of birth, had subsided. She turned back with the incandescence in her eyes at a further level. "Suddenly he was entirely himself and left such feeling with me. I'm the only one who understands it right now, but you will, you will! My only regret is how I failed you."

"You came through it like a pro, I heard."

"No, no, he's gone. I know. I lost him. They told me. He died."

"You haven't failed me, I'm the—"

"I've failed you. You wanted him so badly."

He realized now that he had. "You haven't failed me. It's my fault."

"I was afraid you'd say that. I knew you would. Don't, please, for me. Please. I wanted to see him, but Harner wouldn't let me. 'I guess he just couldn't wait,' he said. All I wanted to do was see him. It wouldn't have bothered me. If I could only have seen just his hands. But maybe it's better. Maybe I'd have nightmares. They rushed him away, and then I saw Harner and another doctor, across the room by the windows, working with him. Their backs were to me. I couldn't see him. The nurse was so great. She—"

"The blonde one?" He wanted to get this all straight, as if for the terrible recompense to come.

"Yes, she was great! Back in the recovery room, well, here, I said, 'I just wanted to see him. I don't care how ugly he was.' And she said, 'There wasn't a thing wrong with him. He wasn't ugly. He was a beautiful baby. He was simply too tiny.' Can you imagine how intelligent he must have been to have done this?"

"What?" The talons in him flexed.

247

"He wanted to bring us closer together, and this was the only way. He knew that. He was so much like you, really—ready to give up everything to make things right."

"Kath."

"I'm in a different perspective. It's from the feeling he left. I know that time and events can't really destroy love. It's something you can't understand by reading about it. I had to learn that, and he knew it. We both had so much to learn from him!"

She laughed with an openness he seldom heard in her, and he began to shrink from this and her growing vision of the event. He was diminishing by degrees, he felt, until he had to take hold of the stretcher at her head to keep himself from being drawn into her, consumed. Then she pulled him down to her and kissed him on the mouth, and whispered with the intimacy of their bed, "No doubt about it. We've had our first child."

Then the perineal bottle in the bathroom of their apartment, in the stilled and grayish light through frosted glass; the green dress she never wore again, in shadow at the back of their closet; the barrenness of her secretary, as if she'd cleared it of even the essentials; the crescent-shaped planter of flowers he'd brought to her room in the hospital, with an eighteenth-century figurine in brown knee breeches and a long yellow coat with lace cuffs and lace froth at the collar, fixed in a contemplative pose, standing among the blossoms, which the florist at the last moment had set in place, and which Charles was unable to look at from the first without Nathaniel registering in him, followed by a tickling trill down his throat; the few articles they'd got for the child, chiefly a red-and-blue banner imprinted with stylized Buckingham Palace Guards, which followed them through every move (like the figurine he kept gluing and regluing until one day it was gone, with no explanation from her) and would suddenly appear out of a box, like another presence, striking them speechless; her feeling of betrayal that he'd signed the body away without telling her, and her depression that remained so long it seemed it would never leave, and when it did it would reappear without warning and set up further silences within her, making her mistrust her ability to work as she once had; his anger at Harner and the hospital, which kept revolving in him and reached its peak in the fall, so that more than once he started toward a lawyer to sue, but found himself foiled each time as if by the season, his favorite, in a release of grief and melancholy—for he was never able to bear the loss with equanimity, or with her wholly physical sense of loss.

It wasn't until after they'd had not only a second child but a third, and then a fourth, graced by this heritage, and he was leaning under the hood of a pickup on a fall afternoon with gold-red trees around awash in a wind and a son underfoot, running off with his tools, that he finally coughed out, "Good God, forgive me." And felt freed into forgiveness, for himself, first, then for her, the rest falling into place—for her because she'd never explained her experience during the birth and what she'd learned from it, as she'd said she would. But he knew now that the child had always been with him, at the edges of his mind and in his thoughts, as much as any of their living children (more, he thought, as he set aside the wrench in his hand and watched the tops of the trees above him springing in the wind), and he began then to look out on those children, on this boy with his hair going back in the wind, and on Katherine and on others, with less darkness in his eyes; that is, he began at last to be able to begin again to see.

LARRY WOIWODE is one of the most distinguished writers in America, a highly respected author who has received a multitude of awards, and whose work has illuminated readers since the publication of his first novel, *What I'm Going To Do, I Think*, in 1969. His other works of fiction include *Silent Passengers: Stories, Indian Affairs, The Neumiller Stories, Born Brothers, Poppa John*, and *Beyond the Bedroom Wall*. His nonfiction includes *Acts*, his meditation on being a writer and the book of Acts, and *What I Think I Did: A Season of Survival in Two Acts*. A native of North Dakota, he lives on a 160-acre farm near Mott, where he continues to write.

ACKNOWLEDGMENTS

"What We Knew When the House Caught Fire" by David Drury. © 2004 by David Drury. This story originally appeared in *Little Engines*. Reprinted with permission of the author.

"Dosie, of Killakeet Island" by Homer Hickam. © 2006 by Homer Hickam. Printed with permission of the author.

"Loud Lake" by Mary Kenagy. © 2006 by Mary Kenagy. This story originally appeared in *Image: A Journal of Arts and Religion*. Reprinted with permission of the author.

"Resolved," by Marsena Konkle. © 2006 by Marsena Konkle. Excerpted from the novel *A Dark Oval Stone*, Paraclete Press. Printed with permission of the author.

"An Evening on the Cusp of the Apocalypse" by Bret Lott. © 2005 by Bret Lott. This story originally appeared in *The Difference Between Women and Men*, Random House.

"Landslide" by David McGlynn. © 2006 by David McGlynn. Printed with permission of the author.

"Ax of the Apostles" by Erin McGraw. © 2004 by Erin McGraw. This story originally appeared in *The Good Life*, Mariner Books. Reprinted by permission of the author.

"Exodus" by James Calvin Schaap. © 2006 by James Calvin Schaap. This story originally appeared in *The Other Side*. Reprinted with permission of the author.

ACKNOWLEDGMENTS

"The Results of a Dog Going Blind" by Rebecca Schmuck. © 2004 by Rebecca Schmuck. This story originally appeared in WORLD Magazine. Reprinted with permission of the author.

"The Virgin's Heart" by A. H. Wald. © 2006 by A. H. Wald. This story originally appeared in *Image: A Journal of Arts and Religion*. Reprinted with permission of the author.

"Firstborn" by Larry Woiwode. © 1989 by Larry Woiwode. This story originally appeared in *The Neumiller Stories*, Farrar, Straus and Giroux. Reprinted with permission of the author.